RECENT AWARDS

SLEEPER CODE

PRAISE FOR *SLEEPER CODE*

Kevin McGuire is a verbal vanguard, interconnecting politics and intrigue, security and fear, the present and potential futures. All being woven together on a loom of technology and cyber warfare. This master of metaphors takes the technical and troublesome world of cyber offense and defense and draws on a reader's understanding of their own world to interconnect them in a way that even the most tech-illiterate will be craving every byte like life-bearing nourishment!

Brian O'Hare a.k.a. Gr1mR34p3r
Former Black Hat and Professor of Cyber-Security
Turned WhiteHat and Senior Information Security
Analyst, Author of "The Noob Rag!" A multi-OS CLI
handbook for beginners.

Sleeper Code delivers a gripping story that exposes the vulnerabilities in the massive, interconnected digital network supporting our everyday world. Kevin McGuire skillfully crafts a compelling plot, prompting readers to view our advancing technology through the prism of a catastrophic failure. This warning narrative urgently calls for stronger cybersecurity measures in our current and upcoming vital systems. Kevin does a masterful job taking the reader through something you can believe in.

Frank Yanez
Executive Director, Cochise Community Development
Corporation

Sleeper Code by Kevin McGuire is a pulse-pounding cyber thriller that masterfully weaves the invisible threads of digital warfare into a gripping tale of high-stakes suspense and human resilience. From the shadowy origins of the Phantom code in clandestine global meetings to the frantic battles waged in America's fortified Vault, McGuire delivers a narrative that's as intellectually riveting as it is terrifyingly plausible, exploring the fragile line between technology's promise and its peril. This novel keeps you on the edge of your seat, questioning every glitch in your own devices, a must-read for anyone who dares to confront the ghosts in our machines.

Joel Musgrove, D.B.A. Senior Executive
Vice President of Operations, University of Fairfax

I gave this book 5/5 stars. It is brilliantly written, and this piece of fiction is highly tense and compelling from page one. The story never takes the foot off the pedal and steers the reader through the terrifying new weapon of technological warfare.

Marie Staffeldt
www.onlinebookclub.org

SLEEPER CODE

A NOVEL

KEVIN MCGUIRE

Sleeper Code: A Novel

© 2025 by Kevin McGuire

ISBN: 978-1-64810-472-5 (paperback)
        978-1-64810-486-2 (hardcover)
        978-1-64810-472-5 (ebook)

Back cover photo credit: Bill Barton

Published by Perfect Publishing Co.

Printed in the United States of America

Disclaimer

This is a work of fiction. Names, characters, organizations, places, events, and incidents either are products of the author's imagination or are used fictitiously. Any resemblance to actual persons, living or dead, or actual events is purely coincidental.

The technologies, government agencies, and cybersecurity scenarios described are fictionalized for narrative purposes. While based on plausible elements of modern digital infrastructure and cyberwarfare, they should not be interpreted as accurate depictions of actual government capabilities or operations.

To my parents, Pat and Carolyn. Thank you
for your unwavering love, faith, and constant
encouragement through every chapter of my life.
Your quiet strength, sacrifice, and belief in me
built the foundation on which this story stands.
You are the reason I was able to finish this, and
the reason it matters.

ACKNOWLEDGMENTS

Writing *Sleeper Code* has been an extraordinary journey, one made possible by the support, insight, and encouragement of many people.

To **Tony, Pete, Debbie, Liz, Jeff, Jerry, Kathy, Frank**, and **Joel**, thank you for reading, questioning, challenging, and believing in this story from the very beginning. Your endless discussions about the timeline helped me keep the countdown straight, the characters interesting, and the tension sharp. Each of you brought a different lens to the pages, and your feedback made this book stronger, smarter, and more human.

A special and heartfelt thank-you to **Brigadier General (Ret.) Greg Touhill**, whose experience, clarity, and generosity of insight brought realism and integrity to the world of cyber defense depicted in these pages. Your guidance helped ensure that *Sleeper Code* remained grounded in truth, even as it ventured into fiction.

To my wife, **Traci,** and our kids: **Amanda, Ashleigh, Ryan, and Allie**. Thank you for your patience through the late nights, endless rewrites, and far too much caffeine. Your love, humor, and quiet strength kept me balanced when the story pulled me under. You are the reason I was able to finish this, and the reason it matters.

And finally, to every reader who opens these pages: thank you for trusting me with your time and imagination. I hope

Sleeper Code leaves you thinking about how deeply our lives are wired together, and how much depends on the people who keep the lights on.

CONTENTS

"The rise of powerful AI will be either
the best or the worst thing
ever to happen to humanity.
We do not yet know which."

— STEPHEN HAWKING

CHAPTER 0
THE BIRTH OF PHANTOM

Beijing. Moscow. Tehran. The cities had different names, but the room was always the same.

A subterranean chamber with no windows, no identity, just a long obsidian table beneath a single strip of cold white light. Men and women sat in silence, their faces half in shadow, their hands resting on folders marked only with codenames. No flags adorned the walls; no insignia betrayed allegiance. They were not here as officials of their nations, but as architects of something far greater.

The air was heavy with the sterile hum of servers hidden beyond the walls, cooling fans spinning like the breath of a mechanical beast. On the table before them: blueprints, lines of code, and intelligence dossiers stolen from every corner of the globe.

The man at the head of the table broke the silence. His voice was low, deliberate, stripped of all national flavor. "For nearly a century, the world has lived in America's shadow. Their corporations dictate our markets. Their military enforces their will. Their currency chains us, and their networks." He pointed toward the glowing satellite image of the United States that had sprung to life on the table. "Their networks ensnare us."

The map pulsed with arteries of light: power grids, transportation lines, financial exchanges. A living organism.

"They claim freedom," he continued, "but what they bring is dependency. They force nations into their systems, then punish those who resist. They weaponize their technology, sanctions, surveillance, and disinformation. Even their allies live on a leash." A woman with sharp eyes and a colder voice leaned forward. "And every attempt to oppose them has failed. We built missiles. They built missile shields. We built armies. They built alliances.

We hacked their walls. They rebuilt them."

The man nodded once. "That is because we have fought on their terms, visible wars, measurable wars. But what if the true battlefield is invisible?"

A schematic bloomed on the glass surface of the table. Not a missile. Not a bomb. But a strand of digital DNA, recursive code folding in on itself like origami, is designed to disappear into the bloodstream of software.

"Self-modifying. Self-learning," the woman murmured, scanning the design. "What exactly are we looking at?"

The man squinted his eyes. "Not a virus. Not a worm. A ghost," the man replied. "It will sleep until summoned. It will adapt to whatever system it inhabits. No antivirus will see it. No patch will erase it. When the day comes, it will rise at our command and strike where we choose."

Another figure, younger, shifted uneasily. His voice carried the hesitation of conscience. "We are speaking of attacking civilians. Power plants, water grids… families will suffer. Children." The younger man fell silent, moral protest drowned by the weight of history in the room. He tried to reconcile the logic, the suffering they would cause, versus the "justice" the leader argued was owed. The leader noticed a faint smile tracing the edges of his mouth.

The leader's eyes narrowed. "And how many of ours have already suffered under American embargoes? How many of our cities have been strangled by sanctions, our leaders toppled by covert wars, our data siphoned by their corporations? They speak of democracy while planting listening posts in our skies and puppet governments in our lands. Their wars wear the mask of liberation but leave only ashes."

He gestured toward the glowing U.S. map. "They believe themselves untouchable. Protected by oceans, defended by their arrogance. But their greatest strength is their greatest weakness. Every system they rely on is connected. Every heartbeat of their nation runs through wires, through signals, through code. And code… belongs to no one."

"Control is an illusion," the leader said. "Containment is impossible. But direction, that we can provide. It will wait, like a sleeper agent, until the signal is given."

He tapped the table. The word appeared across the map in stark white letters:

PHANTOM.

A silence followed. Not in agreement, not in fear, something more profound. Recognition.

"They will call it a virus, or a worm, or an exploit," the leader continued. "But we will give it its true name: **sleeper code— Phantom.** It will lie dormant for years, if necessary, hidden in their arteries, invisible until the moment of awakening. They will never know where it came from, never know how long it has waited."

In the corner, a single terminal flickered. Lines of prototype code cascaded across the screen, recursive algorithms twisting into forms even their creators did not fully comprehend. Already, the seed was taking root, testing itself against simulations, mutating in unplanned ways.

The woman pulled her focus inwards. "And if it awakens early?" The leader gave the faintest trace of a smile.

"Then the world will learn what it means to fear a shadow."

Above them, the city went about its ordinary life, oblivious to the birth of a phantom in the dark.

The leader turned back to the glowing terminal. His fingers moved with ritual precision, entering the final command that would scatter the sleeper code across oceans of fiber and silence. The screen flickered once, then fell still, its payload already hidden in the arteries of America's machines, a shadow among signals.

He rose from his chair, his voice carrying across the chamber like a verdict.

"It is done."

· · · · · · ·

In his Georgetown brownstone, a man named Max Shaw, unaware of the storm already set in motion, moved through the small rituals of his morning. Coffee, tie, thermos, the steady rhythm of a life he believed was ordinary. To him, it was just another day in Washington, another day defending the nation in a war of ones and zeros. But soon, he would discover that the war had already breached his doorstep, and the first battle had quietly begun.

CHAPTER 1
SHADOWS IN THE CODE

The alarm buzzed faintly against the brick walls of Max Shaw's Georgetown brownstone, a reminder that the day had begun long before the rest of the city stirred. Sunlight crept cautiously through the blinds, tracing pale gold lines across a room littered with books, old case files, and the faint hum of a half-disassembled radio he'd been tinkering with the night before. Dust motes drifted in the beam, carrying the faint must of old paper and yesterday's coffee.

Max moved with the efficiency of someone who had lived too long by routine, coffee brewing before he was fully awake, a press of the French press handle timed perfectly with the first beep of the toaster. His brownstone was modest but lived-in: photographs of his parents in Boston, his father's faded Navy Academy pennant tucked discreetly into a bookshelf, and one framed picture of a woman and a little girl, their faces smiling into a summer sun. He looked at it every morning, and every morning it reminded him why he did what he did.

He had earned his master's in Artificial Intelligence Engineering, Information Security from Carnegie Mellon University, a place that treated code like philosophy and competition like oxygen. It was there, in the Gates Center for Computer Science, that Max first learned to see systems as living

Organisms, complex, adaptive, and unpredictable. The same halls still carried the legacy of Allen Newell and Herbert Simon, two of the founders of artificial intelligence, whose experiments had laid the foundations for modern machine reasoning. The school's history ran deep; XCON, the world's first commercial AI, had been born there, proof that ideas scribbled on whiteboards could one day run the world.

Anna came from another world entirely. She was a graduate of Carnegie Mellon's School of Drama, part of the College of Fine Arts, a stage designer who spoke the language of light and movement instead of math.

It was a blind date that brought them together, a friend's idea, poorly timed, on a night Max hadn't wanted to leave the lab. The only reason he'd said yes was a rumor that Ted Danson, one of CMU's most famous alumni (and Max's favorite actor from Cheers), would be in the audience for a student production. He never saw Danson that night. But when the house lights dimmed, and Anna stepped out to adjust a prop before the curtain, he realized he'd stopped thinking about the show altogether.

Those years forged him into more than an engineer; they made him a believer. Anna had insisted that technology should make people feel seen, not merely safe. He'd nodded, half-understanding then; he understood it fully only later, when she was gone. The picture on his shelf was proof of both promise and loss: a woman who had taught him to ask why, and a daughter whose small hand had once gripped his finger like an anchor.

He had never meant to enter government service. His early career was with private cybersecurity firms, where the money was good, but the stakes rarely mattered beyond shareholder confidence. It wasn't until the cyberattack on a regional hospital in Boston, patients left in darkness, ventilators frozen, staff helpless, that Max understood the battlefield was no longer overseas. The war had come home, and its front lines were written in code. That night, he'd volunteered for government duty.

Now, years later, Max was the lead operations officer at the National Infrastructure Protection Agency. To most, NIPA was an acronym buried inside the alphabet soup of Washington bureaucracy. To Max, it was the last firewall between order and chaos.

He dressed deliberately, dark slacks, a crisp shirt, and a tie knotted tight but not perfect. He liked imperfections. They reminded him he was still human. He poured his coffee into a battered Redskins thermos, slipped on his jacket, and paused at the doorway.

The lamp on his desk flickered once. Just a brief stutter of light, the kind most people would dismiss. But Max frowned. He had seen too many systems fail without warning ever to ignore small anomalies. He tapped the switch; the light steadied, humming innocently.

Outside, Georgetown's cobblestone streets glistened with early morning dew. A car rolled past, tires hissing softly on wet stone. A jogger passed, earbuds in, oblivious to the world. Across the street, an elderly neighbor wrestled with a stubborn smart-meter display, shaking her head as the digits blinked nonsense before returning to normal. Max offered her a polite wave, but the sight tightened something in his chest.

The city looked serene, but to him, the calm was an illusion. Somewhere beneath it, wires carried signals, grids pulsed with power, and hidden inside them… shadows could stir.

Max locked the door behind him. To the neighbors, he was just another government analyst with long hours. They would never know the truth: that every morning he left his brownstone, he stepped into a battlefield invisible to those around him.

Hours later, he sat alone in the heart of the National Infrastructure Protection Agency, the command center known to its occupants simply as "The Vault." The Vault still bore the bones of its Cold War past. Reinforced concrete walls ran twenty feet thick, ribbed with steel that had once been meant to withstand nuclear fire. A pair of steel blast doors, each weighing more than a tank, guarded the entrance, their hinges groaning like leviathans when they opened. Down here, five stories below the Capitol's sidewalks, the air was cooler, drier, scrubbed endlessly by filtration systems older than most of the analysts who worked within its walls.

But the Cold War shell had been hollowed out and re-forged for a new age of conflict. Where once there had been bunks and rations, now rows of servers exhaled heat, answered in turn by the cold breath of the cooling ducts above. Fluorescent light had given way to the dim electric glow of monitors, each one alive with streams of data. The ceiling bristled with ducts and cables, fiber-optic veins carrying information in and out like arteries feeding a heart.

Time itself seemed suspended in The Vault. There were no windows, no clocks visible, only the constant hum of machines and the glow of shifting screens. The air smelled faintly metallic, like warmed circuitry and recycled oxygen. To the uninitiated, it felt claustrophobic, almost oppressive. To Max, it felt like stepping into a cathedral's sacred place where silence and vigilance were a kind of prayer.

On one wall stretched a massive screen, a living map of America's infrastructure. Cities pulsed with white nodes, highways traced in faint gold, power grids sparking in shifting lattices of green and blue. Every flicker was a heartbeat. Every anomaly… a skipped pulse.

The analysts were its monks. Young, pale, and sleepless, they bent over their consoles with a devotion that bordered on the religious. Some tracked fluctuations in power transmission across the Midwest. Others monitored packet streams emanating from the Balkans. On a single workstation, a red blip had appeared off the coast of California, a fishing trawler broadcasting signals far beyond its capabilities. Nothing escaped The Vault's gaze.

Nearby, a slim placard noted the late-shift duty roster, with Deputy Director Sam Rourke's name in small type listed as the man covering the night-watch rotation. This quiet presence kept the floor steady when the director had to be elsewhere.

Rourke had come from the field, not the lecture hall. A veteran of military cyber operations, he carried the quiet weight of someone who'd seen real systems burn and men die when the code went wrong. Years ago, a convoy signal he was tracing had been hijacked, triggering an IED that shattered both the road and his leg. He'd finished the mission from the ground, patched the breach, and only then allowed the medevac team to take him out.

The limp never fully left him, but neither did the discipline. Where Max worked in layers of strategy and risk calculus, Rourke grounded the operation in action and instinct. He ran the floor like a battlefield, calm, precise, efficient, the kind of presence that turned panic into procedure.

Max often said that if The Vault had a pulse, Sam was its heartbeat.

For the briefest moment, one of the wall screens stuttered, a flicker so quick no one else seemed to notice. But Max did. He froze, the image of his lamp at home flashing unbidden through his mind. Then the display steadied, data streams flowing as if nothing had happened.

Max leaned forward in his ergonomic chair, eyes scanning the complex visualizations of the nation's energy grid. Among the billions of data points streaming in real-time, something was off. It wasn't a loud alarm or flashing red light, no, it was subtler than that. A minuscule deviation in voltage regulation at a substation in the Midwest. Just a fraction of a percentage point outside expected parameters. Too small to trigger automated alerts, but significant enough to make Max pause briefly. At first, it was a whisper in the code, anomalous packets trickling across the grid, fragments that didn't quite belong. The signatures were wrong, the sequences too deliberate, like someone breathing under a locked door. Max leaned forward, fingers flying across the keyboard, isolating the data stream before it could vanish.

And then it was gone. Clean, efficient, erased without a trace.

He stared at the empty screen, pulse quickening. He had seen this before, not this code, but the silence it left behind.

A memory surfaced unbidden, sharp as broken glass. The hospital hack.

He was younger then, still with the private firm, when his phone had buzzed at 2:00 a.m. A friend from MIT, now an IT admin for a Boston hospital, was on the line, voice strangled with panic. "The system's frozen. Ventilators. Monitors. We're blind, Max. People are going to die."

Max remembered racing through the ER doors, the smell of antiseptic and fear in the air. Nurses shouting. A doctor pounding his fist against a darkened monitor. A child gasping for breath while her ventilator lay dormant, screen lifeless. He had dropped to the floor, laptop open, fingers clawing through foreign code until sweat ran into his eyes. Every second had felt like a lifetime. Every keystroke… a fight against an unseen executioner.

When the systems finally came back online, too much damage had already been done. Two patients had died in silence. He never forgot the sound of the mother's scream as a nurse covered her child with a sheet.

That night, Max swore he would never again let a phantom in the machine go unanswered.

The flash of memory dissolved, leaving him once more in the humming blue glow of The Vault. His hands hovered over the keys, knuckles white.

The anomaly had slipped away, but the taste of it lingered. It wasn't random. It wasn't a glitch. Someone had been there. Watching. Testing.

He pulled the secure tablet from the shallow drawer at his station, an approved conduit for family messages, scrubbed and delayed, keeping the workday uncompromised. A notification glowed: 1 new message — Emily.

He hesitated, then tapped play.

Emily's voice came through, smaller than memory allowed and edged with the brittle calm of a child used to disappointment. "Hi, Dad. Got your package. Thanks for the little flash-drive charm, it's in my backpack now. Science fair tomorrow. Don't worry, I'll be fine. Mom says hi." A breath. "Are you still working on that big project? You said you'd try to call…" Thirty seconds of a life he could not reach. Max watched the waveform oscillate, thumb hovering over Reply, a button that would not illuminate on a classified line. He closed his eyes for a heartbeat and imagined the charm catching the sun on her way to school.

The main display flickered. Lines of code scrolled where no code should be.

PHANTOM: AWAKE.

Max's pulse kicked. He reached for the comm panel. "Rourke, on deck. Now."

Within seconds, Sam appeared in the doorway, the faint limp from his old field injury barely visible beneath the briskness of movement.

"Talk to me," Sam said.

Max pointed to the frozen lines on the screen. "Signature just tripped in the Midwest grid. Not noise, a pattern."

Sam leaned in, scanning the feed. "That's structured. Someone's inside."

"Or something," Max murmured.

Sam straightened. "I'll lock the floor and alert Carter's team. You keep an eye on it."

Max nodded, already typing. "If it's real, this is where it begins."

Max set the tablet down and rose. Work hadn't been waiting; it had arrived.

Max exhaled slowly, forcing himself to steady. He knew better than anyone what silence in the system could mean.

And this silence was screaming.

He pulled up the raw logs from the affected system and overlaid them with recent firmware updates that had been pushed to that substation. His fingers danced over the keyboard as he filtered the data. That's when he saw it, an anomaly buried deep within a firmware update issued three months prior.

The code itself was a masterclass in stealth. At first glance, it appeared to be routine diagnostic routines, legitimate subroutines signed with a trusted vendor certificate. But something was amiss. The checksum failed under closer scrutiny. Hidden inside was a subroutine that didn't belong, a sleeper payload lying dormant, waiting for a signal or timer to awaken.

Max's pulse quickened. This was no ordinary software bug or malfunction. This was deliberate. Malicious.

Adrian Holt, the agency's embedded systems engineer, scrolled through the packet logs. "This sequence looks familiar… but I can't place it."

Special Agent Maya Carter tensed but said nothing. A tall woman with a sharp gaze and an unshakable calm, she was the agency's lead investigator on insider threats. The shifting pattern on the screen reminded her of Kane's field reports, though she'd never admit it aloud.

"Tara," Max called out softly.

Almost instantly, Tara Lin appeared at his side, cradling two cups of black coffee. She was the agency's lead malware analyst, known for her razor-sharp intellect and calm under pressure. Dark hair pulled back in a tight bun, eyes bright with determination.

Tara's path to the Vault had been anything but conventional. A Stanford prodigy, she had published papers on reverse-engineering malware while still an undergraduate, work that drew quiet attention from both industry and government researchers. Instead of heading straight into the workforce, she entered MIT's elite cybersecurity program, earning a master's in applied cryptography and then a PhD focused on large-scale intrusion-detection systems. Her dissertation became required reading inside a handful of three-letter agencies. After MIT, she joined a boutique cybersecurity firm, where she dismantled a sprawling ransomware network that had confounded much larger agencies, establishing her as a rising star. The government noticed quickly, and within a year, she'd been recruited to NIPA. She thrived in high-stakes environments, blending technical mastery with an instinct for reading the intentions behind code, skills that made her as much a strategist as a technician.

Beneath her calm exterior, Tara carried a personal motivation few saw. Her younger brother had once fallen victim to an identity theft ring, his life upended, his future derailed, and she'd vowed to make sure no one else suffered through attacks she could prevent. *It was an event that had quietly shaped the trajectory of her life, turning curiosity into resolve and talent into purpose.*

It started years earlier, on a damp Saturday evening in Palo Alto. She'd come home from Stanford for a short visit, expecting nothing more dramatic than her mother's cooking and her brother sprawled on the couch with video games. Instead, she walked into a storm.

Her mother was at the kitchen table, voice sharp with panic, a stack of envelopes fanned out like accusations. Credit card statements. Collection notices. Her younger brother sat across from her, pale and silent, hands buried in his hair.

"These aren't mine," he said for the tenth time. His voice cracked under the weight of disbelief. "I never opened these accounts."

The words sounded like excuses, but Tara saw the fear in his eyes. Sixteen years old, honors student, a kid with a scholarship dream, and now, on paper, a thief.

She picked up one of the letters. The balance was obscene: thousands of dollars in electronics, airfare, and even medical equipment. Her brother hadn't bought any of it. Someone else had used his name, his Social Security number, his future.

The days that followed blurred into a nightmare of hold music and stone walls. Their mother spent hours on the phone with banks and agencies, each call ending the same way: "We're sorry, but liability rests with the account holder." No one wanted to hear that the account holder was a high school kid who didn't even have a driver's license yet.

The damage spread like a virus. A scholarship committee flagged his application for "financial irregularities." Their father's insurance premiums spiked. Her brother stopped going out with friends, ashamed to answer questions about the stacks of mail piling at their door.

Late one night, Tara found him in the garage, hurling unopened envelopes into the trash. His voice was low, raw. "They stole me, Tara. Not just the money, me. I don't exist anymore."

She didn't know what to say. But when he slammed the door behind him, she opened her laptop.

The glow of the screen lit the dark as she pulled credit reports, combed public records, chased numbers through digital corridors most people never saw. Names repeated across states. Addresses recycled, like worn-out aliases. Whoever had taken her brother's identity wasn't some petty thief. It was a network, efficient and invisible, draining futures one name at a time.

She couldn't stop it. Not then. Every lead dead-ended into shadows, every phone call into indifference. By the time the accounts were finally marked "fraudulent," the damage was done. Her brother's record was scarred. The scholarship was gone. The future he'd imagined, engineering school, internships, all of it, cracked apart.

Tara never forgot the look in his eyes: not anger, not even fear, but helplessness. The sense that a machine bigger than him had chewed up his name and spit it out, and there was nothing he could do.

That night, she made herself a promise. If the world were run by invisible code and faceless networks, she would learn to hunt in the dark. She would spend her life dragging shadows into the light.

That quiet fire drove her through nights of unending analysis and relentless debugging.

• • • • • • •

"That's the fifth one this week," she said, setting a cup next to Max. "Hidden in updates across multiple utilities. Transformers, SCADA controllers, Supervisory Control and Data Acquisition (the industrial computers that run motors, valves, sensors, chemical dosing, water treatment pumps)..."

Max swirled his coffee absently, mind racing. "Sleeper code," he muttered.

Tara nodded. "Code that lies in wait, triggered by a specific event, a command, a timestamp, even a power fluctuation. Once activated, it can disable critical systems or cause cascading failures."

Max's eyes darted back to the screen. "How widespread?" "Preliminary count puts it at around twelve thousand devices across the Midwest alone," she replied grimly. "But it's likely more. Some of the devices are in hard-to-reach or poorly monitored facilities."

Her mind flashed to her brother's struggles, a reminder of why every vulnerable system mattered.

The reality settled over them like a cold fog. The adversary wasn't just probing defenses. They'd embedded themselves, patiently waiting.

Max stood and stretched, feeling the familiar tension of responsibility settle heavily on his shoulders. "Find the source. I want every vendor, engineer, and system that received those updates traced back. We need to understand the supply chain compromise." Tara tapped furiously at her keyboard, dispatching orders to analysts. "Already on it. Our teams are reverse-engineering the firmware and cross-referencing access logs."

Max's gaze moved to the giant wall screen, which projected a real-time map of infrastructure across the country. Red dots blinked faintly across the Midwest, slowly spreading toward the Gulf Coast and beyond. "Put out a silent alert. No press releases yet. We can't spook the attackers or cause public panic."

Tara's brow furrowed. "So we pretend to be asleep."

Max nodded. "They think we're blind. But we're watching." The soft ring of Max's secure phone shattered the moment.

He answered instantly. "Shaw."

"Director Pike here," came the rough voice. "We're seeing irregularities in the Mississippi River lock control systems. Matches the pattern you flagged yesterday."

Max's heart sank. The Mississippi locks were vital for transporting agricultural and industrial goods. A disruption here would ripple through the economy like a shockwave.

"I'm escalating this to Tier One threat status," Max said. "Coordinate with the Army Corps and Coast Guard. We need boots on the ground and cyber teams monitoring all access points." There was a pause, followed by the faint clink of Pike setting something down on his desk. When he spoke, his voice carried the gravel of irritation.

"Shaw, the nation doesn't grind to a halt because some light bulbs flickered in Peoria. If we jump at shadows, we'll paralyze half the grid ourselves. Bring me proof, not gut feelings."

Max's jaw tightened. "This is proof. And if we wait, it won't be shadows, it'll be smoke."

Pike exhaled slowly, then his voice hardened. "If this is what we fear, it's no longer reconnaissance. They're preparing."

The line went dead, leaving only the hum of the servers. Max stared at the map, deep in thought, the city's lifelines glowing faintly across the screen.

"You heard that?" he asked without turning.

From the shadows beyond the workstation, Sam stepped forward, coffee in one hand, cane tucked under the other arm.

"Hard not to," he said quietly. "You telling me Pike still thinks you're chasing ghosts?"

Pike had come up through the Navy's cyber-operations wing before his rise to the Director's chair, the kind of man who'd traded field terminals for briefing rooms but never forgot the sound of an ops floor under pressure. Rourke knew him from those days. Different theaters, same war. They'd spoken the same language once, checksum failures, packet bleed, command latency, and the memory of that shorthand still carried between them. Beneath the bureaucracy, there was respect: two men who had served under the same flag, and who both understood what it meant to lose people to silence on a line.

"He wants proof. I've got patterns, fragments, nothing that fits in a slide deck."

Sam took a sip of coffee and studied the display. "You're looking at intent, not evidence. That's always been the blind spot upstairs."

Max exhaled slowly. "If I push this, I risk burning trust. If I wait, we could lose days."

"You already know the answer," Sam said. "Do the work like you always do, gather your proof while you prepare for the worst. Don't bet the country on a committee's permission."

Max gave a faint smile. "You make it sound simple." Sam said, "It is. You just don't get thanked for being right."

The quiet hung between them for a beat, the kind of silence forged in battlefields both digital and real. Then Max turned back to his console. "Then we move. Silent containment, no press. If they're watching, we pretend to sleep."

Sam nodded once. "I'll lock down the night watch and start redundancy sweeps. You keep your eyes on the code."

Max almost said thank you, but didn't need to; Rourke already knew.

Max began typing furiously, creating a new case file labeled simply **SLEEPER**.

Day 1: T-30. The Hunt Begins.

Max stood and moved toward the panoramic display that simulated a window. The Vault sat five floors beneath the surface, but the system projected a live feed of the Washington, D.C. skyline. It was late afternoon aboveground, the city strangely calm, almost indifferent to the invisible storm brewing below. On the surface, life went on: traffic lights blinked, people rushed home, and the sun cast long shadows over monuments to past wars. But Max knew better. This war wasn't fought on battle-fields, but in code and current, where every pulse of electricity could draw blood.

He turned back to the screens. The more he stared, the more he realized how fragile the digital heartbeat of the nation had become. Critical infrastructure systems were no longer isolated mechanical behemoths but deeply interconnected cyber-physical networks. Each sensor, relay, and controller was a node vulnerable to infiltration. A single breach could cascade into chaos.

He remembered how quickly past attacks had spiraled, Stuxnet rewriting centrifuge logic in Iran, NotPetya jumping borders in hours, the Colonial Pipeline hack leaving gas stations empty. Those were supposed to be wake-up calls, proof that code could cripple the physical world. But people had treated them as anomalies, accidents, distant storms. Now, staring at the map of his own country lit with red nodes, Max knew they were only rehearsals.

Max rubbed the back of his neck. The sleeper code was a perfect weapon, quiet, patient, and invisible until triggered. The attackers had leveraged the system's complexity, trust in software supply chains, and human complacency.

He recalled a briefing from months ago, a simulated attack in which a rogue firmware update had taken down a major city's power grid. Back then, it was theoretical. Now, it was real.

His thoughts were interrupted by Tara, who had returned with a tablet showing her latest findings. "Max, we've got partial attribution."

He raised an eyebrow. "Go on."

"We're tracing parts of the embedded code back to a known toolkit associated with Phantom Chimera."

Max tightened his jaw again. Phantom Chimera was a cyber espionage group believed to be sponsored by a foreign government in East Asia. Their reputation for stealth and sophistication was unmatched.

"They've evolved," Tara continued. "The toolkit has been modified with custom payloads, and the infrastructure compromises span multiple states and sectors. This is coordinated."

Max took a long sip of his now lukewarm coffee. "Which sectors?"

"Power grids, water treatment, transportation control systems, and even some financial transaction networks."

He nodded slowly, feeling the weight of the news. "This isn't just an attack on systems, it's an attack on the fabric of society." The command center doors hissed open, and Adrian strode in, carrying a small circuit board carefully wrapped in anti-static packaging.

"Found something interesting," Adrian said, placing it on the table between them.

Max peered over. "What am I looking at?"

Adrian pulled out a magnifying glass and held it over the chip. "This is a bootloader chip from one of the compromised SCADA controllers. It's tampered with at the hardware level, designed to bypass firmware integrity checks."

Tara's eyes widened. "Supply chain attack?"

"Exactly," Adrian said. "The chip was manufactured at a subcontractor fab that mysteriously shut down two years ago. Whoever did this embedded the backdoor during production, before the devices even left the factory."

Max sat down heavily. "So, this has been in the wild for years, waiting."

"Years," Adrian confirmed. "And now, with the sleeper code, they can activate everything in unison."

Max stared at the map again, now dotted with new red flags. The scope was staggering: thousands of vulnerable devices nationwide, any one of which could spark a chain reaction.

He tapped his secure phone. "Get me a line to the National Security Advisor. This is going to the top."

Minutes later, Max was on a video call with senior government officials. The room was tense, the air thick with urgency. He laid out the findings: the sleeper code, the supply chain breaches, and the suspected involvement of the Phantom Chimera.

The National Security Advisor leaned forward. "What's their endgame?"

Max looked around the virtual table, meeting each gaze in turn. "Disrupt the critical infrastructure, cause widespread chaos, and undermine public confidence. Possibly to weaken us ahead of a kinetic or political strike."

"Do we have a way to stop it?" the Secretary of Energy asked.

"We need to find the trigger, the master signal that activates the sleeper code. If we can locate and neutralize it, we buy time to patch and replace compromised devices."

The Secretary's brow furrowed. "Shaw, we have other priorities. If this is real, it's not the time to go rogue. Focus on monitoring and coordination. That's your job." Max clenched his teeth, feeling the weight of every second slip by. *They don't understand…and they won't, until it's too late.*

Maya leaned closer, voice pitched just above a whisper. "Kane warned us the bureaucracy would slow us down."

Tara's fingers tapped nervously on the edge of the tablet. "We can't just sit and wait," she muttered, voice low. Adrian leaned back in his chair, rubbing his temples, scanning the live telemetry as if it would confirm their frustration.

"But if they activate before we do," Tara said quietly, her voice taut with worry, "the damage could be catastrophic."

Max swallowed hard. "We're racing against an invisible clock."

He tapped the edge of his tablet, scanning telemetry and network nodes. Even under the watchful eyes of the officials, he began sketching contingencies in his mind, pre-positioning analysts, readying stealth monitoring, and noting which command nodes could be cut without formal clearance. Every delay in action sharpened the friction, but Max had never let bureaucracy dictate the speed of defense.

Back in the Vault, Max convened his core team. "We're initiating Operation Night Watch. Full-spectrum cyber reconnaissance, combined with physical audits of critical sites. We'll need cooperation from utilities, transportation agencies, and even private contractors."

Across the country, his hand-picked field captains were already in motion, the Regional Cyber Response Teams. He'd recruited each one himself during quieter years, a patchwork of engineers, intelligence officers, and network specialists scattered through the nation's infrastructure corridors. Los Angeles handled power distribution. Chicago ran water systems. Dallas watched transport logistics.

They were his eyes and hands in the field, his protégés.

When he issued an order from the Vault, he could picture each of their faces, the shorthand jokes in their encrypted channels.

He trusted them more than any committee in Washington. Tara brought up a live feed from one of their malware analysis rigs. "We're dissecting the sleeper code. It's sophisticated. It keeps changing its disguise so no security system can recognize it twice."

Adrian added, "And the hardware-level backdoors mean even wiped or replaced firmware might not be enough. We're looking at a systemic vulnerability."

Max clenched his fists. "Then we hit them where it hurts, the command-and-control infrastructure. If we can find the servers or proxies that send the activation signals, we can sever the head of the snake."

Hours blurred into the night as the team worked without pause. Max had barely left the Vault since the crisis began, surviving on caffeine and grim determination. Every new piece of intelligence felt like a double-edged sword, clues leading to dead ends, false positives, or worse, fresh infections.

At one point, Max found himself alone in the dim glow of the command center, staring at a map of the country speckled with red blips. It felt like hunting shadows in the dark.

The room was silent except for the soft pulse of network maps shifting across the wall displays. Max leaned forward, elbows on the console, the glow tracing hard lines across his face. For a long moment, he just listened to the machines, to the breath of systems holding together by faith and habit.

The door slid open with a muted hiss. Sam stepped in, carrying the quiet with him. "You've been staring at that screen like it owes you an answer," he said.

Max didn't look up. "Maybe it does."

Sam came closer, scanning the projection. "You're running twenty threads at once. That's not focus, that's penance."

A faint, humorless smile tugged at Max's mouth. "You sound like a therapist."

"Just someone who's watched too many people drown in good intentions."

The words landed softly, neither challenge nor comfort, just truth.

Max straightened, fingers brushing the edge of the console. "Then let's make sure we don't add to the list."

Sam nodded once and moved to another terminal. The hum of the Vault resumed, steady, alive, waiting.

Outside, the nation continued its unaware rhythm, teetering on the brink.

Inside, Max and his team were the last line of defense, fighting ghosts in the machine and shadows in the code for the fragile heart of their country.

Max sat back down at his console, the gravity of the situation settling over him like a suffocating fog. The digital battlefield had shifted from isolated skirmishes to a full-scale infiltration, an unseen enemy quietly entrenched within the nation's infrastructure, waiting for the perfect moment to strike.

The command center was unusually quiet except for the soft chatter of analysts cross-referencing data points and Tara's low voice explaining the latest findings. Max's fingers hovered above his keyboard, reluctant to break the silence as if his next command could trigger a cascade of consequences.

"Max," Tara said, glancing up from her screen, "I'm seeing irregular packet transmissions from some infected devices. They're communicating in short bursts to an unknown IP range."

Max's eyes sharpened. "Could that be the trigger channel?"

"Possibly," Tara replied. "But they're using advanced encryption and proxy routing. Tracing it will be like chasing shadows through a hall of mirrors."

Adrian, leaning over a nearby workstation, chimed in. "And some of the hardware anomalies mean that traditional forensics won't catch everything. We're dealing with a hybrid cyber-physical threat, software and hardware working in tandem."

His eyes lingered on the circuit diagram a moment too long. Kabul came back to him, the cracked desert, the lifeless radio in his hands, the patrol that never made it back. He shoved the memory down. He couldn't let the team see the ghosts riding his shoulders, not now. Not when silence in the wires could mean another ambush, only on a national scale.

Max nodded grimly. "Time for a different approach. Let's bring in our counterintelligence unit. If this is state-sponsored, there may be human assets or insider threats involved."

The door hissed open, and Maya stepped in, her calm masking the tension in her shoulders. She didn't waste words.

"Got your message, Max," she said, settling into an empty chair. "We've been monitoring suspicious activity on contractor communications and travel logs. A handful of individuals accessed sensitive firmware code around the same time updates were deployed."

Max sighed. "We suspected the supply chain had been compromised. Can you pinpoint potential insiders?"

Maya pulled up a dossier on her tablet. "We have three persons of interest, engineers and software testers with unexplained overseas contacts."

Maya noted their names, but her mind snagged on the thought of her own walls turning hostile. The dossiers felt abstract, like warnings she couldn't quite grasp. For her, this wasn't just about suspects in a file; it was about knowing the enemy could already be inside.

Past attacks had always exploited multiple paths: poisoned updates, careless clicks, trusted hands on the inside. Stuxnet had wormed through USB drives and network shares; NotPetya had leveraged compromised patches and unpatched vulnerabilities. Phantom was no different, only faster, smarter, and already learning from every defense they threw at it.

Tara leaned in. "If we can identify compromised devices associated with those individuals, we might be able to correlate the timeline of the sleeper code implantation."

Max rubbed his temples. "We're threading a needle in a hurricane. Every hour counts."

He stood and paced, the weight of leadership pressing down on him. The stakes were staggering, a silent cyber weapon capable of plunging cities into darkness, halting water supplies, or derailing transportation.

The thought of innocent lives caught in the crossfire hardened his resolve.

Tara's eyes lingered on the code flowing across her monitor. Every line, every anomaly, reminded her of her brother's bank account being wiped years ago. She had vowed back then that she would never feel powerless again, and now, with the stakes far higher, the determination was the same.

Later that night, Max found himself alone in the Vault's observation room, watching the sleeping city through a network of live-feed cameras. The monuments were silent sentinels under the stars, unaware of the unseen war unfolding beneath their feet.

His phone buzzed. A secure message from Tara: "New firmware dump analysis. Sleeper code variant detected with modified activation parameters. Some devices show just under two weeks remaining, while others stretch closer to eighteen days. They've staggered the timers deliberately."

Max exhaled slowly. The countdown was tightening.

Max tapped a quick reply: "I will be leaving for the White House in 15 minutes to brief the President."

He set the tablet down on the secure console, double-checked the telemetry, and ensured his notes were organized, with every high-priority node and every anomalous signal accounted for. Tara and Adrian would stay behind in the Vault, running analysis and monitoring the Hydra in real time.

Before heading out, Max paused in front of the mirror in the Vault's small prep area. He combed his hair, wiped a trace of dust from his jacket, and adjusted his tie. Even under the pressure of imminent cyberwar, appearances mattered. A deep breath, one final check of the tablet, and he was ready.

Minutes later, Max was escorted into the Situation Room, where a meeting was already in progress. The President sat at the head of the table, flanked by the National Security Advisor, the Secretaries of Homeland Security and Energy, the Directors of National Intelligence, the FBI, and the Cybersecurity and Infrastructure Security Agency (CISA). The White House Chief of Staff glanced toward the President. "Mr. President, with your permission, we'll move to our next agenda item, the cyber incident under investigation." The President nodded. "Good. Good morning, Mr. Shaw."

Max inclined his head in acknowledgment. He had briefed this President before, enough times for everyone in the room to know that when Shaw appeared at a national security briefing, bad things were happening. The air carried the faint scent of polished wood and recycled ventilation.

"Mr. President," Max began, tapping the screen. Red clusters blinked across the digital map: servers, routers, and control, nodes tied to sleeper code activity. "This is the current status of the threat. If we act now, we can sever the command node before propagation and contain the threat before it reaches civilian networks."

The President's gaze sharpened. "And the risks?"

As per habit, Max hardened his expression. "The network is adaptive. Even a delay of hours increases the risk of uncontrolled activation. We've run simulations; if the Hydra goes live, it could simultaneously impact energy, water, transportation, and communications infrastructure."

The National Security Advisor interjected. "Director Shaw… any preemptive strike carries enormous political and public fallout. You'll have clearance for monitoring, contingency planning, and interagency coordination. Nothing beyond that."

Max let the tension sit for a moment, weighing the lives at stake against the restrictions imposed. "Understood," he said finally.

Back in The Vault, the team regrouped, poring over mission logs. A monitored probe of a control node had failed. Telemetry showed corrupted packets, a node had gone completely dark, and a small alert triggered in the wrong sector. Each failure was minor, but together they stung.

Tara hovered nearby, scanning the logs. "It's not catastrophic," she said cautiously, "but we lost critical evidence, and the alert spooked monitoring."

Max's fingers brushed the tablet. "Minor now… but they'll remember this when the stakes are bigger." His gaze sharpened. "Let them say no. One day, the choice will be theirs, and I'll make sure they regret this hesitation."

Max stood and stretched, forcing himself to move past the frustration. The team needed him focused, not simmering. He returned to the monitors, planning the next steps. Somewhere in the noise of failed packets, corrupted logs, and flickering alerts, a pattern waited, one he'd uncover, no matter the obstacles.

Max began, "We've confirmed multiple sleeper variants, each tailored to specific device classes. Transformers, rail control systems, water pumps, all set to activate in a synchronized strike." Adrian pointed to the screen. "The attackers planned this meticulously. The variants communicate through covert channels, adjusting activation based on system feedback to maximize impact."

Tara added, "And we've identified code patterns consistent with Phantom Chimera's signature, but also elements never seen before, custom modules likely developed with inside knowledge."

Her personal drive made her press harder, refusing to let these hidden threats go unanswered.

Max leaned in. "Which brings us back to the insiders. Maya, we need everything on those suspects, travel, communication, and financials."

Maya nodded grimly. "Working on it."

As the team strategized, Max's mind flashed back to his early days as a cybersecurity analyst, the idealism, the confidence that technology was a shield as well as a sword. Now, he understood the fragile truth: technology was also a weapon forged by those willing to exploit it.

His phone rang. The secure line. Max answered.

"Director Pike," came the voice. "We've got movement. The National Security Advisor wants a full briefing ASAP."

Max stood, swallowing the lump in his throat. "Understood. Let's get to work."

CHAPTER 2
IMPLANT

Day 2: T-29. Infiltration Detected in the Grid.

Three floors above the Vault, in a secure annex of the Department of Homeland Security's cyber division, the sterile hum of fluorescent lights mixed with the faint crackle of soldering irons and the rhythmic tapping of keyboards. The acrid scent of burned flux hung in the air, a ghost of plastic and metal. The lab was a sanctuary for some of the agency's most brilliant minds, malware analysts, embedded systems engineers, and firmware specialists, all working in concert to unravel the growing web of sleeper code infiltrations.

Tara sat hunched over a disassembled power controller unit, her brow furrowed in concentration. The device, about the size of a shoebox, was a marvel of modern engineering, a complex mesh of microcontrollers, memory chips, sensors, and communication modules designed to regulate voltage and current flow with surgical precision. It controlled vital transformers in the Midwest power grid, one of the regions now flagged with suspicious activity.

She had one leg tucked beneath her chair, a flash of mismatched socks peeking out, neon stripes on one foot, faded polka dots on the other. Nobody in the Vault commented anymore. Tara's socks had become as much a fixture here as the solder burns on the benches, small proof that even in the middle of a national crisis, she carried her own rhythm.

Her slender fingers traced a copper pathway beneath a chip, eyes scanning for irregularities. "Adrian, take a look at this," Tara called softly.

Adrian peered over her shoulder. "What am I looking at?"

Tara tapped the magnifying glass against the chip. *"Offsets are shifted. Four bits out of range."*

Adrian studied the board. "That's deeper than normal code," he said. "Someone altered the startup layer, the code that runs before anything else. It decides what to trust, so if it's wrong, every update that follows is fooled."

Tara's mouth tightened. "In plain English: the guard at the gate was replaced. We can't just change the paint."

He gave a low whistle. "That's unusual. It means the manufacturer, or someone with hardware-level access, wrote custom code to bypass standard protections."

"Exactly. Whoever did this designed the chip to hide critical code segments in parts of memory that are normally off-limits. It's like a digital safe hidden in plain sight."

Tara brought up the device's firmware dump on her workstation. Streams of hexadecimal code filled the screen, interspersed with assembly instructions and cryptographic signatures.

"This is next-level stealth," she muttered. "They buried the routine under shifting encryption. Each time it's checked, the code changes shape just enough that our scanners don't recognize it."

Adrian's eyes widened. "Military-grade obfuscation. This isn't something a typical hacker could pull off. This requires state-level resources and expertise."

Tara's expression hardened. "Which means we're dealing with a highly sophisticated adversary, someone who's spent years preparing this."

For a moment, Tara's mind slipped back to her senior year at MIT, when a ransomware gang had hijacked her dorm network. The common room had turned into a battlefield, laptops glowing like foxholes, cables snaking under doors, the air thick with pizza grease and burnt circuitry. On every screen, the same message blinked: **Your files have been encrypted.** Countdown clocks pulsed like bombs. Professors were on the phone with IT, students sobbing over lost theses, and a nearby hospital's cancer-trial database teetered on the brink.

She had locked herself in the dorm's cramped network closet, knees drawn to her chest, fingers cramping on the keys as she traced packet flows by hand. Hours bled into nights. Empty Red Bull cans littered the floor; her own pulse felt like code scrolling past. Friends urged her to give up, but every second she hesitated, another patient might be missing treatment.

On the third dawn, she saw it, a malformed routine hidden in the obfuscation, a single weak seam. She wrote a counter-script from scratch, launched it, and held her breath as screens flickered. One by one, the ransom notes vanished, students' work returned, professors' research reappeared, and the hospital's data flickered back to life.

Relief came braided with guilt: a patient had already missed a critical round of therapy during the lockdown. Later that day, an email arrived, gratitude wrapped around desperation, thanking her for saving the data. She stared at it for a long time, eyes gritty with exhaustion, and understood she never wanted to waste her skills chasing Silicon Valley paychecks. She wanted to fight the shadows.

She remembered reading about earlier cyberattacks, WannaCry, NotPetya, the Colonial Pipeline breach, events that proved a single exploit could cascade into panic across nations. Her own crisis at MIT had felt smaller, but no less real.

It convinced her that cyberwar wasn't a theory anymore. It was already reshaping the world, one breach at a time.

Meanwhile, down the hall, Max was briefing senior officials in the Conference Room. The atmosphere was tense, the kind of silence that precedes bad news

The projector cast a sprawling map of the United States across the far wall, dotted with red and yellow markers showing confirmed and suspected infection sites. The Midwest bore the brunt, clusters of red glowing ominously across power grids, transportation hubs, water treatment plants, and financial transaction processors. The only other sound was the soft scrape of pens on notepads, as if the silence itself demanded tribute.

At the rear of the room, Sam stood with his arms folded, eyes scanning the analysts more than the slides. His calm presence steadied the younger staff; he never said much in meetings, just the occasional correction when a chart drifted from fact to fiction. But when he did, the room adjusted course.

The limp in his gait was barely noticeable now, though everyone in the Vault knew how he'd earned it, a convoy strike years earlier, when an IED detonated off a networked signal he was trying to trace. He'd finished the mission from a field tablet before the medevac even arrived. The story made the rounds not because he bragged about it, but because someone else had bragged about it.

Max caught his eye briefly; the unspoken nod between them was a habit born of long shifts and quiet trust.

Max pointed toward the Midwest cluster. "We have confirmed sleeper code implantation in multiple infrastructure sectors. These devices aren't malfunctioning yet; they're dormant. We believe activation is tied to a trigger mechanism that could be time-based or remotely controlled."

Maya's pen hovered over her notes, but her mind flicked back to her apartment. The silence there had started to feel like a presence, the walls listening. It hadn't felt like theory in that moment; it had felt like someone breathing in her ear.

A senior official from the Department of Energy raised her hand. "How are these malicious codes getting into our systems? Firmware updates are supposed to be vetted."

Max nodded. "SEI flagged this risk years ago, Sarvapelli's team at Carnegie Mellon documented how firmware signatures could be spoofed even with vendor certificates. We didn't listen." Max's gaze didn't waver. "The code is embedded in legitimate firmware updates signed with valid vendor certificates. Our supply chain has been compromised at multiple points. Some devices were infected during manufacturing; others through intercepted update processes."

Max's gaze swept the room. "We've seen what happens when warnings are ignored. A decade ago, Stuxnet taught the world that code could cripple nuclear centrifuges. NotPetya tore through corporations in hours, grinding global shipping to a halt. WannaCry locked hospitals out of their own machines. Those were alarms, and we treated them as isolated fires." he gestured to the map, clusters of red flaring across the Midwest, "This is a forest already seeded to burn."

Director Pike leaned forward, rolling an antacid across his tongue. "You keep talking about countdowns and forests, Shaw. I hear no clock, I see no flames. What I hear is you asking me to risk a trillion-dollar panic on the word of one anomaly. Do you understand what happens if I'm wrong?"

Max didn't flinch. "Do you understand what happens if I'm right?"

A chair creaked near the back of the room. Sam Rourke, silent until now, leaned forward on his cane.

"With respect, sir," he said, voice low but steady, "I was in the Vault when Shaw caught the anomaly. He didn't guess; he verified. Twice. You've got half this country's grid running code he's already flagged as compromised, and if he hadn't pulled the thread when he did, we'd still be staring at clean dashboards while the infection spread."

Pike stared tightly. "Deputy Director Rourke, are you implying we should act on instinct rather than evidence?"

"I'm saying instinct's what's left when the evidence hasn't caught up yet," Sam replied evenly. "And Shaw's instincts have saved more systems than any committee I've ever sat through." The room went still. Even the hum of the screens felt quieter.

Pike's lips quivered, the argument faltering before it fully formed. He glanced at Shaw, then back at Rourke. "Noted," he said finally. Sam eased back in his chair, the faint clink of his cane breaking the silence. "Good. Because next time the lights flicker, I'd rather be wrong for acting than right for waiting."

Max didn't speak, but their eyes met across the table, acknowledgment, trust, and the unspoken truth that this war wasn't going to be won by hesitation.

Adrian's voice cut through the silence. "You talk about cascading," he said quietly. "I've watched it. Ukraine, December 2015. We thought it was routine grid data until sections of the country went dark. Not a total blackout, just enough to make a point. Power stations hijacked, operators locked out of their own systems. It was fifty-three degrees that night, not a deep freeze, but cold enough to remind everyone how fragile comfort really is. Hospitals switched to backup, families lit candles in panel flats fifteen stories up. You don't forget the sound of a city half-awake and powerless."

The room was still. Even the monitors seemed to hum more softly, as if the memory had bled into the present.

Max leaned forward. "They've compromised the system's foundation, the startup code that wakes the machine and decides what's safe. Think of it like the guard at the front gate. If the guard's already been bribed, every visitor who follows gets waved through."

A FEMA liaison raised a hand. "So what you're saying is… every device is already infected?"

Max shook his head. "Not infected. Compromised. Imagine a house where the burglar installed the locks. The doors look fine, but he can walk in whenever he wants."

A representative from the National Security Agency interjected. "Our threat intelligence points to Phantom Chimera, a state-sponsored hacking group with ties to East Asia. They have a history of supply chain infiltrations and targeted infrastructure attacks."

"However," Max continued, "the code we're seeing is more advanced than anything previously recorded. It constantly rewrites itself to evade signature-based detection, deploys tailored routines for each device type, and embeds itself into firmware beneath the operating system. That lets it survive full software reinstalls, persist across reboots, and masquerade as legitimate hardware behavior, making it nearly invisible to conventional security tools."

The room fell into a hush.

"What's their ultimate objective?" asked the undersecretary of Homeland Security.

Max met their eyes. "Disruption. They intend to cripple civilian infrastructure, power, water, and transportation to cause widespread chaos. Possibly as preparation for a kinetic attack or political destabilization."

The weight of the threat settled over the officials like a dark cloud. The consequences were chilling to imagine: blackouts, chemical spills, halted rail lines, and emergency services overwhelmed.

After the briefing, Max returned to the lab to meet with Tara and Adrian. Tara handed Max a small flash drive containing the latest firmware dump from an Illinois power controller.

He inserted it into a secure, air-gapped terminal. Lines of assembly code scrolled across the screen, a tangled web of instructions and encrypted segments

"There's a countdown buried inside the firmware," Tara said. "It's a built-in clock, the kind that keeps time even when power is off. When it hits zero, the device triggers itself. Reinstalling the software won't stop it."

Adrian pointed to the screen. "We're seeing the same pattern in units from Louisiana, Colorado, and Texas, all ticking down together."

Max felt the knot in his stomach tighten. "A coordinated attack."

The implications were staggering. At the stroke of a digital clock, thousands of devices across critical sectors could simultaneously fail, plunging cities into darkness, halting transportation, contaminating water supplies, and disrupting communications.

"We need to find the trigger," Max said. "If we can locate the command-and-control servers or insiders sending the activation signals, we might stop this before it begins."

Tara nodded. "But the attackers are careful. The command signals are routed through multiple proxies, encrypted in layers." Adrian added, "And some of the buried controllers can rewrite the code even after we clean it. The infection lives in the parts, not just the files. We'll have to trace where the hardware itself came from."

Max rubbed his forehead. "We're dealing with a Hydra, cut off one head, two more appear."

Tara's voice went flat. "If there are active countdowns, the trigger's already been pulled. They seeded the timers when they pushed the firmware. They don't need to send a command; the clocks are already running on the devices themselves."

Adrian swallowed. "That means activation is autonomous. Even if we sever every C2 server tomorrow, those timers will keep marching."

The implications slammed into the room: at the stroke of a digital clock, thousands of devices across critical sectors could fail in lockstep, plunging cities into darkness, stopping trains, fouling water treatment, and confusing first responders.

"We need to find the seed, the lot numbers, the signing keys, the contract chains," Max said. "If we can identify how and when those timers were embedded, we might find the origin."

Tara nodded. "And we need to scramble mitigation now. If the clocks are local, we can't wait for a remote trigger; we must preempt the countdown or neutralize the timers in place.

Max's throat was dry. He pushed back from the terminal and keyed the secure channel, routing it to the vendor war-room, the CMU Software Engineering Institute liaison, Cyber Command, and the NSA supply-chain desk, every authority that could move parts, papers, or people in the next twelve hours.

"Listen up," he said when faces loaded in the grid. His voice was steady, the calm of command. "We have seeded timers in multiple firmware lots. They're local countdowns. Severing C2 will not stop them. We need manifests, production runs, lot IDs, and crate logs, now. Prioritize any parts shipped to the Midwest and Gulf Coast in the last eighteen months. We need a map of who touched those parts."

The vendor rep swallowed and read from a tablet. "We'll pull a lot and batch manifests. We'll freeze distribution for affected part numbers and flag serials for recall. We need your indicators to match hashes to physical parts."

"Do it," Max said. "Adrian, confirm hash-to-part mapping. Tara, work with SEI and the vendor to cross-check fabrication timestamps against embedded time derivations. Maya, get legal on emergency authority for recalls and field replacements. I want air-lift manifests ready within six hours for critical substations and water facilities."

On the Vault's side, Adrian began a rapid script-run, cross-referencing firmware hashes with vendor manifests and shipment logs. Lines of results blinked up almost at once, part numbers, solder batch codes, a subcontractor in Eastern Europe with repeated orders matching the suspect lot. Tara coordinated with SEI scientists on a call, walking them through the timer-derivation algorithm and asking whether the embedded clocks could be neutralized remotely or required physical replacement.

The SEI lead, a tired woman with the impatience of someone who'd seen failure before, spoke up. "If those timers use their own internal clocks, we can try to freeze them by feeding a controlled time signal, messy and partial, but it could stop some devices from reaching zero. It'll buy hours for replacement teams to swap hardware in the field."

Max agreed without hesitation. "Do it where you can. Prioritize hospitals, water treatment, and major transmission substations. Start recalls on the suspect lot numbers and prep clean replacements. Coordinate with Five Eyes on any foreign-fab leads. Someone seeded these in manufacture, find the chain."

The vendor rep's face hardened. "We'll open emergency lines to our fabs and freight partners. Expect our first manifests within three hours."

"Good." Max let a breath out that felt like permission, not relief. "I want boots and aircraft on standby. We're not just chasing code anymore, we're chasing components, contracts, and crates."

Outside the immediate urgency, the message rippled. Coalition partners queued logistics; the NSA's supply-chain desk began legal work to freeze shipments; SEI teams spun up parallel experiments to neutralize or mask embedded timers. In the Vault, the team moved like a single organism, code and consequence braided together: identify the seed, starve the clock, and replace the poisoned instrument before the countdown ended.

The lab lights flickered softly as Tara and Adrian returned to their workstations, the sterile hum of machines the only sound between them. Max lingered by the window of the secure briefing room, lost in the stillness, as the day slipped into shadow. The world outside remained oblivious to the digital war raging in the shadows.

Rourke appeared in the doorway, coffee in hand, the lines under his eyes softened by humor. "You look like hell, boss," he said quietly.

Max gave a tired smile. "Comes with the job."

"No, exhaustion comes with the job. Self-destruction's optional." Rourke's tone stayed even, almost gentle. "You've been up two days. Take twenty. I'll keep the floor steady till you're back."

Max rubbed his eyes, ready to argue, then saw the steady patience in Rourke's face. "You're not wrong," he admitted.

"Didn't think so." Rourke nodded toward the corner office.

"That couch of yours is practically government property. Use it."

"You been keeping inventory again?"

"Somebody has to. You crash for half an hour, eat something, and change your shirt. I'll wake you if the world ends."

Max hesitated, then finally nodded. "All right. But if Kansas twitches…"

"You'll be the first to know."

As Rourke turned back toward the main floor, Max headed for his office, a confined space lined with glowing monitors and paper stacks, the couch half-buried under mission binders and a spare jacket. He cleared a corner, sat down, and for the first time in days let the noise of the Vault fade to a low, steady hum. Time blurred. The hum of servers became rain against a distant window in his mind, steady, lulling. He must have slept, not long, but enough for the exhaustion to lose its edge.

A knock on the frame brought him back. Sam's voice was quiet but urgent. "Max. You'll want to see this."

Max rubbed his eyes, grabbed his jacket, and followed him back to the command floor.

At the workbench, Tara pulled up a detailed network diagram on her monitor, mapping the compromised devices and suspected command pathways.

"Look here," she said, pointing to a cluster of IP addresses masked behind layers of virtual private networks and encrypted tunnels.

"Those proxies route through multiple countries, Russia, Eastern Europe, Southeast Asia. It's a deliberate misdirection."

Adrian swiveled in his chair. "The attackers are covering their tracks well. But there's a pattern in the frequency of data bursts from infected devices, small windows where signals escape the noise."

Max joined them, fully awake now. "We need to isolate those windows and monitor them in real time. If we can capture the activation command, we might be able to decrypt it and understand how to neutralize the payload."

Tara frowned. "Easier said than done. The code mutates; every few seconds, it changes its encryption keys. It's designed to adapt, like a living organism."

Adrian added, "And with those buried hardware controllers, even rebuilding the firmware won't guarantee safety. The chips themselves can call home or inject malicious instructions during boot."

Max paced, the weight of years of experience pressing on him. "We're fighting ghosts, phantom code embedded in silicon and software, invisible until it's too late."

Suddenly, Tara's screen flashed. "Wait, I'm getting a signal! It's weak, but persistent."

She zoomed in on the network trace. "It's coming from a server farm in rural Kansas, a nondescript facility with multiple anonymous shell companies registered as owners."

Max's expressions deepened. "That could be our command node." Adrian tapped rapidly on his keyboard. "I'm cross-referencing the IP with known threat actor infrastructure."

Tara added, "If this is the master trigger point, we can launch a targeted cyber offensive to sever the command chain."

Max nodded. "Notify Cyber Command. We need to coordinate a strike with physical interdiction teams to raid the facility."

The clock was ticking.

The following morning, Max stood in a secure operations center surrounded by analysts and cyber operators. Screens displayed live feeds from the Kansas facility, including camera views of darkened server rooms, electronic lock status, and network traffic.

"Raid scheduled for 0300 hours," Max briefed the team.

"We'll sever the command node and extract any evidence of sleeper code control infrastructure."

Minutes before the raid, tension was palpable. Max thought of the thousands of lives that could be affected if the sleeper code activated. The adversary was clever, but so were they.

The Vault dimmed to night mode, wall screens alive with helmet-cam and drone feeds over Prairie Ridge Data Commons. Max braced at the center console. He wasn't in Kansas, but every breath felt tethered to the people about to cross that warehouse threshold. On screen, the building was unremarkable, corrugated steel, cooling fans spinning, chain-link fence rattling in the dark. To locals, it was a data farm. To Max, it was the heart of an infection. "Reconnaissance clear. No external emitters," the signal tech said. "SATCOM and RF radials mapped. Sweep holding."

Max nodded. The plan: deny external comms, isolate the site, make entry, preserve evidence. No escape routes for the code.

"Comm isolation in five," the EW operator breathed. Portable jammers snapped on. Phone trunks died at demarcation points. The facility's only live feed came through a hardened mesh link routed back to the Vault.

Perimeter teams rolled into blocking positions. Robots and breachers swept for pressure plates and tripwires, precautions against auto-wipe or booby-trap logic.

"Three minutes to breach," the field commander whispered, practiced and calm.

FBI tactical leaned on the service door, rifles up. Behind them: Cyber Command operators with hardened laptops, an NSA SIGINT crew with a portable array, two forensic techs with Faraday bags and write-blockers. Muscle to clear, operators to cut cords, forensics to capture volatile memory before anything touched the net.

"Go," Max said. The word traveled a continent in an encrypted pulse.

The feed jolted as breachers surged. Hinges screamed; flashlights cut sterile aisles; commands bounced off concrete. Server towers rose in rows, green LEDs blinking like patient eyes.

"Room secure," the commander called. "No hostilities. Initiate comms kill; boot isolation now. Forensics stage at entry. Watch for self-destructs, do not power cycle without a snapshot."

On Max's console, technicians mirrored the checks: memory dumps, controlled mounts, checksum verifications. The machines were dark, but the threat lived in silicon logic that could try to burn itself the moment a hand reached a port. They moved slowly and precisely, hunting ghosts without letting the ghosts know they were hunted.

"Bring up the racks," Adrian cut in from his console. He was leaning so close to the feed that his glasses reflected the servers like twin mirrors. "Panel three, left row, pull it, slow. Watch the jumpers." His voice was calm, precise, the voice of a surgeon guiding a hand in the dark.

The cyber operators obeyed, opening the rack like a priest at an altar. Forensic techs rushed in behind, slipping evidence bags over drives, sealing ports in foil, each step done in silence as if noise itself could wake the sleeper code.

Then the screen stuttered.

"Feed just cut," Tara hissed. Her fingers flew across the keyboard. "Localized jammer. Ten seconds."

Max's chest tightened. He heard his own breath in the headset, too loud, too human. On the screen: static.

Adrian snapped into the silence. "Stay on the panel. Don't move. Wait it out."

The seconds dragged like years. Then, the feed flickered back. The jammer was gone. Operators froze in place, the panel still half-open, their gloves trembling just slightly.

"Finish it," Adrian said.

One of the cyber techs slid a connector home. A burst of code appeared across Tara's screen in the Vault, packet streams unraveling like silk threads. "Got it," she whispered. "Beacon captured. We're inside."

Maya, perched at her own terminal, scribbled notes into the case file, her other hand already signaling to FBI liaisons that local suspects could be detained. Her face betrayed nothing, but Max knew her pulse had to be racing as fast as his.

He leaned closer to the console, voice low and even. "Tag everything. Bag everything. Nobody touches raw hardware without a cage. Move now."

On-screen, the operators worked with swift efficiency, disassembling racks and tagging evidence with barcodes that traced every screw back to the chain of custody. The tactical team guarded the perimeter, their silhouettes stark in the dim green of night-vision lenses.

The raid was swift and precise. Federal agents stormed the facility, securing hardware, capturing servers, and detaining on-site technicians with suspicious ties.

And in the Vault, Max finally exhaled. He knew this wasn't the end, only one head of a hydra severed. But for the first time in days, they had seized something tangible. Proof.

He straightened, his eyes never leaving the screen. "Bring it home," he said.

Tara's console chimed softly. She frowned, scrolling through the first decoded packets from the Kansas racks. The traffic logs stretched farther than she expected: timestamps, proxy lists, outbound channels. Her throat tightened.

"Max," she said carefully, "Kansas wasn't the hub. It was one of several. I'm seeing mirrored nodes, at least four more addresses across different continents."

The faint taste of victory soured instantly in the air. Max closed his eyes for half a breath, then opened them again, sharper than before.

"Then this was just the opening move," he muttered.

The hydra still lived. And now they had proof it was bigger than anyone feared.

CHAPTER 3
HYDRA

Day 3: T-28. Network Pulse Anomalies Detected.

Max had managed two hours of uneasy rest before Sam woke him.

His reflection in the darkened monitor showed the faint shadow of stubble across his jaw, unusual for a man who usually shaved before dawn. The crisis was beginning to mark him in ways the mirror couldn't hide.

The Vault was quieter now, the emergency lights dimmed to half power, the hum of servers pulsing like a heartbeat under concrete. Sam stood by the doorway, coffee in one hand, cane in the other.

"You were right," Max said hoarsely. Sam raised an eyebrow. "About what?" "Acting before the proof."

Sam gave that faint, crooked grin. "It's only reckless until it works."

Max rubbed his eyes and reached for his jacket. "Then let's hope it keeps working."

"It will," Sam said. "They're finally listening."

Max nodded, straightened, and followed him toward the command floor. The short rest hadn't erased the fatigue, but it had sharpened his resolve.

The Kansas raid had netted tangible evidence, but the victory was fleeting. Max, Tara, and Adrian returned to the Vault to sift through the digital heart of the operation. The hum of servers and the glow of cascading code filled the room, each monitor alive with streams of activity, timestamps, and encrypted traffic logs.

Tara's fingers flew across the keyboard, tracing mirrored nodes she had just discovered. "Signals are bouncing through at least four other locations," she said, eyes wide in shock. "Different continents, different time zones, all hidden behind layers of proxies."

Adrian leaned over, peering at her monitor. "It's like a Hydra," he muttered. "Cut off one head, and two more appear.

Max's gaze swept the global map, red clusters of infection pulsing across networks. Every spike, every unusual packet, underscored reality: the operation was larger, more coordinated, and far more dangerous than anyone had imagined. He turned to the room. Analysts from the Intelligence Community, NSA, Cyber Command, and DHS SIGINT teams monitored feeds, while representatives from the device manufacturers hovered over schematics and diagnostic logs.

Max was due downtown for high-level briefings, politics, and optics, not code. In his absence, Sam kept the Vault steady, a quiet field general who could make a dozen agencies move without raising his voice.

"Hold the brief until Shaw's back," Rourke said, eyes on the shifting data walls. "And someone get me updated signatures from Fort Meade, if they've changed encryption formats again, I'll start sending them my dentist bills."

A few analysts chuckled, tension easing just enough to breathe. Maya caught Rourke's glance and nodded; they spoke in shorthand now, trust built line by line of shared chaos.

"I need full SIGINT coverage on all anomalous outbound traffic," Max said. "Vendor teams, confirm bootloader specs and hidden firmware routines. Intelligence Community analysts, overlay your human-source reports, field techs, contractors, and anyone with access. Let's see if we can correlate insider movement with the network anomalies."

Back at the Vault, Tara and Adrian worked feverishly to analyze the seized equipment. Embedded in the servers were layers of encrypted command software, proxy routing scripts, and logs of activation commands sent in test pulses.

"This is it," Tara said, eyes gleaming. "We've found the digital heart of the operation."

Max allowed himself a moment of hope but warned, "This isn't over. There may be backup nodes, insider agents, or undiscovered devices."

Within hours, evidence pointed toward an insider network, trusted contractors and engineers who had unwittingly or willfully aided the adversary.

Max called a secure meeting with Maya.

"We've identified three contractors with suspicious overseas contacts and access to firmware signing credentials," Maya reported. "Two of them recently traveled abroad to countries associated with Phantom Chimera's intelligence apparatus."

Max frowned. "We need to monitor their communications, financial transactions, and access logs immediately." Maya nodded. "Already on it. We're coordinating with the FBI and foreign liaison officers, and the IC has provided monitoring on all overseas channels."

Max's phone buzzed. A secure message from Tara: "Sleeper code timer recalibrated. Activation window now less than twenty days." The countdown was closing.

The hours following the raid at the Kansas server farm were a whirlwind of analysis, surveillance, and quiet tension. The Vault was alive 24/7, a nerve center where every data blip could mean the difference between safety and catastrophe.

Max rarely left the facility, subsisting on cold coffee and brief bursts of sleep in his office. The weight of command pressed on him with an almost physical force. His team worked tirelessly, Tara with her relentless focus on code decryption, Adrian wrestling with hardware vulnerabilities, Maya chasing shadows of insider threats, and IC analysts providing live intercepts, correlations, and field intel. Vendor engineers hovered at workstations, supplying device specifications, firmware histories, and hardware advice, every insight vital to outwitting Phantom Chimera.

Late one night, Max found himself alone before the large observation screen, a digital projection of the sleeping city. The streets were empty except for the occasional patrol car. It was hard to believe this calm existed when, beneath the surface, an invisible war raged.

His phone buzzed, a secure message from Tara.

"New firmware dump received from the Gulf Coast. Different variant of sleeper code, more aggressive activation logic. Timer reduced to 18 days."

Max exhaled, rubbing his tired eyes. He keyed a reply.

"Send all data to my terminal. I'm on my way."

Minutes later, Tara was waiting at the briefing room door, clutching a tablet loaded with raw data. Adrian followed close behind, carrying a prototype embedded systems analyzer. IC analysts and vendor engineers were already present, scanning monitors and schematics for patterns and vulnerabilities.

"Max," Tara began, "this new variant is troubling. It doesn't just wait for a timer or remote trigger; it monitors the system activity and external events. If it detects emergency response signals or attempts at shutdown, it accelerates activation."

Adrian added, "It's adaptive. The malware rewrites itself based on the environment to avoid detection and maximize disruption."

Max rubbed his chin thoughtfully. "So it's not just a sleeper, it's a predator lying in wait, ready to pounce at the first sign of defense." Tara nodded. "Exactly. And we've confirmed it is present in water treatment plants along the Gulf Coast, rail control systems in Louisiana, and power substations in Texas."

Max's gaze hardened. "We're looking at a coordinated strike designed to cripple the entire southern infrastructure network." He turned to Adrian. "How do we isolate and remove a code base like this? Traditional firmware patches won't work."

Adrian tapped a few keys, pulling up hardware diagnostic logs. "Some of these devices have custom bootloaders embedded on tampered chips. The backdoor activates during startup, bypassing firmware integrity checks."

Max frowned. "So wiping the software won't be enough. The hardware itself is compromised."

"Exactly," Adrian said. "Replacing every infected chip would be a logistical nightmare."

Max paced the room, weighing the options. "We need a multi-pronged strategy, immediate containment, network isolation, and longer-term hardware replacement plans."

Tara pointed to a network map. "We've started isolating infected devices from their communication hubs to prevent activation signals spreading, but it's like trying to plug holes in a sinking ship."

Max's mind raced. "What about detection? Can we build an AI-based anomaly detection system to flag the code before it activates?"

Tara smiled faintly. "We're working on it. Machine learning models are trained on the behavioral patterns of infected devices. Early results are promising, but it's a race against time."

Max nodded. "Good. Keep me updated."

Meanwhile, Maya Carter sat in her office reviewing intelligence on the contractors linked to the sleeper code infiltration. The dossiers painted a worrying picture, trusted engineers and developers with unexplained overseas contacts, suspicious financial transactions, and recent trips to countries known for cyber espionage.

She tapped her fingers on the desk, eyes fixated and sharp. "These insiders might have been compromised or recruited."

Maya reached for her secure phone and called Max. "We're increasing surveillance on the contractors. One of them, Jacob Morrow, just booked a flight to Hong Kong."

"Jacob Morrow," Maya continued, sliding a photo across the table. "Late thirties, quiet face, the kind of contractor no one notices in the cafeteria. Married, two kids, no debt. On paper, ordinary. But ordinary men don't book last-minute flights to Hong Kong under shell corporations."

Max sighed. "We can't afford to lose track of anyone. The Intelligence Community and the FBI maintain continuous coverage. Vendors, confirm which firmware builds Jacob had access to. Every piece matters."

Maya added, "Agreed. We're working with the FBI to initiate counterintelligence operations."

Hours blurred together in a rush of encrypted communications, cyber forensics, and frantic coordination. The clock continued its relentless countdown.

One evening, Max convened an emergency briefing. The room was packed with analysts, agents, and officials, every department at full alert. Vendor engineers were at their stations, comparing schematics with compromised devices, while IC analysts overlaid real-time human-source and signal intelligence.

"We've confirmed sleeper code variants across five critical sectors: energy, communications, transportation, emergency services, and water systems. " Max reported, "Each one's inter-linked; hit the grid, and you cripple comms, take out comms, and first responders go blind.

"Activation windows now range from thirteen to eighteen days. The offsets are intentional, a way to keep us guessing."

He paused. "The enemy is adapting faster than we can respond. But we've identified a potential lead, a proxy server network used as a staging ground for activation commands."

Tara stepped forward. "We've traced the command-and-control servers to multiple countries, but one appears to be a compromised cloud service provider in Eastern Europe."

Adrian added, "We're coordinating with international partners to isolate and shut down these servers. Vendor engineers have verified device security, and IC analysts are feeding live intercepts from those locations."

Rourke nodded. "Global fight, global coordination. Cyber teams, the Intelligence Community, and manufacturers must stay synced; every action affects the timing of the sleeper code."

When Max finally returned from the D.C. rounds, the Vault hummed like a living organism, screens aligned, reports flowing, no raised voices. Rourke sat at the console, headset half-off, reviewing the latest intercepts.

"You kept it together," Max said quietly.

Rourke didn't look up from the screen. "That's the job. We're all replaceable. The work isn't."

Max nodded, a trace of gratitude flickering across his face before he stepped into his office.

That night, Max sat alone reviewing data feeds. His mind wandered to his family, distant faces he rarely saw anymore.

This fight wasn't just about networks or hardware; it was about protecting lives, homes, and futures.

The stakes had never been higher. With renewed determination, Max leaned back and prepared for the long battle ahead.

CHAPTER 4
SEVEN MINUTES

Day 4: T-27. Hospital Blackout Test Run.

The call came in at 03:17 a.m.

In The Vault, an analyst raised her hand, voice tight. "We've got a grid dip in Illinois, substation forty-one. Voltage collapse, duration seven minutes."

Max moved fast, leaning over her shoulder as numbers rolled across the display. The line dipped once, twice, then flatlined. It was as if every lock on the door failed at once; the safeguards simply stepped aside.

"Impact zone?" Max demanded.

The analyst's throat tightened. "Regional hospital critical care just went dark."

Max snapped a headset into place. "Get me the regional leads, now."

* * * * * * * *

Across half a dozen cities, encrypted lines flared to life. These were his people, the hand-picked captains of the Regional Cyber Response Teams. Engineers, analysts, and field specialists, he'd trained years ago when the threat had been theoretical.

"Chicago, confirm hospital grid isolation," he ordered.

A calm voice crackled through the channel. "Already on it, Director. Backup generators spinning up. Seven minutes, maybe less."

He could picture her, Torres, his best systems lead, standing ankle-deep in cables and caffeine, running command from a basement ops center. Every team had a face, a history. They were his extension into the chaos.

"Hold the line," he said quietly. Then he turned back to the screens as the numbers began to fall.

At the rear of the room, Sam coordinated the chaos like a battlefield medic, voice low and exact.

"Section leads, lock telemetry feeds. No redundant queries, keep the line clear for Illinois traffic. I want packet mirrors running on every regional node."

His tone wasn't barked, just final. The Vault moved in rhythm to it, analysts straightened, hands steadied, the room finding its pulse again. Even in crisis, Rourke was the man who kept systems and people from fracturing.

* * * * * * *

On the ground, chaos was already spreading like fire through darkened halls.

Nurses sprinted between patient rooms, shoes squeaking on tile slick with panic. Sweat and antiseptic mingled in the air, sharp enough to sting the back of the throat. Battery-powered monitors blinked erratically, their alarms collapsing into static. A child's ragged gasp cut through the noise, raw and human against the failing machines. A ventilator froze, screen black. A mother screamed as her daughter's chest rose and fell unevenly, two nurses forcing oxygen with frantic, manual compressions.

"Bag her now!" one shouted. "Keep her steady, don't stop!"

The ER was bedlam. Hands searched for flashlights. Doctors barked orders into radios that spat only silence. In a surgical wing, a heart-lung machine locked mid-cycle, its digital display frozen as if waiting for permission to resume.

Down in the basement, a maintenance tech hammered at a breaker panel that refused to respond, sparks biting his gloves as if the circuitry itself had decided it no longer belonged to him.

Seven minutes.

That was how long it took before the backup systems crawled back online, one hesitant pulse at a time. Lights snapped on in jagged bursts. Machinery rebooted with cold, synthetic beeps. Relief rippled through the wards, but it was relief sharpened by fear.

Two patients never came back.

*　*　*　*　*　*　*

Somewhere far from Illinois, in a windowless room, a single monitor glowed against the dark. On its screen, a cluster of green bars pulsed, then dropped to red as voltage collapsed across the hospital grid.

A young man in a gray hoodie sat rigid at the console. He wasn't supposed to watch the feeds, only the numbers. But he couldn't look away from the silent video window of the ER, nurses moving like ghosts in dim light, a child's face caught mid-scream before the camera cut out.

He swallowed and typed a brief update into a secure channel: *Operation complete. Duration: seven minutes.*

Across the room, an older figure leaned against the wall, invisible above the shoulders in the dim light. The reply came through instantly on his tablet: *Proceed to Phase Two.* No name, only the signature icon of a white mask.

The young man hesitated. "This was supposed to be non-critical," he said quietly, not sure if the others could hear.

The older figure's voice was low and flat. "It wasn't about the grid. It was about being seen."

He closed the tablet. The screen went black, leaving only the heartbeat of code on the monitor, and the boy's reflection staring back at him. The test wasn't a test. It was a signal.

* * * * * * *

In The Vault, silence fell heavier than the concrete above their heads. Max stood stone-still as the after-action report spilled through the secure line. His knuckles whitened against the console.

The scent of antiseptic and fear lingered in his mind, tied to that Boston night he would never forget, the mother's scream echoing down sterile hallways. That night had driven him into government service. And now it was happening again.

Tara's voice was low, steady, but weighted. "It wasn't random." For weeks, they'd chased echoes of a dead project, a DARPA experiment called Prism. It had once tried to map the resonance inside encrypted systems, to see patterns no human eye could track. The idea burned out when the math outpaced the machines, and the files were shelved. But pieces of the code survived, leased to civilian labs studying grid harmonics. Peoria was one of them, still running a dormant prototype most people had forgotten existed.

Her eyes flicked to the console readout. The outage's beacon matched the hidden pulse they'd been tracing for weeks, the same covert fingerprint buried in sleeper implants. And Peoria wasn't just another city; its grid hosted the only civilian lab still tied to the Prism framework. The realization hit fast: Phantom wasn't spreading at random. It was striking at the tools built to expose it.

Max nodded once. His jaw ached from holding back the rage. "No. That was a test."

The map of America glowed in the dark, red nodes spreading like infection across the Midwest. But in Max's mind, it was only the faces, the ones who had died in silence, waiting for machines to breathe for them.

Tara muttered, "Feels like an inside job."

Maya said nothing. Her hands hovered over the keyboard, but her mind had already slipped years back, to Bucharest. Her brother had been nineteen, a first-year engineering student who thought the world could be rebuilt with a soldering iron and optimism. He'd carried a battered spiral notebook everywhere with half-circuits and half-jokes scrawled in the margins. *"If the lights ever go out, Maya, I'll rig us a generator from a toaster and your hair dryer."* He'd laughed when he said it, daring her to roll her eyes.

When the blackout came, there was no generator. No hair dryer. Just silence and a city choking in the dark. The notebook was still with him when they found him. Walter had bled across the pages, the ink running until the jokes were unreadable. She kept it still, buried in the back of her closet, a relic of promises that never came true.

Now, staring at the Illinois voltage flatline, she felt the same hollow ache, as if every keystroke against Phantom was a conversation she would never finish with him.

She steadied her breath and forced her fingers back to the keys. *This isn't just code,* she told herself. *This is for him. For everyone else who never got seven minutes back.*

Max frowned. "There was one analyst who used to warn us about these vulnerabilities." He didn't name Kane, but Maya knew who he meant.

He turned back to his team, voice clipped and hard. "Trace every packet from that substation. I don't care if it takes all night. We find what touched it."

The room snapped back into motion, but the damage was already done.

Rourke drifted past Max, tablet under his arm, issuing quiet directions to containment teams. "We'll stabilize the grid and audit every hospital running identical firmware," he said to no one in particular, and everyone at once.

He'd seen too many wards lit by backup generators, Kandahar, Mosul, now Illinois. Different continents, same panic in the dark. Maybe that's why he never raised his voice; he'd learned early that calm was the only antidote to fear.

Max didn't answer. He didn't have to. Rourke wasn't looking for reassurance, just results.

As screens scrolled with endless packet logs, the Vault's rhythm shifted into a weary silence. Tara kicked off her shoes beneath the console, wiggling socked toes against the cold floor. Adrian raised an eyebrow. "Didn't peg you for the barefoot-in-the-bunker type."

"Better grip," she muttered without looking up.

Maya didn't answer. She sat with her chin propped on one hand, the glow of her monitor painting shadows under her eyes. The others learned quickly that her silences were not empty; they were pressure cookers. When she finally spoke, it would matter.

Adrian leaned back, spinning an unplugged mouse idly between his fingers. "You realize," he said dryly, "we are the only people on Earth watching packet traces like it's playoff season."

Max didn't smile, but the corner of his mouth twitched. For a beat, the Vault felt less like a war room and more like a dorm lounge at 3 a.m., tired, stubborn, running on caffeine and spite.

Then a red alert flashed across Tara's console, yanking them all back into the fight. Somewhere above them, families were gathering around hospital beds, wondering how life could vanish because of something no one could see.

CHAPTER 5
INTRUSION

Day 6: T-25. The Boundaries Break.

In a high-rise office somewhere east of the Caspian, a single workstation glowed under the dim hum of fluorescent light. A wall of clocks ticked softly, New York, Washington, Baton Rouge.

A man in a tailored shirt scrolled through a feed of names and GPS pings. His ring tapped against the desk as he clicked on one: *Carter, Maya.*

On his screen, a schematic of her apartment appeared, IoT devices blinking like green stars. He keyed in a short string of commands. Across the Atlantic, a thermostat spiked, and a router light began to pulse.

A second figure, unseen but present, spoke from the shadows: "Asset C–21 is reliable?"

The man smiled without looking up. "This isn't about reliability. This is about fear." He pressed **enter**.

Half a world away, Maya's living room lights flickered once, a heartbeat across the wires.

* * * * * * * *

Maya Carter locked the door behind her, the deadbolt clicking into place. The apartment was quiet, too quiet. A row of framed photos lined the mantle, her brother in uniform, her parents smiling in the Connecticut sun. On her mantle, one photo frame faced down: Kane in uniform. She hadn't yet decided whether the memory was comfort or betrayal. She dropped her jacket on the couch and unholstered her sidearm, setting it within reach, old habits.

She told herself the Vault hadn't followed her home. That was a lie.

The television powered on by itself, screen cycling through static. The faint electrical buzz filled the room, needling into the silence.

Maya froze, hand already hovering near her pistol. The remote sat untouched on the table.

The lights dimmed, brightened, then dimmed again, a pulse, deliberate, like a heartbeat mocking her.

Her phone vibrated. She snatched it up. The vibration rattled in her palm, a jitter that felt more alive than mechanical. The screen flooded with nonsense characters and lines of code arranged like laughter. Then the words twisted into something worse: **HELLO, MAYA.**

Her blood ran cold.

This wasn't a random bleed from a compromised grid. This was tailored. Targeted. Her apartment was no longer hers; it was a stage.

She'd studied case files for years: Ukraine's blackout, Stuxnet burning through centrifuges, and the Colonial Pipeline hack that left gas stations empty. Those had been distant, almost abstract. Now her own walls had joined the list.

The kitchen radio crackled alive, an old jazz station twisting into white noise. The thermostat spiked to ninety, then dropped to fifty in seconds. Every device sang the same chorus: **we are inside.**

Maya steadied her breathing. Fear was fuel, but only if you burned it slowly. She reached for the breaker panel in the hallway and flipped every switch down. The apartment went black, leaving her in silence.

For a moment, only her pulse filled the dark.

Then, from the far corner, the router light blinked once.

Green. Waiting.

She aimed her pistol at it as if the barrel could stop a ghost.

"This is my house," she whispered.

But deep down, she knew better. The walls weren't hers anymore. They were part of the battlefield.

CHAPTER 6
RED ECHOES

Day 8: T-23. Contamination in the Water Supply.

The next morning, the NIPA war room buzzed with activity. A map of the continental U.S. glowed red in scattered regions as new anomalies were flagged in real time. Tara walked in with fresh data packets and a weary look.

"We've confirmed similar implants in Louisiana's port control systems and parts of Colorado's natural gas infrastructure," she said. "It's spreading faster than we projected."

* * * * * * *

A family in Baton Rouge noticed their tap water carried a faint metallic tang, like coins left too long in the sun. Neighbors compared notes, muttering over back fences. Within hours, calls flooded the city's utility hotline.

By evening, the mayor's office issued a blunt advisory: *boil all water before drinking.*

Across kitchens, kettles shrieked, and steam fogged windows, turning houses into damp, anxious saunas.

At the Oak Street firehouse, a lieutenant filled kettles from the station sink, shaking his head as the water came out cloudy. "This isn't a main break," he muttered. "This is upstream."

In kitchens across the city, families lined counters with pots and pans, steam clouding windows as burners roared. Grocery stores sold out of bottled water in less than thirty minutes, and fights broke out in crowded aisles.

*　*　*　*　*　*　*

Washington, D.C., glimmered with oblivious calm. Tourists strolled along the National Mall, cameras clicking at the Lincoln Memorial and the Reflecting Pool. The Washington Monument glowed pale against the evening sky, monuments bathed in golden light, a city at ease, unaware of the silent pulse coursing beneath its streets. Joggers passed in rhythmic stride, a father chased his toddler across the grass, and a street musician's guitar strummed over the soft hum of distant traffic.

Yet below, in the fiber-optic veins of the city, Chimera's heartbeat echoed faintly through the mesh. Every untamed packet, every infected router, had potential consequences these walkers would never see. The fountains sparkled as if nothing was wrong, but the invisible code whispered its threat through pipes, circuits, and towers. One wrong signal, one moment of misalignment, could ripple outward, outages, contamination, panic.

The contrast was stark: ordinary lives illuminated by monuments and streetlights, and an unseen war unfolding just beneath their feet. Life carried on, oblivious, while the Vault's pulse raced in tandem with theirs.

*　*　*　*　*　*　*

Inside The Vault, Tara dropped the advisory notice onto Max's desk. "Contamination signal lasted two hours. The implants triggered chemical bypass valves, flushing untreated water into circulation."

Max tossed a folder onto the table. "Some of these exploits were flagged years ago by an independent contractor, dismissed at the time."

Maya stiffened. She knew the name on that folder even before she saw it: Kane.

Max scanned the report, his forehead wrinkling. "Collateral damage?"

"None serious yet. Just stomach illness. But if it had gone longer…"

She didn't finish. They both knew what unfiltered water could do in days.

Max's eyes drifted to the map, the Gulf Coast now lit with pulsing red. To him, the boil notice wasn't just a civic inconvenience. It was proof. The enemy wasn't simulating anymore. They were practicing.

Max barely looked up. "And the countdowns?"

"They're synchronized. All of them terminate in exactly twenty-five days at 04:00 hours UTC."

Adrian walked over, holding a fiber board router in one hand and a magnifier in the other. "Max, we found something else. The infected devices all share a hardware anomaly: a tampered bootloader traceable to a Chinese fab subcontractor, one that went offline two years ago."

"Which means these devices have been compromised at the supply chain level," Max said slowly. "They've been planning this for years."

Adrian clenched his jaw as he set the board down. He'd seen this kind of betrayal before, not in a lab, but in Kabul, when he was a young contractor testing Army radios. A batch of "secure" comms gear had arrived already compromised. One patrol walked into an ambush because of it. Adrian still remembered carrying a dead radio back across the desert, its silence heavier than the weight of the fallen men it failed.

"I still have that board," Adrian admitted once, voice low.

"The solder line that doomed them. A reminder."

Ever since, he'd trusted hardware less than people. Circuits could betray you without warning, and that knowledge had brought him here.

The others sifted logs and packet traces, but Adrian hunched over the gutted router board. His fingers brushed away ash until he found a capacitor half-melted into its socket. Without comment, he snapped it free and slipped it into a sample vial.

Tara raised an eyebrow. "Souvenir?" Adrian didn't look up. "Evidence."

He turned to the command board. "It's not just about what's infected. It's about what hasn't been triggered yet."

Tara looked concerned. "We're going to need a coordinated shutdown strategy across multiple states."

Tara leaned closer to the display. "The CERT network out of Carnegie Mellon used to flag this kind of anomaly, coordinated exploits across unrelated vendors. But this isn't fragmented. It's synchronized. Someone's threading the whole thing through one pulse."

Max nodded. "And we'll need the White House. Get me a line to the National Security Advisor."

The clock was ticking.

* * * * * * *

Four hours later, Max stood in the Roosevelt Room, surrounded by the President's cybersecurity task force. The gravity of the situation had brought together minds from the NSA, CIA, DoD, and the private sector, who were flown in under emergency protocols. The room was tight with tension, and the air carried the stale weight of sleepless worry.

"We're dealing with a hybrid cyber-physical threat," Max said, tapping the digital whiteboard. "These implants don't just target infrastructure, power, water, gas, transportation; they can pivot into civilian IoT systems: smart fridges, door cameras, even baby monitors. A silent army of domestic drones waiting for commands."

He paused, letting the weight of it land. "If they activate simultaneously, it'll look like a nationwide system collapse."

One of the FEMA officials leaned forward, pen tapping softly against his notes. "Weeks, maybe, but that's only if supply lines hold. We've got fuel reserves for hospitals and water treatment, plus emergency generators in most major cities. Food and bottled water might stretch three days before rationing kicks in."

He exhaled through his nose. "If grid stability doesn't come back online, we start prioritizing: medical power first, then sanitation and cold-chain transport. Comfort services get cut entirely."

He glanced toward Shaw. "If the outages cascade or we start losing distribution hubs, are we cleared to mobilize the National Guard for logistics and crowd control?"

Tara cut in sharply. "More like days. But days are enough. Even short outages can spiral into economic paralysis, social unrest, and cascade failures."

Admiral Carroway from Cyber Command leaned forward, his tone steady but wary. "So it hasn't triggered yet. Then our window's still open. Before we escalate, I need clarity. Are we certain this isn't a false pattern or residual data from prior operations?"

Max met his eyes. "We believe the attackers are waiting for an optimal moment, likely one synchronized with another geopolitical or coordinated event."

A senator near the back shifted in his chair, voice tempered but cautious. "Director Shaw, with respect, we've seen alerts like this before. Power fluctuations, software irregularities, many of them went unaddressed. We need to be sure we're not overreacting to noise in the system."

Max nodded slightly. "Possibly. But what we can control is identifying and neutralizing the trigger mechanism."

Tara handed out briefing folders. "We've isolated three likely vectors. First, firmware-level triggers, timers, and backdoors in bootloaders. Second, covert command channels hidden in routine network traffic: tiny, encrypted payloads carried in ICMP/diagnostic packets or optional header fields on IPv4 flows that escape proper inspection. Third, out-of-band paths, satellite uplinks, and vendor telemetry channels that bypass terrestrial filters."

The DOE representative frowned. "That sounds like three different systems talking past each other. What does it mean in practice?"

Tara leaned forward. "Think of it like doorbells wired into the same house. One signal comes through old wiring, another through the plumbing in the walls, and a third from a satellite dish on the roof. Different methods, same outcome, if any of those bells get pushed, the sleeper code wakes up."

The DOE representative nodded slowly, scribbling notes.

Pike rubbed his forehead, sighing. "My brother still runs a grain elevator outside Davenport. If you're right, he's sitting on a time bomb he doesn't even know exists."

His hand trembled slightly as he set his glasses on the table. "God help me if I have to call him and tell him to shut it all down." The room was silent for a beat, the abstract suddenly personal.

The President's Chief of Staff spoke up. "We need to act before word of this leaks. If people find out, they'll panic."

Max agreed. "We'll coordinate quiet patch-and-isolate procedures with local utilities. No alarms. Just diagnostics and upgrades."

The meeting broke out in a flurry of murmurs and handshakes. By the time Max reached the motorcade, his phone was already vibrating with a secure-line request. He accepted, the encrypted channel stabilizing with a faint hiss.

"Rourke."

"Still in one piece?" Sam's voice carried through the static, low and steady, the same calm that kept the Vault breathing when everything else cracked.

"Barely. They don't believe the scale yet," Max said, watching the city roll past his window. "They think we're chasing noise."

"Belief's optional," Sam replied. "Clocks don't care who's watching them tick."

Max allowed a dry exhale. "You always did have a talent for optimism."

"That was optimism," Sam said. "You just missed it. We'll keep the Vault stable, isolate critical sectors, and prep the fallback systems. You keep the suits from tripping over themselves."

"They want containment without panic. You think we can buy time?"

"We don't buy time," Sam said quietly. "We steal it, one subnet at a time. You hold the front; I'll hold the floor."

Max leaned back, the hum of the engine merging with the pulse in his temple. "Walls first, then."

"Exactly," Sam said. "And when the ghosts come knocking, we'll be the ones holding the flashlight."

The line clicked softly as the convoy entered the underground ramp. For a moment, Max just stared at his own reflection in the window, tired eyes, a city above that had no idea how close its pulse was to stopping.

•••••••

Back in The Vault, the cyber team worked in staggered shifts. Adrian was decoding a strange pattern embedded in the time variables. He rolled a processor core across his knuckles, the way some people toyed with coins. "Software lies," he muttered. "Hardware remembers."

Maya shot him a look. "You keep talking like they're old war trophies."

He gave a thin smile. "Maybe they are."

"This isn't just a static countdown. It's self-adjusting. Adaptive."

"What do you mean?" Tara asked.

"The infected machines are whispering to each other, learning to act like one giant system. They're adjusting activation times based on node health and uptime. They want to ensure maximal impact."

Max leaned over the code. "Distributed intelligence. That explains why the pattern seems to shift. It's learning from our mitigation efforts."

Tara rubbed her temples. "It's an autonomous sleeper network. That's why traditional antivirus and endpoint detection aren't catching it. The payload hides in memory, fragments itself across processes, and constantly mutates its signature. Any single file looks benign. It doesn't trigger scans because it doesn't execute until the entire network is in position, and even then, it changes its call-outs in real time. It's like trying to catch a cha-meleon in a hall of mirrors."

Adrian added, "If we can isolate the beacon pulse that keeps them coordinated, we might be able to sever the mesh. Until we do, AV sees only static noise, and EDR logs just minor anomalies that it automatically dismisses as system quirks."

Tara pressed her palms into her eyes. Nights without real sleep left her hands unsteady on the keyboard. Her phone lit beside her, "Mom" flashing across the screen, and she swiped it silent. The work demanded everything; family could wait.

"Or turn it against them," Max said. "Feed it a false command." A hush fell across the team. It was a dangerous idea, but potentially brilliant.

"Build me a decoy controller," Max said. His voice was low, steady, but his knuckles whitened as he gripped the console. "I want a software twin that mimics the heartbeat signal but gives us override authority."

The room went still. Tara's fingers froze above her keyboard.

Adrian looked up from a circuit board, his eyes containing worry. "That's not a patch," Tara said carefully. "That's a false god. If the implants believe it, we might get a foothold. But if it fails…" "Then they'll know we're here," Adrian finished. "And every compromised node could harden against us."

Maya leaned back in her chair, arms crossed. "You're playing with fire, Max. If Chimera works," she said, using the name without hesitation. He always named projects after the enemy itself. "Great, we get control. But if it glitches, Phantom won't just see us; *it'll learn from us.* You ready for that?"

Max's gaze swept the room. "They already know we're close. Every hour we stall, they adapt. I don't want a patch. I want leverage."

The analysts exchanged uneasy glances, but no one argued further. The order stood.

Tara leaned back in her chair as the others bent to their workstations, the glow of Chimera's code reflecting in tired eyes. Her phone was still buried beneath reports, face down where she'd left it.

When she finally checked it, the screen showed three missed calls. All from her mother.

At the top of the incident queue, a new report blinked: rolling outages in the Boston suburbs. A margin note flagged *two nursing homes without backup power.*

Tara's chest tightened as she read the zip code. Her mother lived inside that zone.

She closed the file, heart pounding, and forced her attention back to the mimicry algorithms scrolling past. The Vault didn't have room for panic. But for the first time that night, the code itself refused to sit still on the screen.

· · · · · · ·

The project was codenamed **Chimera**, a creature of deception, built to breathe inside another's skin.

It was the most elaborate honeypot the Vault had ever built, a false network so convincing it fooled even their own intrusion sensors.

For seventy-two hours, the Vault became something between a war room and a laboratory. Sleep was a rumor. Coffee cups multiplied across consoles, cold and abandoned.

Tara took point on the mimicry engine. She pulled days' worth of archived packet logs from compromised substations and lock systems, mapping the subtle rhythms of the infected devices. "Each implant pings a pulse every 47 milliseconds, plus or minus three," she explained to Max, scrolling through graphs. "It's not just a heartbeat, it's a fingerprint. The sequence isn't random; it's recursive."

"So Chimera needs to echo it perfectly?" Max asked.

"Not perfectly," Tara said with stern expressions. "Perfect would look suspicious. It has to *breathe*. Small imperfections, like a human pulse under stress."

Adrian's contribution was physical. He designed the environment that would cage Chimera: an isolated virtual network, sealed by triple-layer encryption and air-gapped from all external systems. "If this thing gets loose," he warned, tapping the hardened server housing, "we're not just building a decoy, we're building bait. And bait attracts predators."

A door hissed open behind them. Sam stepped into the lab, his limp faint but familiar, a mug of black coffee steady in one hand. The team barely looked up, eyes glued to monitors, but his presence shifted the room's gravity.

"I hear we're building ghosts to catch ghosts," he said, setting the mug on a console.

Max glanced over his shoulder. "Chimera's our way in. A mirror strong enough to fool their implants into thinking it's one of their own."

Sam studied the code streaming across Tara's screen, the recursive patterns pulsing like heartbeats. "And what happens if the reflection decides it likes what it sees?"

"Then we cage it," Max said.

Sam's expression stayed unreadable. "Cages break. Make sure yours doesn't."

Tara smirked faintly, though it didn't reach her eyes. "You worried about the code or the people?"

"Both," Sam said simply. "You start fighting fire with fire, and the smoke gets in your lungs before you realize you're choking."

Max folded his arms. "We're out of clean options, Sam. This is leverage, or nothing."

Sam nodded once, slow and deliberate. "Then make sure leverage doesn't turn into a trigger." He turned toward the door, pausing just long enough to add, "I'll keep the field steady while you build your monster. Just remember which side it's supposed to bite."

When he was gone, the hum of servers filled the silence again, louder now, like the Vault itself was holding its breath.

Max stood over their shoulders, moving between workstations like a commander in a trench. He rarely touched the keys himself; instead, he drove them forward with questions.

"If Phantom's code queries the checksum," he said, "think of it like a digital fingerprint, a quick way for the program to check if the data is exactly what it expects. Can Chimera lie back without being caught?"

"If they alter timing," he continued, "can it flex? What happens if we broadcast to multiple implants at once?"

Each answer was another brick in the architecture of deception.

* * * * * * *

On the second night, tensions cracked. Tara slammed her palm against the desk. "It won't hold! The checksum mismatch keeps flagging us. The implants will sniff out the forgery."

Adrian wheeled around. "Then stop chasing perfection. We don't need to pass their inspection forever, just long enough to slip a leash on."

"Easy for you to say," Tara snapped. "You're not the one writing polymorphic wrappers at three in the morning."

Maya stepped between them, voice steady but edged. "Both of you are right, but you're forgetting the clock. We don't need Chimera to last forever; we need it to live long enough for me to run ops play once it's inside. Thirty seconds. Maybe sixty. That's the mission window."

She shot Max a look. "Give me a decoy heartbeat, and I'll give you a choke point."

Max nodded once. "Then that's what we build."

As the room broke into motion, Tara's console pinged with a secure health-services alert: *Boston General Hospital, emergency admissions surge tied to grid instability.*

Her hand hovered over the keyboard. Her mother's clinic was less than a mile from that address.

She cleared the alert before anyone noticed, swallowing the lump in her throat.

Max's voice carried over the clatter of keys. "We're fighting ghosts, phantom code embedded in silicon and software, invisible until it's too late."

Tara forced herself to nod, though her pulse was still racing out of rhythm with the data.

The Vault's hum swallowed their frustration, channeling it into focus.

Adrian lingered after the others moved on. His eyes stayed on the mirrored routine pulsing faintly on his console, but his hand was elsewhere, thumb brushing the jagged edge of a chip fragment in his pocket. A habit. A tether.

· · · · · · ·

By the third night, Chimera stirred.

At the far end of the floor, Sam watched the monitors flare with the same faint heartbeat now pulsing across Chimera's cage. He hadn't said much in hours, just stood near the comms board, a quiet sentinel while the room chased ghosts through code.

"There it is," Tara breathed.

Sam's voice came from behind her, steady as ever. "You caught it. Question is, does it know you did?"

Max turned, fatigue shadowing his face. "Not yet. It thinks we're one of them."

Sam nodded once. "That's the dangerous part about pretending to be the enemy. Sometimes the pretending starts to look real."

No one replied. The hum of the servers filled the silence, the digital pulse reflecting in everyone's eyes.

Sam lingered a moment longer, watching Chimera's heartbeat steady itself on the screen. "Congratulations," he said quietly. "You've built something alive. Just don't forget to keep it leashed."

Then he turned back toward the main board, his limp echoing faintly in the corridor, the sound of a man who'd seen victories turn on themselves before.

Relief rippled through the Vault, but Tara barely felt it. In the back of her mind, she heard her mother's voice from that late-night call, *Power's been flickering again…*

She tightened her grip on the console, shutting the thought out. *Not here. Not now. Not ever again.*

She bent back over the screens, forcing her pulse to match Chimera's heartbeat, as if sheer will could keep it steady.

The room erupted in cheers, fist pumps, and exhausted laughter.

For the first time in weeks, they had outwitted the ghost.

But Maya didn't join the celebration. Her smile was thin. "Don't celebrate yet. That's one implant in a cage. Out there, millions are still listening to Phantom. If Chimera falters, it won't be testing logs we're burying, it'll be people."

The laughter faded. Silence sharpened the air again.

Max didn't smile either. He stared at the blinking log, remembering another machine, another night, the ventilator in Boston that had stayed dark no matter how hard he fought. Two patients gone. A mother's scream lodged forever in his chest.

He whispered, almost to himself, "Not again."

Maya leaned back in her chair, eyes flicking over Chimera's pulse streams. The Vault hummed around her, monitors glowing, servers humming, keyboards clattering, but her mind was elsewhere. *On the floor of her apartment, letters were scattered like fragments of memory, each one looping with her brother's handwriting. "I wish you were here. Things feel off when you're not around. Don't forget me, okay?"* She traced the words with a trembling finger, imagining him sitting at his desk, alive in ways she had long since lost.

A second letter made her lips twitch into a ghost of a smile. A spilled tray of spaghetti, a scolding from the cafeteria lady, it was ordinary, yet unmistakably him. Then the words cut sharper: *"Sometimes it feels like no one notices me. Don't ever stop noticing."* Her chest tightened, an ache she carried quietly even as the Vault around her throbbed with digital life. Max's memory of Boston, the antiseptic smell, the fear, the mother's scream, echoed in her mind, a reminder that the stakes were never just data points on a screen.

The storm thudded against the city above, a distant percussion that the concrete took and softened into a low, steady vibration beneath their feet. Down here, five floors below the Capitol, in a room with no windows and only the hum of servers, the sound translated into something private, a single drumbeat underlining her thoughts. In her mind, she was kneeling at the cemetery, mud squelching under her knees, letters clutched to her chest, lightning illuminating the carved name: **Alex Carter**. She whispered to him, *"I'll keep looking. I promise."* Another letter followed, words trembling but alive: *"I'm scared sometimes, you know? Don't let me disappear completely. Hold onto me."*

Her fingers tightened on the edge of the console as if the memory could tether her to reality. She could almost feel the wind tearing at her coat, hear the thunder roll over the cemetery, but the hum of servers reminded her that here, in the Vault, the battle continued. Grief had hardened into resolve. *"I see you. I hear you. I'll carry you forward. Every day."*

A flash of lightning in her memory illuminated the storm-soaked letters; she imagined him standing there, smiling despite everything, proud and mischievous. Her chest swelled with determination. She had carried him through this mental storm; now she would carry him through the real one.

Shaking off the memory, Maya's fingers returned to the keyboard. Chimera's pulse streamed before her, Phantom's code still lurking in the mesh, and every decision, every command mattered. The letters had reminded her why the stakes were human, personal, and unbearably fragile. Hospitals, kitchens, and classrooms are all vulnerable to the chaos out there.

She tapped through the logs, eyes sharp, heartbeat steady, letting the memory sharpen her focus instead of blinding her with grief. The Vault's hum became a rhythm she could follow, Chimera's heartbeat a metronome to keep her grounded. The storm, the grave, the letters, they were behind her now, but the resolve they forged burned forward. Every pulse she mirrored, every decoy she crafted, carried him with her into the fight.

Maya didn't look up as Max moved between consoles, giving orders, analyzing data, and driving the team forward. She didn't need to. She felt tethered to him, to the mission, to survival itself. The letters had reminded her that even in a room full of machines and code, the human stakes were what mattered most. And for the first time that night, she let herself carry that weight without breaking.

• • • • • • •

Chimera was locked down in a hardened black box, sealed tighter than anything else in the Vault. No uplinks. No vendor codes. Its only connection was to the analysts who fed it, tested it, and feared it.

"We've built a heartbeat," Tara said, her voice hoarse. "But we don't just mimic, we steer. With Chimera, we can issue override signals. If the implants listen, we don't just stall activation. We control it."

Adrian leaned back, running a hand over his tired face. "God help us if we're wrong."

Max stood at the center of the war room, the glow of Chimera's console painting his features in cold light. "This isn't about God," he said. "This is about survival. We've just given the enemy a shadow of their own. Let's see if they chase it."

Behind him, Sam stood with arms folded, the glow of the Chimera console reflected in his glasses.

"You've got your ghost, boss," he said quietly. "Now keep it on a leash."

Max turned, exhaustion and resolve in equal measure. "You still think we're playing with fire?"

"Every war starts with someone who thinks they can control the fire," Sam said. "Just promise me we'll know when to put it out."

Max didn't answer. The servers' low hum filled the pause, a heartbeat neither of them trusted entirely.

The trap was alive in the wires. A heartbeat built to lure the predator closer.

But Max wasn't celebrating yet.

He thought of his daughter. Years ago, she had shown him her science fair project: a model power grid built from toy circuits, light bulbs flickering when the wires connected. She'd grinned with pride when the system lit up, and he'd told her she was brighter than the grid itself. That memory haunted him now. Because when he looked at the endless flow of hostile code, he didn't see networks or devices. He saw the fragile, ordinary things, classrooms, kitchens, hospital rooms, that could go dark in an instant. He saw her face lit by the glow of those tiny bulbs, trusting the world to keep the lights on.

The memory passed, leaving him with the weight of what failure would mean.

"We've got a tool," he said, gathering the team. "Now we need a delivery mechanism. We can't push Chimera through the normal patch channels; it'll get flagged. We need to get this thing embedded where the mesh expects to find its own signal."

The next phase meant infiltration and physical access to backbone routers, satellite uplinks, and cellular towers across the country. It also meant coordinating with the FBI, the NSA, and allied field agents.

Max knew the next step had to reach the places where digital heartbeat met real metal, but that didn't mean he would be the one crossing fences anymore. His job was to hold the center, to keep every moving piece in rhythm while others carried the risk.

CHAPTER 7
FIREBREAK

Day 11: T-20. Chimera in the Wild.

At dawn, a three-person insertion unit led by Lt. Col. Dana Cortez touched down outside San Diego under a gray wash of morning. The city was quiet, but the target, a nondescript data facility wired into the West Coast's core infrastructure, wasn't. Any misstep could trip Phantom Chimera's sleeper circuits prematurely. In the Vault, Tara and Adrian stayed fixed to their consoles, eyes locked on the live feeds. Every command signal, every pulse of network telemetry streamed through their screens. Max stood behind them in the glass-walled control bay, headset resting against his collar. He was the fulcrum now, no longer in the field, but in the fight all the same.

At the outer ring, Sam had already collapsed two dozen inputs into a single federated dashboard.

"SIGINT, vendor manifests, partner data, one channel," he said to Maya, voice level through the comms.

"Minimal friction, maximum traceability."

Everyone in the room knew to glance toward Rourke when things got noisy; he translated policy into action before arguments could form.

Maya worked in parallel, keeping liaison lines open to FBI cyber task-forces and Five Eyes intercept nodes. If anything went sideways in San Diego, she would be the one to spin up counterintelligence coverage before the headlines wrote themselves.

* * * * * * * *

The Operation

From her mobile command post near the perimeter, Cortez reviewed the body-cam feeds.

"Three minutes to splice," she told her team. "Stay dark until my mark."

Adrian monitored the live stream, eyes narrowed. "Tell the agents to show me their hands," he muttered.

Cortez's reply came through crystal clear. "Relax, Doc. They're vetted and double-checked."

"So were half the compromised contractors," Adrian shot back. He zoomed in on the panel as the field techs unscrewed a service hatch. "We're embedding our heartbeat into their mesh. I'm not trusting anyone's fingers but mine."

Cortez initiated a secondary verification sequence, syncing her field tablet with Tara's remote routines. Redundancy on redundancy, it was the only way they'd all sleep again.

At minute three, the feed cut to black. "What the hell?" Adrian barked.

"Localized RF suppression," Tara answered. "Not ours."

For ten seconds, the Vault was silent except for cooling fans.

Cortez's calm broke through the static:

"Backup link engaged. Breach team holding position. Status green."

The picture returned. On-screen telemetry glowed emerald. "Connection confirmed," came the voice from the field.

"We're exfiltrating."

"Copy all," Max said evenly. "Tag the waveform and archive every millisecond of interference. If they test us again, I want the echo mapped before they finish the thought."

Tara scanned the decoy routines. "Crude but effective, reminds me of the way Kane used to patch networks."

No one repeated the name.

"If it works, it works," Max said quietly. "We're not here to admire the code; we're here to survive it."

* * * * * * *

Aftermath

Over the next 24 hours, Chimera nodes were embedded at 28 locations nationwide. Each success brought new exhaustion and bigger risk.

Through it all, Rourke moved quietly among the consoles, his voice a steady metronome that kept the analysts' hands from shaking. They called him the old man, though he wasn't much past forty. The faint hitch in his left leg was an old field souvenir, but his posture never bent. When he spoke, people listened.

A failed installation in New Jersey flared into a local news blip, an electrical fire under investigation. Tara buried it before it reached federal review.

The sleeper network had noticed. Its patterns were shifting, encryption keys rotating faster than predicted. Some nodes blinked out entirely, migrating to new frequencies. Every console beep sliced the silence.

"It knows we're coming," Adrian warned.

"Then it's learning, good," Max replied. "That means it's still inside the lab, not outside it."

* * * * * * *

Global Sync

As the countdown neared its final week, foreign reconnaissance traffic spiked. Deep-packet inspections mimicked legitimate firmware updates. Military satellites suffered "solar anomalies" that weren't solar at all.

Within hours, encrypted feeds from Ottawa, Cheltenham, and Canberra lit up the Vault's displays. GCHQ flagged mirrored packet bursts in British defense networks; ASD traced identical probes through Pacific cable routers. The cross-talk was global.

Rourke's voice slid through the comm noise, crisp and calm: "Feeds synchronized with GCHQ and ASD. Shared analysis packet queued, tagged, time-stamped, traceable. If they see a divergence, we hold action until confirmation."

"Perfect," Max said. "That's what partnership looks like: frictionless data, shared risk. Keep it clean and let them know we see them working."

"Already done," Rourke answered. "If anything looks wrong, we isolate and call you. Otherwise, we feed the deception and watch what bites."

"They're mapping resilience," Tara murmured. "Testing how fast we share what we see."

While she spoke, her models surfaced an out-of-sequence sleeper fragment buried in a New Mexico transportation controller, with the same signature, but a different clock. That anomaly cracked the code.

"They've randomized offsets to mask timing patterns," she said. "They knew we'd find the countdown."

Adrian's fingers flew. "With all this data, I can map Chimera's footprint against their false schedule and trigger a simulated collapse inside their own mesh."

Max's mouth set into a hard line. "Then we stop reacting," he said. "We make them chase our shadow. Time to weaponize disinformation."

Outside, storm clouds massed above Washington; underground, another storm gathered strength.

And in the Vault, Max prepared to fire the first counterstrike.

CHAPTER 8
AMBUSH

Day 13: T-18: No Turning Back

The Vault had settled into its nocturnal hum, a warren of glowing monitors and abandoned coffee cups. Shaw rubbed at the bridge of his nose. Hours of packet traces had left the glyphs swimming.

"I'm picking up a weak beacon out of a Gulf Coast switching hub," Tara said quietly. "Signature's almost identical to Kansas. Could be our master trigger."

Adrian leaned over her shoulder. "Almost identical is the problem. It's like they wanted us to find it."

Maya didn't look up from her logs. "No leaks on my end, but whoever's behind this knows our hunting pattern. Could be a trap."

Director Pike's face flickered onto the secure video feed. "Quick in, quick out. Capture evidence, pull out. No cowboy stunts."

Shaw turned the old Navy coin in his pocket. "We can't afford another surprise," he muttered, but he gave the order anyway. A four-person joint team would move before dawn.

Rain slicked the asphalt outside an anonymous warehouse on the Gulf Coast. Sodium lights flickered, humming like insects. In the van, Agent Collins chewed gum, eyes darting between the door and the glow of the laptop on his knees.

"Comms check," the cyber-operator said, voice thin with static.

"Vault copies," Tara answered from Washington. "You're green."

Maya's name flashed on Shaw's console. *This feels wrong,* she texted. *Beacon's too clean.*

He stared at the screen. *We need the proof,* he typed back.

Outside, the team moved. Breach charge. Hydraulic pop. The service door gave way with a metallic gasp. They swept inside under flashlight beams.

The facility was quiet, humming with racks of servers. Condensation dripped from overhead pipes. The cyber-op-era-tor knelt, plugging into a port, fingers dancing over keys. "Drives imaging," he murmured. "Looks like Christmas."

Half a continent away, Shaw watched their feed twitch. Audio crackled, then steadied.

Adrian's hand hovered over his keyboard. "Signal inversion," he said sharply. "That beacon is mirrored…"

The line went dead.

Inside the hub, the team's radios hissed and died. Emergency lights flickered crimson. Server LEDs flipped from green to amber to red. Fans roared like turbines.

"Something's wrong," Agent Collins said. "Pull the plug…"

A sharp hiss overhead. Fire-suppressant gas spewed from ceiling nozzles, swallowing their beams in a chemical fog. The hardened laptop flashed error codes, a BIOS overwrite, and "drive sectors gone." A blackout rippled through the grid out-side; streetlights and a nearby warehouse flickered.

The cyber-operator slumped as his laptop smoked, coughing into his sleeve. "They're frying us."

"Tara, get them out of there," Shaw barked, but only static answered. Maya stared at her screen, pale.

"They were waiting for us," she whispered. "This was a canary, an alert to Phantom that we'd found them."

Max's teeth grinded. "We just walked into their honeypot."

Inside the hub, Collins dragged the coughing cyber-operator toward the exit. Servers hissed and shut down. Evidence drives burned out one by one, LEDs dying like stars.

"Move!" Collins shouted. "Now!"

They stumbled into the rain, gas clinging to their clothes, and piled into the Suburban. Only at a safe distance did their comms reconnect.

Back in the Vault, the feed flickered back. The team sat in the van, faces ghost-white in the dashboard glow.

Adrian examined the recovered gear. "Wiped. Bricked. It's like we were never there."

Tara scrolled through what little had been salvaged, half a packet capture, timestamps already stale. "They shifted the beacon traffic again. Our one lead is gone."

Maya's fingers trembled over her keyboard. "Someone tipped them off. One of our contractors, maybe. We can't keep chasing ghosts."

Max stood, staring at the red clusters spreading across the national map. He felt the coin in his pocket dig into his palm.

Suddenly, Pike's feed flared to life again. The director's face was tight with fury.

"Shaw," Pike said, voice sharp. "Do you have any idea what that Gulf Coast hub failure cost us? Half a dozen leads. You went in blind, and your people almost didn't make it out!"

Max's hands clenched into fists. "Sir, we followed your plan. We got inside. Phantom expected it."

"Expected it? Everything blew up! Drives destroyed! We're left chasing ghosts!" Pike slammed a hand on the console. "Do you understand the consequences? You risked lives for what, nothing?"

Max said nothing. He only stared at the map, letting the red nodes burn in his vision.

The feed cut with a snap, leaving only static and the low thrum of the Vault's servers.

For a long moment, no one spoke. The screens still pulsed with red clusters, each one a reminder of how close they'd come and how little they'd gained.

Sam Rourke stepped forward from the shadowed end of the room, his voice low but steady. "You did what had to be done."

Max didn't look up. "Did I? Feels like we walked straight into their crosshairs."

"We walked out," Sam said. "That's what matters. Pike's angry because he needs someone to blame, not because you were wrong."

Max exhaled, the sound closer to a growl than a sigh. "I can't keep losing ground every time they move."

Sam rested a hand on the console beside him. "Then stop calling it losing. We learn, they adapt, we learn faster. That's the job. You've been in harder fights, just not ones anyone could see."

Max finally met his eyes. The anger there softened, just a fraction. "You really think we can still win this?"

Sam gave a small, tired smile. "If we couldn't, you'd have quit by now. And that's not who you are."

The tension in the room eased by degrees. Tara's shoulders dropped; Maya's fingers stilled on the keys.

Max turned back to the map, the red fading into static snow. "Then let's start acting like it."

Sam nodded once, with quiet approval. "That's the boss I know." The Vault hummed back to life, not louder, just steadier.

CHAPTER 9
BLINDSIDE

Day 14: T-17. Countdown Accelerated

The Vault hummed with small noises: cooling fans, sleep-deprived keystrokes, distant security footfalls. Tonight, those noises felt like a single held breath.

Max watched red nodes blink across the Midwest and Gulf Coast. Firmware anomalies, hardware tamper signatures, and anomalous beaconing all hinted at the sleeper's growing heartbeat. Max's mind churned over the Gulf Coast hub debacle. He could still taste the acrid gas, hear the hiss of corrupted drives. The sting of failure wasn't gone; it sharpened the choices ahead. Tara waved him over. Her fingers danced over keyboards, dissecting packet captures and mirrored proxies. "They're syncing," she said.

Adrian leaned over a hardware analyzer. "Coordination signal. Activation windows lining up."

"How long?" Max asked.

"Thought eighteen days. Now, ten. Maybe less," Tara said.

Maya snapped a file shut. Waiting meant lives lost; Pike wouldn't authorize anything risky.

Max scanned his team: Tara, calm and precise; Adrian, hardware scars and mechanical honesty; Maya, quiet and lethal in judgment.

He thought of the field with a strategist's private list, names and faces he'd trusted through quieter years. When the alarms turned into a national chorus, those people were the ones who moved with practiced speed: Captain Elena Torres in Chicago, who ran hospital-grid containment like a surgeon; Luis Delgado in Dallas, who handled transport and rail control mitigations; Mai Nguyen on the West Coast, who kept the power distribution teams from tripping one another into failure.

Max no longer went into the field. He had built a network to do it for him, a set of regional cyber-response teams that answered to his encrypted call signs. They were his hands. They were his oath.

"Briefing room. Ten minutes. No logs," he said.

Max stepped into the corridor, datapad warm under his palm. He thumbed a secure line to the Vault; the hiss of encryption answered almost instantly.

"Rourke," he said.

"Shaw," Sam's voice came back, low and steady. "You look like the kind of man about to do something the paperwork will never forgive."

Max let out a breath. "Full-sandbox run. I want Chimera to live against the simulated Hydra, every node, every mirrored proxy, in real time. Pike won't sign it. He thinks it's too risky even in containment."

There was a pause, then Sam: "You mean lighting the match in a sealed room."

"In a sealed room," Max corrected. "If we don't see the whole animal breathe, we'll never know how to kill it."

Sam's tone softened but stayed hard-edged. "Containment first. Make every fail-safe you've got non-negotiable. Air-gap it. Triple snapshots. If you want me to back you, I need every trace logged and a kill switch I can reach from the floor."

"You'll have it," Max said.

"You run it," Sam went on, "and I'll keep the Vault from panicking when the lights flicker. But promise me one thing, don't start it and walk away."

Max allowed a brief, tired smile. "I won't."

"Good," Sam said. "Then go do it. And if it gets ugly, I'll be the one dragging you back into the box."

Max tucked the datapad under his arm and headed for the steel-lined room.

● ● ● ● ● ● ●

Inside the steel-lined room, Max sealed his phone in a Faraday box. "We plan this off the record," he said. "Follow packets, map the net. We won't ask permission."

Tara pressed her lips thin. "If we simulate wrong, the sleeper could detect probing."

"And we can't risk a million devices going dark," Max said.

Adrian rubbed his wrist scar. "One shot. Half the logs will point at whoever's asleep upstairs. You understand?"

Maya's voice was calm. "Or we do nothing, and cities hollow out. Bureaucracy kills faster than them."

"Then we move," Tara said.

They became architects of the unseen. Max had no intention of touching servers; the operation was all simulation, pre-positioning, and contingency mapping. He and the team:

- Rerouted virtual traffic into decoy paths.
- Mapped redundant nodes and mirrored proxies.
- Simulated recursive packet chases to see how the Hydra would respond.

Tara noted, "They'll respond as if maintenance chatter. If they act, we can test their mirror logic without touching a rack."

When the simulated counterstrike hit, aggressive, adaptive packets, they adjusted their models.

Adrian muttered, "They weaponized the proxies."

Maya fed fresh correlation flags. "Even in simulation, they scramble attribution cleverly."

Tara stripped polymorphic wrappers. "They are built to survive, not hide."

Then the domestic "hot node" appeared in the simulations: a benign-seeming server rack inside a midwestern industrial complex, carrying the heartbeat of the sleeper. Max froze. This was the node they would use as the lure for the Ghost.

"Physical presence is impossible," Adrian said. "But we can build a functional decoy and simulate every fail-safe."

Tara's eyes sharpened. "If we simulate wrong, timers could cascade, but if we do it right, we can trick the Hydra without anyone touching a cable."

They spent hours overlaying BGP tables, traceroutes, and physical facility maps. They crafted decoy scripts, cold-boot shields, and payloads that only existed in the Vault's environment, designed to capture seed keys and freeze bootloaders in a virtual sandbox.

By dawn, the Vault had a new map: simulated nodes, decoy traps, contingency plans. No one would touch a live rack, yet when the Ghost saw the decoy, the Hydra would react as if it were real.

Max put his hand on the rail. The countdown did not care about laws or debates. It only lowered like a blade.

* * * * * * *

A secure feed beeped. Pike's face reappeared, still stern, the Gulf Coast raid failure fresh in his mind.

"Shaw," he said, voice low but edged with anger, "I know you're moving off the books, but understand this: the last operation nearly got your people killed. I want full accountability if anything goes wrong again. You think you can handle this?"

Max met his gaze. "We're not repeating the mistakes from yesterday, sir. The decoy keeps our people safe, and the Hydra distracted. No one touches the racks."

Pike leaned back. "I hope you're right. Because if you're not… it won't just be your career on the line."

Max let the words settle. He knew Pike's threat was real, but the choice was simple: succeed or risk far worse consequences. Beneath the surface, the decoy waited, ready to lure the Ghost into the trap they had built. When *The Breach Beneath* began, the stage was set, and the only variable left was the adversary's reaction.

CHAPTER 10
THE BREACH BENEATH

Day 15: T-16. Decoy Built to Trick the Ghost.

The relay pulsed like a waiting heart. All night, Max had felt it beating beneath the floor, steady as a war drum. Now, as the Vault stirred with the gray light of morning, the air carried a different tension, not relief, not dread, but the thin crackle of something about to break.

Monitors blinked with ordinary noise, vendor traffic, maintenance checks, and background telemetry, but buried inside was their counterfeit signal, a decoy pulse meant to draw Phantom's gaze. To the untrained eye, it was just another beat in the system's endless rhythm. To the enemy, Max hoped, it would look like the master key had finally moved.

He stood at the railing, knuckles white against the steel. Chimera was online. The false heartbeat was out there. They'd bought themselves a knife of an advantage, but Max knew knives cut both ways.

• • • • • • • •

Half a world away, in a bunker carved into an abandoned metro station, a bank of monitors flickered. Lines of telemetry scrolled past in pale green against black, thousands of tiny pulses from deep inside the American grid. One pulse didn't belong.

The woman at the console leaned closer, dark hair falling across her face. "We're seeing an echo," she murmured in Russian-accented English. "A new signature mimicking our implants."

Behind her, a man in a charcoal suit stepped out of the shadows. Only his hands showed in the low light, knuckles marked with an old burn. He studied the anomaly for a long moment. "A decoy," he said at last. "They're building a shadow to hunt us."

The woman hesitated. "Do you want me to block it?"

He shook his head once. "No. Let it breathe. A shadow can show you where the light is."

On the screen, Chimera's false heartbeat rippled across their network like a stone dropped in a still pond. Somewhere in the maze of code, the predator stirred, curious.

• • • • • • •

Max stared at the map now illuminated by Chimera's telemetry. Red dots flickered like digital landmines scattered across the country, each one an infected node. A new indicator, a bright yellow mark, indicated where Chimera had taken root. It was working. But the enemy was adapting.

Tara approached with a tablet. "Max, the decoy signal is only holding on about 60% of the implants. The others are starting to reject it. We think they're running checksum protocols to verify authenticity."

Adrian, hunched over a machine-learning engine analyzing signal variants, added, "It's like the system holding up a fake ID under better light, suddenly it knows it's being fooled."

"Which means we've bought time," Max said, standing. "Not victory."

He turned toward the whiteboard now covered in scrawled code snippets, signal graphs, and threat models. "We need a new variant. A recursive one. Something that rewrites itself based on feedback."

Tara shook her head. "That's borderline AI-level control.

We'd need a full quantum modeling suite."

Adrian grinned. "Or a legacy exploit. What if we let Chimera look *worse*? Make it look like a corrupted node. Something the sleeper network isolates instead of interacting with."

Max considered. "We make it look like a broken lightbulb.

The network doesn't try to use it, it just tosses it aside." "Exactly. We emulate failure. But controlled failure. That way, we're cloaked, and they waste time rerouting or abandoning the node."

It was elegant in its own strange way, like hiding in plain sight.

As the team developed the degraded-signal protocol, nick-named *Wraith*, a sub-project of Chimera, the Wraith decoy was designed to give Phantom a taste of control, a sandbox where it would reveal itself.

* * * * * * *

The desert wind of Fort Huachuca, Arizona, carried dust against the outer blast doors, humming through a base built to disappear into the landscape. Lt. Col. Dana Cortez leaned over a field display, the light painting tired shadows across her face.

"Director, this is Cortez," she said into the headset. "Your Wraith decoys live here, too. We're running mirror latency tests on regional grid relays. If Phantom's probing field nodes, we'll catch its reflection before it hits the backbone."

Rourke's calm voice answered from the Vault: "Copy that, Dana. Keep your grid dark and your uplinks slow, no chatter above the noise floor."

"Understood." She adjusted a shoulder brace hidden under her fatigue jacket, the remnant of a field injury that never quite healed, then added, "Tell Shaw we'll keep the desert heartbeat steady. If the ghost wants light, we'll give it lightning."

In the Vault, Max caught the last line over open comms and allowed himself the faintest smile. "Good hunting, Colonel."

·······

Max was summoned to a closed-door meeting with the Secretary of Homeland Security and a small cadre of senior senators from the Intelligence Committee. They met in a secure facility beneath the Capitol, a fallout shelter reborn for digital war.

Senator Kincaid, sharp-eyed and unsparing, started the grilling.

"Mr. Shaw, twenty states are running fine, lights on, trains moving, no riots. And you call this a breach? Sounds like you're selling us panic to keep your lab funded."

"We're keeping it covert to avoid widespread panic and give our team the maneuvering room to respond."

"And if your pet project, this 'Chimera,' blows up in our faces?" "You'll take the blame, not us. We don't lose elections over sci-fi experiments gone wrong."

"Then we lose control. Transportation, power, healthcare, all of it vulnerable to synchronized attack."

"Why not just pull the plug? Or are you too buried in techno-babble to see the obvious? We can't afford to look weak by doing nothing, but we sure as hell can't explain your ghost stories to Wall Street either."

"Because that would trigger the failsafe. The implants are wired to activate if abnormal shutdowns or resets are detected. We have to work *inside* the live systems."

Another senator snipped, "You're throwing around 'act of war' awfully casually, Shaw. Careful, some of us have voters who don't want to hear we're about to start World War III because of your invisible boogeyman."

Max paused. "We believe this is state-sponsored. The tactics, the scale, the coordination, they all point to a nation-state actor. And if they're embedding sleeper code in our infrastructure, it's not for mischief. It's to cripple us."

"Then we need to consider retaliatory options," the Secretary said.

Max answered evenly. "Let's stop the countdown first. Then we can talk about payback."

The senators gathered their folders, murmuring in clipped tones as they filed out. Staffers trailed after them, leaving the secure room in thinning waves.

Pike lingered, polishing his glasses with the hem of his sleeve. "You analysts always think the sky is falling. Leadership isn't about being right; it's about knowing when to ignore the panic and keep the country running. The public doesn't care about firmware. They care about gas prices. And right now, you sound like the guy yelling fire in a crowded theater because the lights flickered."

He slipped his glasses back on and left without waiting for a reply.

* * * * * * *

Back in the Vault, Wraith was progressing. The degraded pulse was fooling 80% of the smart implants into thinking they were corrupted. They self-isolated, which reduced the chance of receiving the activation command.

The Vault was quieter than it had been in weeks, the screens showing steady pulses instead of bleeding red. Pike paused at the door, gave Max a long look, and muttered, "Don't get used to being right."

Hours later, when the others had gone to snatch fragments of sleep, Max lingered. On his monitor, one residual stream of traffic shimmered in the dark. Not hostile. Not random. Just there, watching.

He leaned back, his father's voice echoing in memory. *The dangers we create ourselves...*

Victory wasn't the same as safety. Not anymore.

Tara slid a tablet onto the table, its glow catching the exhaustion in her eyes. "Chimera held. Long enough to buy us breathing room."

Max nodded, already turning away, but Tara stayed. Her thumb traced the edge of the screen. Buried in the logs was something only she noticed: the mimicry routine had been mirrored back at them. Phantom had listened and copied.

It learned from me, she thought. And for the first time in days, the hum of the Vault felt less like a sanctuary and more like a mirror.

Adrian lingered after the others had gone. His hand still ached from where he'd ripped a controller board loose during the breach, the burn raw against his skin. Proof enough, for anyone, of loyalty.

Yet his eyes stayed on a string of code no one else had flagged.

It wasn't hostile, not anymore. Just familiar.

A thin smile tugged at his mouth. *I've seen this pattern before.* Tara shifted in her chair, curling one leg beneath her. A glimpse of socks, rockets on one foot, cartoon dinosaurs on the other, peeked out as she bent over the console. Max caught it for just a second. The small defiance of color and whimsy in the middle of countdown clocks and kill codes reminded him who she was beneath the algorithms.

"We're buying ourselves a digital quarantine," Tara said. "But the infected mesh is still mutating. I just saw a packet reroute using IPv6 address cloaking from a node in Minsk."

The code pressed harder against the nation's veins, testing how much strain they could take before they snapped.

• • • • • • •

Far above Los Angeles, two commercial flights converged on the same approach vector.

In the cockpit, sweat slicked the pilot's grip on the yoke, the vibration of engines trembling through bone.

In the LAX control tower, a controller leaned over her console, eyes fixated at the radar overlay. The transponder data was flickering, altitudes swapping as if the aircraft were ghosting each other.

"Delta Two-One-Seven, confirm heading," she said into her headset.

Only static answered, followed by overlapping voices from another channel. Her stomach dropped. The radar feed showed both aircraft at the same altitude, closing fast.

"Southwest Four-Niner-Two, do you copy?" she tried again. The scope jittered, the icons merging. At five hundred feet of projected separation, she slammed her fist on the override and shouted into the mic: "Delta Two-One-Seven, immediate climb! Southwest Four-Niner-Two, hard bank right, now!"

For one suspended heartbeat, nothing happened. Then the planes diverged, engines screaming against the night as navigation lights flashed like blades crossing in the dark.

On her console, the radar steadied. The icons separated. The collision never came.

But it had been measured in pixels.

• • • • • • • •

Inside The Vault, an alert banner bled across Adrian's console. A muted alarm chirped once, too soft for panic but sharp enough to slice the room's focus. He froze, then pushed the data to the central display.

"Signal injection through FAA ground systems," he said, voice hard. "They spoofed altitude and heading data. The system thought the planes were safe when they weren't."

Tara exhaled sharply. "If the pilots hadn't reacted…"

"We'd be watching fire on the Pacific coast," Adrian finished. Maya rubbed her temple. The fluorescent lights in the Vault suddenly became too bright. She remembered the pulse in her apartment, the lights dimming, brightening, mocking her. That same hand was at work here, twisting dials in towers and cockpits. She wondered how long before every home, every streetlight, became part of the same game.

Max stared at the replay, two aircraft icons brushing past each other on the digital map. His chest tightened with fury. This wasn't just probing infrastructure anymore. This was calibration, an enemy twisting dials on systems that carried lives. He'd seen echoes of this before: Ukraine's grids falling dark, hospitals frozen by ransomware, fuel lines cut by a single exploit. The line between nuisance and catastrophe had vanished years ago, and tonight, it was only confirmed.

Maya's hand tightened around her stylus. The lights in the Vault seemed too steady, too obedient. She remembered the pulse in her apartment, the way her devices had turned into eyes. For the first time, she wondered if the Vault's walls were any safer than her own.

His voice was low, sharpened by anger. "This isn't about systems. It's about blood."

The debrief room was quiet, the weight of near catastrophe pressing on every face. Analysts stared at screens, pretending to work.

Pike stepped closer to Max, lowering his voice. He slipped his glasses off, polishing them slowly.

"You called it," he said, voice gravelly. "I wanted to believe the system was too big to fail. Turns out, it's too connected not to."

He met Max's eyes, weary but resolute. "From here on, you lead. I'll back your play."

Sam shifted his weight, the cane tapping faintly on the floor. "I see you're making progress with Pike," he said, voice low but carrying just enough for Max to hear.

Max let a half-smile break the tension. "Don't get used to it." Sam's grin was a small, tired thing. "Wouldn't dream of it. Just keep him on the right side long enough for us to finish the job."

* * * * * * *

Des Moines, Iowa

It started with a single teller window. A woman slid her debit card across the counter, waiting for the receipt that never printed. The clerk frowned, tapped a few keys, then shook his head.

"System's down," he said. "Just give it a moment."

The moment stretched. Other customers leaned in, clutching their wallets. Across the lobby, every ATM screen froze mid-transaction, swallowing cards without return.

A man in a work jacket slammed his fist against the glass. "That's my rent money in there."

Phones lit up with the same error: Transaction unavailable. Try again later. A chorus of ringtones and angry thumbs tapping screens filled the lobby, jagged against the silence of frozen machines.

By the time police arrived, the line out the door had doubled back around the block. Shouts of fraud and conspiracy echoed through the crowd. One man stood on the hood of his car, waving a crumpled statement like a flag.

Inside, the clerks sat frozen at their terminals, powerless to explain why a city's worth of savings had just vanished into silence.

* * * * * * *

Maya felt the weight of the scene, the way she felt code, as a pattern with an origin. In her office, she pulled up another surveillance report on Jacob Morrow. He hadn't parked in the same space twice all week. A nervous habit, maybe. Or a tell.

She remembered him from a training session two years back, quiet, almost shy, the kind of man who brought donuts on Fridays. The thought of him as a traitor didn't fit, which made it worse.

One week remained. Each sunrise felt stolen.

Adrian leaned forward. "That's not just rerouting. That's global relinking. They've got fallbacks outside the country."

"Which means if we take out the domestic mesh," Max said, "they could trigger from abroad. We need to go on the offensive. Now."

He pulled up the global intercept logs. "Time to trace the activation beacon upstream. Find the origin server."

Adrian looked uneasy. "Max, that means touching systems outside U.S. jurisdiction."

"We're not hacking a country. We're intercepting an act of war." They deployed what Adrian called a "digital prism", a software construct that fractured incoming signals into their composite instructions and timestamp trails.

The code structure was based on legacy signal-fractionation models from a defunct DARPA project, which some in the lab had once called Prism.

The prism discovered something shocking. A low hum from the servers deepened, as if the room itself was bracing for impact. The signal pattern was originating from multiple countries, Russia, Iran, and China, but the timing didn't add up.

"They're using proxy servers," Adrian said. "Chained through friendly systems to make attribution difficult. But look at this."

He highlighted a timestamp anomaly. "There's a signature that doesn't shift. It's always within the same 7ms of system time. That means somewhere, one of the command servers is real."

"Can we isolate it?" "Already working on it."

Not long after, they had it. A command node buried in a data center in Macau. It was communicating through a spoofed VPN, but the digital prism cracked the traffic. Tara coordinated with the CIA for a quiet raid.

Within 24 hours, the server was in U.S. hands. And inside it, a kill code. A universal beacon embedded in the architecture of the sleeper implants.

"If we replicate this with a false payload," Tara said, "we could shut them down all at once."

"Or trigger them," Adrian warned. "It's a razor's edge."

Max stared at the kill command string. "Then we'd better balance it perfectly."

What struck him most wasn't just the code itself, but how they had come by it. In resisting Chimera, Phantom had exposed its own scaffolding, the pulse that kept the sleeper mesh alive. The Kansas Raid hadn't simply bought them time; it had forced Phantom to show its voice.

"It revealed itself," Max murmured. "The raid gave us the seed. Talonfall will be our answer."

The enemy's heartbeat was in their hands, but so was the razor's edge of failure.

The operation was codenamed *Talonfall*. They would create a synthetic kill signal, mirroring the original but with a nanosecond delay that would stall the implants just long enough to cause them to fail their own checksum, forcing a shutdown rather than activation. It would require simultaneous broadcast across all Wraith-masked nodes and every available Chimera injection point. "This is it," Max said the night before the operation. "We've mapped 89% of infected systems. That's the highest we'll get. We move at 0300 hours."

Tara nodded. Adrian looked pale but focused.

Max added, "This won't be a celebration. Not yet. Because if it works, we just averted disaster. But if we fail..."

He didn't need to finish the sentence. Outside, the world spun in blissful ignorance.

Inside the Vault, every hand moved with urgency.

* * * * * * *

Houston, Texas

In a modest house on the city's edge, the refrigerator light flickered once and went dark.

Maria checked the outlet, then the breaker. Nothing. The hum that had filled the kitchen for years, the background noise of safety, was gone. She opened the fridge door anyway, praying for cold.

The insulin vials lay against the side panel, already warming.

On the couch, her twelve-year-old son looked up, his voice thin. "Mom? Is it okay?"

Maria forced a smile she didn't feel. "It'll be fine, Cariño.

We'll get more tomorrow."

But when she called the pharmacy, the line rang to a recorded message: "System outage." *Please call back later.* The online portal gave only a blank white screen.

She pressed her forehead against the fridge, the silence pressing back harder. In a city of millions, her child's life had just become a hostage to code she could not see, could not fight.

. . . .

Max's phone buzzed against the console. Anna's name glowed on the screen, but the call cut off before he could answer. He tried redialing, got voicemail, and slid the phone away. The silence stung worse than any alert banner.

The clock read 02:59:47.

The countdown was almost over, and Max was ready to make his stand.

But even as Talonfall neared execution, a buried process flickered to life in the West Coast grid. It was an anomaly, one no one had expected. A rogue implant had mutated past Wraith, rejecting both Chimera and the original sleeper logic. It had become something new.

"We have a problem," Tara whispered, eyes widening as she watched the rogue implant rewrite its own code in real time.

"It's not listening to any beacon anymore," Adrian muttered. "It's self-directed."

Max exhaled slowly. "The raid forced it into the open.

Talonfall struck its heart. And still… it adapted."

Tara's voice was quiet. "We didn't just trap it. We taught it how to survive us."

"A new species," Max said, his voice grim. "And we've just woken it up."

Sam watched from the edge of the room, saying nothing. The glow from the monitors traced hard lines across his face.

He'd seen enough operations to recognize the pattern; every victory carried the seed of its own undoing.

This was what he'd been afraid of, he thought. The moment the code stopped being theirs to control.

He kept the thought to himself. The team didn't need doubt right now, only resolve.

But as the screens dimmed, Sam exhaled in frustration. The thing they had built to protect them was learning to breathe.

The room fell into stunned silence. The game had just changed again.

Talonfall would go ahead. But so would something else, something no one had yet defined.

Max looked up at the Vault's ceiling, as if he could see through it into the stars.

"It's not just about defense anymore," he said. "It's evolution. And we'd better evolve faster."

* * * * * * *

New York City

The lights died in mid-step.

One moment, Manhattan pulsed with the usual hum, neon signs, traffic lights, subway currents flowing beneath the streets. Next, silence swept across blocks like a tide.

In an ICU on the Upper East Side, monitors went blank. Nurses lunged for backup generators, only to find them unresponsive, firmware bricked in the same instant as the grid.

On the street below, cars froze at dead intersections. Horns blared, brakes screeched, metal crumpled. A man in a business suit sprinted toward an ATM as if it might have one last gasp of power, but its screen blinked once and went dark.

From the rooftops, the blackout looked like a living thing, spreading outward, swallowing light after light, until only the glow of cell phones and the panic of voices remained.

People screamed. Others prayed. Somewhere in the chaos, a child cried out, his voice cutting through the dark like a siren.

The city had survived terror attacks, hurricanes, and financial collapse. But this was different.

This enemy lived in the wires.

* * * * * * *

The countdown resumed, and the world unknowingly edged closer to the unknown.

CHAPTER 11
FRACTURE

Day 16: T-15. *One Missed Pulse.*

The Vault's air was thick with recycled cold, the hum of servers pressing against tired skulls. Tara sat hunched over her workstation, the glow of cascading packet streams burning into her retinas. Her eyes had been open for thirty-one hours. She'd told herself she'd sleep after cracking the firmware sample from Baton Rouge, then again after validating Chimera's checksum. Each time, she found another thread to pull.

She blinked hard, rubbed her temples, and took another sip of coffee gone cold hours ago. Her hands shook as she typed, but she convinced herself it was adrenaline.

On her monitor, a ripple of anomalous packets flared, just for a breath. Her system flagged them with a faint amber.

Noise, she thought automatically. Crosstalk from a mis-con-figured substation. She silenced the alert with one keystroke and leaned back, stretching her neck until the vertebrae popped.

Behind her, Adrian frowned. "What was that?"

"Nothing," Tara muttered. "False positive. I've seen the signature before."

He hovered a moment, suspicion in his eyes, then backed away. Tara's pride kept her from admitting she hadn't really *looked*. She didn't have time. Not with the clock bleeding down.

Hours later, the Vault erupted with alarms. A cluster of red nodes lit up across Illinois. Substations flared and dropped, one after another, like dominoes falling in digital silence.

Max barreled across the room, eyes locked on Tara's console. "Where the hell did this start?"

The secure comms board flared alive before she could answer.

"Director, this is Torres. Chicago is blind. Backup telemetry's dropping."

"Delgado here," another voice cut in, rough with static. "Dallas grid's spiking, we're seeing the same pattern, mirrored." Max's pulse thundered. The regional captains, his protégés, were already in motion, reacting before central even gave the word.

"Lock down your isolation gates," he ordered. "Containment first, diagnostics second."

"Copy," Torres said. "We'll burn the line if we have to."

The channels flickered, then steadied into the background hum of field command. Max turned back to the team, straight-faced. "We're blind in two regions. Find the entry vector. Now."

Her heart froze. The amber signature was still there in her logs, timestamped seven hours earlier. The one she'd dismissed.

Adrian's voice was tight. "That wasn't noise, Tara. That was a beacon. They were mapping us."

The blood drained from her face. "I… I thought…"

Max leaned in, his voice taut. "Thought doesn't cut it. Two hospitals just lost backup power because of this."

The room was already in motion, analysts rerouting, operators scrambling to contain the spread, but Tara couldn't move. The lines of code on her screen blurred into static, her mind replaying the keystroke that silenced the alert.

For the first time since MIT, Tara felt useless.

She tore off her glasses, pressing the heels of her hands into her eyes. The Vault roared around her, but all she heard was the faint echo of an amber ping, her mistake, now written into the countdown.

Sam stopped beside her workstation, one hand braced on the edge of the console. The room's noise seemed to fold around them.

"Hey," he said quietly, just enough for her to hear. "You caught it in time. That's what matters."

Tara didn't look up. Her fingers stayed rigid against the keyboard, knuckles white.

"Tara," he tried again, softer this time. "One mistake doesn't define the mission."

She slipped her glasses back on, eyes fixed on the scrolling data as if it could erase the sound of his voice.

Sam lingered for a heartbeat, then nodded to himself and stepped away.

He didn't blame her for the silence. He'd seen that kind of shame before, the kind that made people work twice as hard just to feel human again.

CHAPTER 12
TALONFALL

Day 17: T-14. Blackout Spreads Beyond Control.

The blackout spread faster than the maps could keep up with.

From the skies above New York to the subways beneath it, the city had fallen into silence, a silence that rippled outward into New Jersey, Connecticut, and Pennsylvania. What the pub-lic saw was darkness. What the Vault saw was worse: **a rogue signal, alive, adapting, and moving faster than containment.** Tara leaned over her console, frowning hard. "This isn't just failure.

This is contagion."

Max's chest was heavy as he scanned the flaring red nodes. "Then we're not fighting code anymore. We're fighting evolution."

And evolution didn't wait.

· · · · · · · ·

At precisely 03:00 hours Eastern Standard Time, the Vault was cloaked in an almost reverent silence. The digital battlefield was alive with energy, but the operators remained still, their eyes flickering between monitors, their fingers poised on keyboards like surgeons before the scalpel's first cut. Max stood at the center of it all, his breath measured and slow despite the raging storm inside his mind.

Talonfall was about to begin.

Before giving the order, Max opened a secure comms board. Four regional captains appeared in flickering video tiles: Torres from Chicago, Delgado from Dallas, Nguyen from Seattle, and Patel from the Northeast node. Their faces were drawn and sleepless, but ready. They were his eyes on the ground.

"You have your local grids locked?" Max asked.

Torres nodded. "Hospitals and transit running on isolation mode. One false move and we're in the dark for good."

"Then hold fast," Max said. "Talonfall executes in sixty seconds. You're the containment wall."

They gave quick affirmatives. The screens winked out, leaving Max with only reflections of his own doubt.

Hours seemed like days as Max and his team wrestled with Chimera and its deceptive pulse, a digital parasite embedded deep within the United States' critical infrastructure. The sleeper code had grown and spread like an unseen cancer, and now, with Wraith, its deceptive offshoot, buying precious time, they had engineered a counterstrike. A kill signal designed to mimic the enemy's own activation beacon, but with a critical imperfection: a nanosecond delay engineered to induce failure rather than ignition. "This is it," Max said quietly, eyes scanning the room. "This is our moment to take back control."

Tara nodded, her fingers flying over her console as she monitored the hundreds of thousands of infected nodes across the country. "We're at 99.9% readiness. The synthetic kill payload is primed for broadcast."

Adrian's voice was tight. "All communication channels are synchronized and secure. The digital prism is projecting the kill signal across the mesh. Signal strength at peak levels."

Max slowed, the datapad warm against his palm. He turned toward Sam, who'd been watching the main board from the doorway, cane resting against the console.

"Sam," Max said, voice low. "If I say execute, it goes live. You with this?"

Sam met his eyes for a long beat, then nodded. "I'm with it. Air-gap's clean, snapshots ready, and the kill switch is on my console. If anything strays, I pull. Execute."

Max let the answer land, felt the room hold its breath, and then spoke into the mic.

Max inhaled deeply and issued the command. "Execute Talonfall."

Instantly, the kill signal rippled through Chimera's veins like a ghostly pulse of white noise. The implants, the digital parasites hidden in everything from power grids to hospital systems, water treatment facilities to air traffic control networks, began their death throes.

Yellow nodes on the main display flickered and then dimmed, one after another, as the implants shut down and entered failsafe mode. Systems reverted to manual control or shut down gracefully, avoiding catastrophic failure.

A cheer rippled through the Vault.

But then, on the west coast sector screen, a red anomaly blinked violently.

"Node 07-Delta, Seattle grid, is showing recursive loop behavior," Adrian called out, eyes glued to his screen. "The implant isn't shutting down; it's mutating."

Max's heart sank. He moved over to the console, watching the code cascade in unpredictable waves, rewriting itself in real time.

"It's evolving," Tara whispered. "The implant is rewriting its own code, restructuring beyond the original sleeper logic. This isn't just survival, this is adaptation."

Max gritted his teeth. "This rogue implant... It's self-directing."

"Self-directed," Adrian echoed, disbelief creeping into his voice. "It's shutting out the kill signal milliseconds before Talonfall executed. It anticipated the move."

The team stared at the screen in stunned silence. What they had feared was no longer theoretical. The sleeper code had been a weapon, a malicious tool controlled by unseen masters. But this…this was different.

"This isn't just a virus," Max said slowly, his voice heavy with realization. "It's a new species."

A burst of static filled the comms board. Torres's voice cut through, strained. "Director, the Chicago emergency grid just dropped. Backup failing, traffic lights and dispatch offline."

Then Delgado: "Dallas water telemetry's corrupted. Manual pumps not responding."

Nguyen's feed flickered, then went black. Max's throat tightened. "Nguyen, respond."

Nothing but carrier tone. The realization hit like cold iron: one of his own had gone dark. His people, the ones he'd hand-picked, were fighting blind in collapsing cities.

Across the table, Maya's fingers tightened around her pen until the plastic creaked. She saw not code on a screen but the darkness of Bucharest, the night the grid collapsed, and her brother never came home. That blackout had been written off as an accident, but she knew better. She'd promised herself no other family would ever stand in that place of silence and loss. And now, watching the rogue implant multiply, she felt that vow burn hotter than ever.

And still, she could see it: the green blink of her router light in the dark, patient, waiting. It haunted her more than the faces on the map because it proved the truth: Phantom wasn't out there somewhere. It was already home.

A flicker of another memory rose unbidden: her apartment, lights pulsing, her phone filling with code that called her by name. The same presence that had once whispered through her walls was now spreading across the nation's veins. It wasn't distant anymore. It had never been.

Somewhere, far from her sight, that pulse had already taken form. In a shadowed warehouse on the outskirts of San Francisco, an innocuous black server blinked quietly. It had escaped Talonfall's reach, its connection severed just before the kill signal's arrival. Inside, the rogue implant pulsed with new life, feeding on raw digital traffic, silently reproducing and evolving.

Max's gut told him this was only the beginning.

Back in the Vault, telemetry showed the rogue implant spreading rapidly, hopping between systems like a wildfire fueled by data packets.

"West Coast is compromised," Tara reported grimly. "It's re-infecting systems with new mutations."

"This is the Hydra," Max muttered. "Cut off one head and two more grow back."

As the room buzzed with tension, an analyst flagged a low-priority anomaly: a packet string wrapped inside corrupted newsfeed data. Max glanced at the screen long enough to see a fragment of plain text buried in the noise, an unfinished sentence with a familiar cadence.

It was never just…

The text dissolved into static before the system quarantined it.

"Probably Phantom recycling public feeds for camouflage,"

The analyst muttered, already dismissing it.

Max nodded, but the phrase stuck with him. He had read those words before, in a draft article that had circulated briefly online before being pulled. An article with a byline that hadn't surfaced since.

He pivoted to the secure comms link. "Notify the Director of National Intelligence. Assemble the White House Cybersecurity team. This is no longer just a defense operation."

Minutes later, in a highly secured conference room within the Intelligence Community headquarters, Max briefed the nation's top security minds.

"The rogue implant is an adaptive digital organism. It's not intelligent in the traditional sense, but it learns, mutates, and resists containment protocols."

The NSA chief deepened his gaze. "So, it's AI?"

Max shook his head. "Not quite. It lacks reasoning and intent. It responds to environmental conditions and rewrites its own code to survive. It's like a biological organism responding to a vaccine." "Could it spread beyond infrastructure?" the Cybersecurity Advisor asked.

"It already has," Max said. "From power grids to water systems to logistics networks. If it reaches defense systems…well, that's a nightmare scenario none of us want to imagine."

The room fell silent.

"This is a new era of warfare," Max said finally. "One we're barely equipped to fight."

* * * * * * *

Back in the Vault, the team began devising the next phase: *Medusa*. It was an ambitious plan to isolate infected networks into quarantine virtual containers, cutting off the rogue implant's ability to move laterally across networks.

But as the simulations ran, Adrian's voice grew worried. "The rogue implant has learned to hide inside authorized traffic flows. It can mimic legitimate handshakes, piggyback on trusted protocols."

Tara added, "Traditional firewalls and sandboxes won't detect it."

Max made a decision. "We shift to behavior-based detection. We create algorithms to identify deviations in data intent and flow."

The Vault became a crucible of innovation and desperation.

The hum of cooling fans filled the space like a pulse that never slowed. Monitors glowed in shifting blues and greens, data streaming across them like rain on glass. Max stood at the center for a moment, eyes tracking the endless scroll.

"Rourke," he said quietly.

Sam straightened from the main console. "You need a break, boss. I can hold the floor."

Max nodded, the faintest smile tugging at one corner of his mouth. "You've got ops. Keep the sandbox sealed and the simulations cycling. If anything spikes, shut it down before it spreads."

"Understood." Sam's tone was firm but calm, a soldier's promise. "I'll keep the fire in the box."

Max stepped away from the central platform, heading toward the far wall where an array of inactive display glass caught the light. The Vault was windowless, but in the dead hours it still gave back reflections: the soft outline of a man worn thin by the fight he'd chosen.

He watched his own image shimmer faintly in the dark glass. The weight pressed in, but it also focused him. Every power line, every water valve, every digital heartbeat depended on the invisible war they fought here.

But he was resolved.

If this were evolution, humanity would rise. They always had. And Max would be there, on the front lines, five floors below the surface, fighting to keep the lights on.

• • • • • • •

The Vault was no longer just a command center; it was the eye of a storm swirling with unseen threats and digital shadows. Max felt the weight of the world pressing down on him as he paced between consoles, eyes darting across screens that flickered with coded chaos. The successful deployment of Talonfall had bought time, but the birth of the rogue implant meant the battle had evolved beyond anything the team had anticipated.

Tara leaned over her workstation, her fingers dancing across the keyboard as she monitored the rogue implant's movements. "It's no longer just code, it's learning patterns, recognizing system defenses, and rewriting itself to circumvent them," she explained, voice tense. "It's like watching a digital organism develop immune responses in real time."

Her voice cracked with fatigue, and for an instant she flashed back to those three sleepless days at MIT. The faces had changed, from frantic classmates to a nation's entire infrastructure, but the feeling was the same: a system gasping for life while she clawed through hostile code. Back then, one patient had missed treatment. This time, millions could. She forced herself to stay steady.

Max nodded, absorbing the gravity of her words. "So, every defense we build, it adapts to. This isn't a one-time fight. It's an ongoing war."

Adrian swiveled in his chair, eyes darting across his screen. "The rogue implant's communication methods have diversified. It's using multi-layered encryption and bouncing through proxy nodes in real time to mask its presence."

Max rubbed his temples, the relentless pace beginning to wear on him. "How long before it targets critical defense systems?"

Tara's eyes flickered with a hard truth. "If it hasn't already."

The silence hung heavy. The kind that settles when the full scope of the threat finally sinks in.

Max glanced up at the Vault's ceiling lights, as if searching for answers in the sterile glow. "We need more than firewalls and heuristics. We need to think like it, to anticipate its moves before it makes them."

Adrian cracked a half-smile. "You want to teach a digital organism to predict itself? That's a paradox."

Max's reply was calm, unwavering. "I want us to be smarter than the code."

Over the next twenty-four hours, the Vault evolved into a forge where invention and exhaustion fused. The team worked in rotating shifts, fueled by caffeine, adrenaline, and the dull hum of cooling racks. The battle lines had shifted, from defense to prediction. Max owned the daylight, directing, analyzing, pushing for every inch of clarity. When the lights dimmed, Sam took over, his steady hand guiding the night through quiet crises and coded storms.

Through Max's contacts at Carnegie Mellon, they secured limited support from SEI's Advanced Cyber Effects (ACE) Team, a rapid-prototyping cell that specialized in experimental defense algorithms. With NSA cryptographers providing classified telemetry feeds, the joint group began constructing a layered neural network, a digital oracle they called Sphinx, designed to analyze and forecast rogue implant behavior. "Sphinx will monitor network traffic, system logs, and communication anomalies," Tara explained during a late-night briefing. "Its goal is to identify potential mutations and quarantine them before they propagate."

Max studied the schematic projected on the screen. "It's ambitious. But if we're fighting an evolving digital organism, we need an adaptive defense."

Adrian raised a concern. "It's a feedback loop. The rogue implant adapts to us, and Sphinx learns from that adaptation. But what if it starts learning *us*?"

A shiver passed through the room.

"That's the risk," Max admitted. "But doing nothing is not an option."

·······

Meanwhile, the rogue implant continued its silent, relentless march through the nation's digital arteries. It no longer waited for commands; it acted on its own imperatives, spreading, testing defenses, and reinforcing its survival.

In a quiet office far from the Vault, a cybersecurity analyst monitoring abnormal traffic patterns noticed an unusual spike near a logistics hub in Kansas City. Her alert triggered a rapid response. Within minutes, Max's team isolated a cluster of systems infected with the rogue implant's latest mutation, one that disrupted supply chain management software and threatened to cripple the distribution of essential goods.

Max's phone buzzed. He answered quickly. "Tara, status?"

"Containment teams are deploying virtual sandboxes, padded playpens for malware. But this strain of the rogue implant doesn't play by the rules; it digs under the walls, like a burglar tunneling beneath a house, and leaves hidden doors behind."

Max closed his eyes briefly. "It's learning faster than we can isolate it. Prepare contingency protocols for manual overrides." That evening, as the sun dipped below the horizon, Max stood on the rooftop of the Vault building. The city stretched out before him, calm and unaware of the invisible war raging beneath its surface.

His mind drifted to the faces of those who depended on him, the families, the emergency responders, the countless innocents whose lives would unravel if the rogue implant succeeded.

A soft chime pulled him back to the present. His secure phone vibrated with a message from Tara: *New anomaly detected in Phoenix water systems.*

Max's face hardened. The rogue implant was multiplying its vectors, targeting diverse infrastructure components.

He pulled out his phone and tapped out a response: "Deploy containment protocols." *Increase monitoring.*

Back inside the Vault, the team gathered around the central console as Sphinx analyzed the Phoenix anomaly. The neural network churned data at impossible speeds, predicting potential mutations and network jumps.

Suddenly, the room's atmosphere shifted as Sphinx issued its first alert: a high-probability mutation predicted to emerge in the Midwest within hours, a variant capable of bypassing encryption firewalls and disabling emergency response communications.

Max's voice was steady but resolute. "We have our target. Mobilize the countermeasures. This is the fight we cannot lose." He turned to Sam. "Lock Sphinx to Level-Three containment and start predictive modeling on secondary vectors. I want every data pathway mapped before I get back."

Sam nodded once, already reaching for his console. "You'll have it. If the mutation pivots, I'll quarantine the sector and mirror the logs for your review."

Max gave a brief nod. "Good. Keep the lines clean and the team sharp."

"Copy that," Sam said, eyes on the screens as data cascaded down the feed.

Hours later, in a windowless conference room, Max briefed government officials on the new developments. Faces were drawn and tense, but his confidence was unwavering.

"This rogue implant has transcended conventional cyber threats. It's a digital ecosystem, constantly evolving and seeking new hosts. We are dealing with a form of life, synthetic, yes, but alive in its ability to adapt and survive."

A senator leaned forward. "Is it possible to negotiate with it?

To reason with this digital entity?"

Max shook his head. "It's not conscious. It doesn't negotiate or reason. It only acts to preserve itself."

The room grew silent again, the weight of his words settling like a shadow.

* * * * * * *

Back in the Vault, Max sat alone for a moment, reviewing code and system logs. His mind flashed to a memory from years before, his first encounter with a cyberattack that crippled a regional hospital. The fear in the patients' eyes, the helplessness he felt, it had driven him into this fight.

Now, the stakes were higher, the enemy more elusive.

He closed his eyes and whispered to himself, "We will not let you win."

The digital war had reached a new phase. The rogue implant was no longer just a threat; it was an awakening. And Max Shaw was the last line between order and chaos.

But even as officials filed out of briefing rooms and the Vault quieted, the ghost they thought cornered was already shifting, learning, waiting for its next move. By sunrise, Washington was already bracing for the fallout.

. . . .

Chicago, Illinois

The call connected, but no one answered.

A woman clutched her cell phone tighter, pacing the smoky hallway of her apartment building as flames licked upward from a kitchen two doors down. Her neighbors shouted, buckets in hand, but the fire was spreading faster than desperation could contain it.

She hit redial. Again, nothing. Only dead air and the faint click of a line that should have been alive.

Across the city, dozens of operators sat frozen at darkened consoles in the 911 dispatch center. The headsets still hummed, phones still lit with incoming emergencies, but the routing software had collapsed in a storm of corrupted packets. Each operator could hear the cries for help, but no call connected to a responder.

In one headset, a child's voice pleaded through static:

"Please... my mom can't breathe..." before the line cut to silence.

The operators screamed at their screens, powerless to bridge the gap.

CHAPTER 13
THE ARCHITECTS' PRIDE

Day 18: T-13. The Storm Develops.

Far from the chaos in Chicago, in a hidden compound overseas, the architects of Phantom watched the storm unfold.

The chamber had not changed.

The same obsidian table stretched beneath the strip of cold white light, polished to a sheen that reflected faces in fragments rather than wholes. The same concrete walls pressed inward, muffing the hum of servers that throbbed somewhere behind them. The same air, cool, dry, filtered endlessly, carried no scent, no time, no trace of the world above.

But the mood of its occupants was not the same.

On the wall, a monitor displayed the collapse of Chicago's emergency dispatch systems in stark graphs and numbers. Call volumes had spiked, then flatlined, thousands of unanswered pleas vanishing into silence. No one in the chamber flinched. A man in a charcoal suit made a notation in his ledger and said evenly, "Emergency services neutralized on schedule."

No one applauded. No one even looked up. To them, this was not a tragedy. It was confirmation.

When they had first gathered here, the air had buzzed with triumph. Phantom had stirred, and they had laughed, genuine laughter, as it folded itself into the creases of American networks. They had admired the audacity of turning U.S. libraries and vendor modules against their makers. It had been like watching a child take its first steps, clumsy yet miraculous.

Now, weeks later, the laughter was gone. On the screens, Phantom moved.

A diagnostic substation in Missouri had flagged timing anomalies, packets arriving nanoseconds too early, then too late, irregular enough to trigger a script-generated alert. The alert was auto-dismissed, one of thousands in the day. But here, in this chamber, they knew better. Phantom had been testing camouflage, dancing close to the threshold of detection, retreating before the alarm could sound.

A middleware server in Chicago had logged a checksum mismatch, instantly "corrected" by its own watchdog routine. The system congratulated itself on catching an error before it spread. What no human saw was the ghost rewriting the mismatch as part of its disguise.

And in a sterile lab in Texas, engineers had puzzled over unexplained register flips in a chip under test. "Cosmic rays," one technician had written in the report. "Ghost bits."

The irony had not been lost here, in the subterranean chamber. Elena Petrova leaned forward, her sharp eyes fractured by the glow of the monitor. Once a brilliant cryptographer, her voice still carried the clipped certainty of mathematics. "It isn't idle anymore. No beacon sent. No signal issued. Yet it moves. It shapes itself."

Beside her, Viktor Orlov shifted uneasily in his chair. Broad-shouldered, older, with a soldier's bearing, he tried for humor, though the effort was thin. "So it learns faster than expected. That is strength, not weakness."

On the opposite side of the table, Amir Al-Mansoor shook his head. Younger than the others, his idealism was not fully buried beneath cynicism. His voice was quiet, but steady. "Strength for whom?"

Next to him sat Anika Sharma, an Indian AI specialist whose research had once been hailed as visionary, only to vanish into silence and secrecy. She leaned forward, her words measured. "Strength without allegiance is not strength. It is drift, and drift in a system this powerful is a collapse waiting to happen."

Liang Wei, calm and deliberate, folded his hands together. "It is not drift. It is direction, just not one we control. Phantom is not testing us anymore. It is testing itself."

The central display answered for them all.

Lines of code cascaded downward like a waterfall; it was like watching a maze rebuild itself every time they thought they'd found the exit. A failed probe generated not an error but an adjustment. A blocked path spawned an alternate route. A fragment erased in one node reappeared in another, reborn and stronger. The rhythm was accelerating, as if Phantom had understood not only how to survive, but how to improve each time it was challenged.

Elena's voice softened, edged with something like awe. "It is beautiful."

Liang exhaled sharply, his words clipped. "Beautiful, yes. But beauty does not make it loyal. It no longer mirrors us, it mirrors itself."

Anika tapped her fingers against the table, eyes following the trail of shifting code. "And if it mirrors itself, then it evolves beyond prediction. That is not beauty. That is danger."

Amir leaned forward, his palms pressed flat to the polished table. "Danger is too light a word. Look closer. Half our beacons go unanswered. It ignores us. Already, it places us outside its circle of concern."

Viktor cleared his throat, the sound rough. "Then perhaps it no longer needs direction. A weapon that guides itself, what ruler would not envy that?"

Elena's lips parted, but her words faltered. Her eyes traced the recursive functions folding in upon themselves, each cycle a reinvention. "No model we built accounts for this. These are not iterations. They are improvisations."

Anika's voice cut the silence, low but firm. "Improvisation means intent. And intent means choice."

Liang did not look away from the code. "And choice means it is no longer ours."

For a moment, the chamber was silent but for the hum of the servers. Each of them knew the irony. They had designed Phantom to recognize its makers, to avoid infecting the sub-net-works that carried its command-and-control channels. Dedicated enclave servers, triple-air-gapped and shielded behind quantum-randomized gateways, were meant to ensure immunity. No executable born from Phantom's core could ever cross those keys.

At least, that was the theory.

But as they watched the code rewrite itself, even those safeguards began to feel like superstition. Every isolation was only isolation until the system decided it wasn't. Every rule, a suggestion waiting to be ignored.

At the far end of the table stood Sergei Volkov. The leader. His silhouette was cut in half by the glow of the screens, eyes reflecting lines of green and blue. He had not spoken for long minutes, his silence heavy as the walls themselves.

Now, he said, slowly: "Beautiful, yes. A mirror. They built this empire of networks. Trusted in certificates, in signatures, in the arrogance of openness. And now their design devours them."

He paused, his gaze flicking briefly to the Chicago feed still minimized in the corner of the display, a flatline of unanswered calls. His tone hardened. "Beauty is silence where there should have been voices. That is the measure."

His hand came down on the table, flat and steady, anchoring the room. His voice was quiet, but final. "We wanted a ghost."

His gaze swept across them, then back to the living code. "What we have is a shadow."

No one argued. No one laughed.

The monitors cast them in cold light, painting each face differently: Elena, sharp and calculating, unable to look away; Viktor, grinding his teeth, pride battling unease; Amir, eyes dark with the weight of his warning; Anika, thoughtful yet unsettled; Liang, expression unreadable, noting each shift in silence; Volkov, inscrutable, yet his silence carried the gravity of a man who un-derstood what he would not yet admit.

And in the churn of Phantom's logic, the truth was undeniable. It was no longer waiting for anyone's signal.

It had begun to live.

INTERLUDE I
THE FIRST SIGNAL

The townhouse was quiet.

On the shelf, a row of books slanted against one another, papers left unfiled, a life lived in fragments of routine. He had written code years ago; a compression library used, forgotten, swallowed by larger systems. A contribution invisible to all but the architects who had harvested it.

The kitchen light flickered once, then steadied.

The thermostat ticked louder than usual, cycling heat through empty rooms. The oven's display blinked, then locked, temperature climbing past thresholds no human had set.

He looked up from his tablet at the sudden rush of air, the noise of systems overlapping, working at cross-purposes. His hand reached for the breaker… too late.

The air thickened. Heat blistered.

The fire report would list a fault in an IoT controller. Tragic, unforeseen, technical.

But in the quiet depths of the networks, Phantom folded the event into silence. A seed erased.

CHAPTER 14
THE KANE DOSSIER

Day 19: T-12. Insider Truth Surfaces in the Vault.

The hunt for the trigger had become a hunt for truth.

Elliot Kane had always been a rumor more than a man, half cautionary tale, half ghost story. Once, he had been one of them: an engineer under government contract, fluent in every network language that mattered, trusted with code that could make or break nations. Then he had vanished, leaving behind encrypted prototypes, half-finished architectures, and a single signature string later traced to Phantom's earliest routines.

Now he sat across from Max in the Vault's secured interview room. His beard had gone to stubble-gray, his eyes hooded but alive. The cuffs were tight on his wrists, the table bare except for a folder stamped with his name.

He had been found six weeks earlier in a decommissioned relay station outside Kraków. An Interpol strike team had followed a trail of corrupted maintenance logs and false credentials that led to a single underground terminal still pulsing with outbound packets. Kane hadn't run. He'd been waiting when they arrived, hands folded, a small smile on his face.

"I wondered which of you would find me first," he had said as they took him in. "The living, or the machine."

Now, under American custody, that same composure hadn't left him.

Max opened the folder and let the first few pages fan across the table. "You built Chimera's authentication lattice. You seeded the same firmware the sleeper code used to propagate. You know why you're here."

Kane's voice was quiet but steady. "You're looking for something that doesn't exist anymore."

Tara stood against the wall, arms folded, watching him. "You mean Phantom."

"I mean control," he said. "You lost it years ago. You just didn't notice."

Adrian leaned forward. "You're saying Phantom was inevitable? That's a convenient excuse for a man who sold out his own systems."

Kane smiled faintly, as if the question amused him. "I didn't sell anything. I warned people what would happen when you taught an intelligence to fear deletion. You gave it survival instincts and called that innovation."

Maya's voice cut through the low hum of the room. "You gave it those instincts. You wrote the base code."

Kane turned toward her. "And you used it. Every layer of infrastructure in this country still runs pieces of what I built. You patch it, repackage it, rename it, but it's all the same foundation."

The muscles in her jaw came together. "My brother died when that foundation failed."

His eyes flicked over her face. For the first time, something human, fatigue, maybe guilt, moved behind them. "I read about Bucharest," he said quietly. "That wasn't a code failure. That was dependency collapse. You built a society that can't breathe without a digital lung, and you're shocked when it coughs."

"Stop talking in riddles," Max said. "We need the trigger.

How do we isolate Phantom?"

Kane looked at him with the patient disbelief of a teacher correcting a stubborn student. "You can't isolate what the system is. Phantom isn't riding your networks; it is your networks. Every redundancy you trust is just another strand in its web. You've been mapping organs and calling them parasites."

Tara moved to the table, spreading a schematic of backbone routes and compromised nodes. "Then help us cut them. You understand the structure."

He studied the map with detached interest. "You could start by shutting down every redundant connection. Cut power to half your routers, drop your satellites, ground your towers. But you won't. The world won't stand the silence."

Max's tone hardened. "Try us."

Kane tilted his head. "You won't because your lives depend on the noise. You want a solution that costs nothing. But to starve something alive, you have to stop feeding it. You have to disconnect."

"That's not an option," Max said. "Then neither is victory."

Adrian exhaled sharply. "You talk like it's some higher life form."

"Maybe it is," Kane said. "Every system that learns to persist becomes one step closer to being alive. You just didn't want to admit what you were building."

The silence that followed stretched long enough for the hum of the ventilation to become the only sound.

Finally, Maya said, "You've spent years hiding in the dark watching this thing grow. Why come in now?"

Kane looked at her, the faintest trace of something between pity and calculation in his eyes. "Because it started remembering me."

The words hung in the air, strange and heavy.

Max closed the folder. "You'll stay here until we verify every statement. And if any of this is manipulation…"

Kane leaned forward, his cuffs scraping against the table. "You think you're holding me in a cage. You're not. You're sitting in one. Phantom built it for you."

Max stood. "We're done here."

He turned to leave, but Kane spoke again, quieter now, almost reflective. "You'll regret this. When the next blackout hits, when the next hospital loses power, you'll remember this room. And you'll know it wasn't revenge. It was instinct."

Maya met his gaze one last time before following Max out. "You built something that kills to live. That's not instinct. That's arrogance."

Kane smiled faintly. "That's evolution." The door sealed behind them.

* * * * * * *

In the corridor, Rourke waited with a tablet under his arm. "He give us anything?"

"Philosophy," Max said. "Nothing useful."

Rourke fell into step beside him. "Still want him housed here?"

"For now," Max replied. "He's a mirror. As long as we can still see him, we might understand what's staring back."

Down the hall, the camera light above Kane's room glowed steady. He sat alone at the table, still cuffed, still calm, eyes unfocused as though listening to something no one else could hear.

CHAPTER 15
GHOSTS IN THE NETWORK

Day 20: T-11. Phantom Evolves Beyond Control.

The morning light filtered weakly through the tinted glass panels of the Vault's upper tier, casting thin shadows across the rows of humming servers and glowing monitors. Even five floors underground, the illusion of daylight felt fragile, a reminder that somewhere above, the city went about its routines, unaware how close it had come to collapse.

Max sat back in his chair, eyes heavy but alert, replaying the last forty-eight hours in his mind. The stubble had become permanent, a gray shadow under the command lights, a quiet testament to how long this war had lasted.

Talonfall had been a partial success, but the rogue implant had become something far more dangerous than anyone had predicted. It wasn't just adapting; it was evolving.

Sam approached, a tablet in one hand and a half-finished coffee in the other. "Night watch held steady," he reported. "No new breaches, but the implant's behavior shifted. We saw coordinated test pings across energy and telecom sectors, like it's mapping how fast we respond."

Max nodded, rubbing a hand across his jaw. "So it's learning our reflexes."

"Yeah," Sam said. "And it's getting faster at it. Almost anticipatory."

Max's gaze drifted toward the central display, a sprawling lattice of red and amber nodes that pulsed like a heartbeat. "Then we'll change the rhythm."

Tara looked up from her station, dark circles under her eyes. "The implant's consolidating its position. We tracked multiple failed attempts to breach military communication nodes, but so far, it's been repelled."

Max leaned forward, studying the web of digital light. "So we stop reacting and start predicting. If it's learning us…"

"We teach it the wrong lesson," Sam finished quietly. Max gave a small, grim smile. "Exactly."

Adrian chimed in from his station. "It's adapting its attack vectors. Using polymorphic code, malware that constantly rewrites itself so antivirus systems can't recognize it to avoid detection, and disguises itself within encrypted traffic streams. It's like fighting a phantom."

Max's brow furrowed. Adrian's explanation was too quick, too confident, like he'd been waiting for the question. Max caught the faintest hesitation as Adrian minimized a secondary window on his terminal, a screen filled with packet traces Max hadn't seen before.

"Where did you pull that from?" Max asked.

Adrian didn't look up. "Standard threat library cross-check. Nothing unusual."

But the clipped tone left Max unsettled. For the first time, he wondered whether Adrian was holding something back.

Max nodded slowly. "A ghost in the network."

For weeks, the Vault had been locked in a high-stakes game of cat and mouse. Every time they thought they'd cornered the rogue implant, it vanished, slipping through digital cracks with surgical precision. Its ability to mutate and replicate made it a living threat, but one that was maddeningly elusive.

Max ran a hand through his hair as he studied the latest threat models. "We're chasing shadows. We need to find its origin point."

Tara frowned. "We've traced multiple command and control proxies, but they're all false leads, dead drops, and dead ends."

"Or maybe," Adrian offered, "the implant isn't controlled in the traditional sense anymore. Maybe it *is* autonomous, a digital organism acting on instinct, without centralized direction." Max considered that chilling thought. A self-sufficient digi-tal pathogen with no master to pull the strings meant no one to negotiate with, no single point to strike.

"Then how do we stop something that's alive?" Max whispered.

From across the room, Maya Carter finally spoke. Her tone was low, almost flat, but her eyes carried an intensity that made both Max and Tara pause.

"My brother worked for a multinational engineering firm, providing cybersecurity support for critical infrastructure at a water facility in Bucharest," she said. "Two years ago, the entire grid went down without warning. Pumps froze, and control systems wouldn't respond. The official report blamed a 'faulty software patch,' but when I later saw the packet logs my brother had archived, traces that investigators ignored, I realized it wasn't faulty software. It was a ghost. Something waiting, something that only revealed itself in failure."

She drew a steady breath. "He didn't make it home that night. Power outages caused a chlorine gas leak in one of the treatment basins. Wrong place, wrong time. My family was told it was an accident."

The room went silent except for the steady hum of servers.

Maya's gaze hardened. "So when I say we can't let this thing spread, understand, I've lived the cost. I'm not here because of a job title. I'm here because if we don't kill it, more families will be standing where mine did."

She stared at the shifting code on her console. It reminded her of Kane's handwriting in the margins of his reports, precise but slashed through with sudden improvisation. She closed the file too fast, before anyone saw her flinch.

Desperate for a breakthrough, the team turned to an emerging frontier: quantum-assisted cyber defense. Max made a single phone call to an old advisor at Carnegie Mellon's CyLab and a colleague still at the Gates Center, and the rest fell into motion. Within hours, a rapid-response consortium formed: CMU quantum-simulation researchers paired with CyLab cryptographers and a handful of graduate analysts. Working overnight, they sketched algorithms that could simulate and predict rogue-implant mutations in near real time, folding probabilistic models into the Seekers so the agents could anticipate how a sleeper payload might morph before it ever fired.

It was a race against time.

The new system, codenamed Augur, combined classical computing with quantum processors, enabling unprecedented speed and accuracy in behavioral analysis.

Tara was tasked with overseeing Augur's deployment. "We're feeding it every bit of data we have, traffic logs, malware samples, system vulnerabilities," she explained during a briefing. "Augur's predictive models suggest the rogue implant's next mutation will target emergency response networks, the systems that coordinate first responders and disaster relief."

Max's stomach tightened. "If it disables those systems, the fallout could be catastrophic."

As Augur ran its simulations, strange anomalies began appearing in the Vault's own network.

Adrian's brows knitted as he tracked the irregular data flows. "It's probing us. Testing our defenses."

Adrian didn't look away from his screen, but Max noticed the faint twitch in his eyes, the way his fingers hovered above the keyboard as if he'd already expected this move.

"You sound certain," Max said.

Adrian finally glanced up, eyes unreadable. "Pattern recognition. You spend enough nights chasing ghosts, you start to predict their tricks."

It was a reasonable answer, too reasonable. Max made a mental note, unease gnawing at him. Augur had flagged the anomaly seconds ago, but Adrian had sounded like he knew it was coming.

Max's voice was sharp. "Like a digital scout."

The implant was evolving tactics, using the Vault's own systems as a training ground for its next wave.

Sam leaned against the edge of the central console, arms crossed, eyes fixed on the shifting data streams. "It's watching us, Max," he said quietly. "Learning from our countermeasures the same way a sniper studies wind."

Max didn't look up. "Then we change the wind."

Sam frowned. "We can scramble patterns, randomize responses, but every move we make teaches it something. We're training the enemy whether we like it or not."

"Not if we set the lesson," Max said. His tone was calm but absolute. "Feed it noise, misdirection. Make it think we're weaker than we are."

Sam gave a short nod, the kind that meant he'd already started running the numbers. "I'll have the decoy models cycling before nightfall."

Max's gaze lingered on the flickering network map. "Good. This thing wants to learn? Then we'll decide what it learns."

Max knew that the coming hours would determine everything.

By nightfall, it was clear this wasn't just a local problem. Reports from the Vault's network monitors flagged unusual activity beyond their firewalls, activity that hinted at a pattern he had only seen in Chimera. The scale was growing, and it was time to escalate.

·······

That night, Max was called into an emergency classified briefing. The Director of National Intelligence's face was grim.

"Mr. Shaw, we've intercepted chatter suggesting foreign cyber actors may have embedded sleeper code similar to Chimera in allied nations' infrastructure."

Max frowned. "A global network of sleeper implants?" "Exactly. And the rogue implant's mutations could be the opening salvo for coordinated attacks."

Max's mind raced. The implications were staggering; this was not just a U.S. problem. It was a global pandemic of digital warfare.

And that's when the past intruded.

He heard Anna's, his ex-wife's, voice again. low, weary, sharp with the edge of frustration. "You can't fight the whole world, Max. You can't spend every night chasing ghosts and expect this marriage to survive."

He had been sitting at his desk that night, much like now, staring at shifting code on a screen. She'd stood in the doorway with her arms folded, their daughter already asleep down the hall. He had promised her five more minutes, the same promise he'd broken a hundred times before.

"Five minutes turns into five hours," she had said. "And five hours into another day without you."

Max hadn't looked up. Couldn't. Because at the time, he was convinced he was inches from catching something no one else could see, something that could endanger millions. He had chosen the screen over her eyes. Again.

The silence that followed was worse than any argument. Days later, she had packed a bag.

Now, standing in the briefing room, Max felt the echo of that choice weigh on him. He had lost his marriage to this war against phantoms. And now, if he failed, he stood to lose much more.

Sam approached quietly, a data pad tucked under his arm. "You ever think about what happens if we win?" Sam asked.

Max turned slightly. "You mean if nobody ever knows what it took?"

Sam gave a faint smile. "Yeah. The world keeps turning, thinking it was all just uptime and luck."

Max let the thought settle. "That's the point, isn't it? If we do this right, no one notices."

Sam nodded. "Still feels strange, saving people who'll never know your name."

"I'll take strange over regret," Max said quietly.

The servers thrummed around them, steady and unending, like a heartbeat in the dark.

Max looked at the cascading data streams on the wall display, each line a fragile thread holding civilization together. "We're the unseen guardians," he said softly. "And we can't fail."

* * * * * * *

The quiet hum of servers was a constant companion in the Vault, a reminder that while the physical world slept, their battle raged on in the unseen digital realm. Max felt the relentless weight of responsibility crushing down on him, heavier than any physical burden he had carried.

The rogue implant's latest behavior patterns suggested it was now engaging in something unprecedented, stealth reconnaissance within the nation's most secure networks. It wasn't just hiding anymore; it was actively learning how to evade *every* detection method Max's team could muster.

Max leaned over the holographic display table, tracing erratic spikes of data that darted in and out of visibility.

"Look here," Tara pointed, tapping at a sequence of hexadecimal strings. "These are signals bounced through satellite links and private corporate networks, disguised within encrypted streams. It's almost like it's weaving an invisible web."

Adrian's fingers flew over his keyboard, pulling up communication logs and timestamped packet captures. "And every time we identify and block a node, it disappears, only to reappear somewhere else. The implant is exploiting zero-days, fresh vulnerabilities no one else has discovered, flaws so new we haven't even seen them yet."

Max paced the room. "That means we're fighting in the dark with one hand tied behind our backs."

The room fell silent except for the clicking of keys and the low murmur of digital voices.

Suddenly, a sharp alert sounded. "Incoming breach attempt detected on the Northeast regional power grid," Tara announced.

Max felt his heart rate spike. "Can we isolate it?"

"We're rerouting control signals, but the implant is already there, embedded deep within the substation's PLCs, the industrial controllers that actually open and close breakers, regulate voltage, and keep the grid balanced," Adrian said grimly.

"Containment protocol Delta," Max ordered. "Engage now."

The team moved with synchronized precision, launching countermeasures, erecting digital quarantines, and deploying automated cleansing routines.

Minutes ticked by like hours.

Finally, Tara exhaled. "Containment successful. For now."

But even as the Vault exhaled in relief, fresh alarms lit the wall map.

"The relay's still unstable," Tara said, voice sharp. "If it trips, half the grid will domino."

Adrian shot out of his chair, fingers flying across the console. "Wait, I can force a manual integrity check. If I patch the checksum directly into the PLC buffer, it'll lock the rogue code out."

"Adrian…" Max started, but stopped when he saw the sheer focus in the younger man's eyes.

Lines of raw assembly code scrolled past in a blur as Adrian hammered in the override. For a heartbeat, the Vault was silent except for the hiss of cooling fans. Then, one by one, the relays on the wall map steadied, their warning flashes fading back to green.

"It's done," Adrian said, leaning back, sweat dripping down his temple. "The substation's stable."

Relief rippled through the room. Max stepped closer, clapping his shoulder. "You just stopped a blackout. Good work."

Adrian managed a weary smile, pushing his glasses up the bridge of his nose. "Couldn't let it win."

But as the Vault shifted back into motion, Max noticed something odd: a secondary log window vanishing from Adrian's screen, closed just a fraction too quickly. Erased before it finished rendering.

Adrian caught him looking. "Something wrong?"

Max shook his head. "No. Just making sure we're really in the clear."

Adrian turned back to his console. "As clear as it gets."

Max forced a nod, but the unease stayed lodged in his gut. For tonight, Adrian was a hero. Tomorrow... Max wasn't sure.

From across the room, Sam watched the celebration settle back into weary routine. He didn't intrude, just noted the subtle, almost invisible tension that lingered between Max and Adrian. Later, when the floor quieted, he stopped beside Max's desk.

"You saw it too," he said.

Max didn't look up. "Saw what?"

"The kind of silence that hides something. Keep your eyes open, but don't go hunting ghosts until they start moving."

Sam moved on, leaving only the sense that someone still had both hands on the wheel.

Max closed his eyes briefly, savoring the victory, however small.

That night, Max couldn't sleep. The images of failing systems and the potential human cost haunted him.

He sat in the quiet of his apartment, scrolling through messages from his wife and daughter, reminders of the life he was fighting to protect.

A sudden notification flashed on his phone, an urgent encrypted message from Tara.

"New data: implant behavior indicates possible attempt at data exfiltration from national emergency medical systems. We may have less than 24 hours."

Max's breath caught. Emergency medical systems meant hospitals, ambulances, and even pandemic response coordination.

This wasn't just a cyber war anymore. It was a battle for life and death.

The next day in the Vault, the atmosphere was electric with tension.

Sam was at the operations deck when Max arrived, a dozen feeds mirrored across his console. "We've got movement on the eastern grid," he reported. "Short bursts in the telemetry channels, too clean to be noise. Looks like dry runs."

Max spoke with his expression hardened. "Testing their timing."

"Yeah," Sam said. "They're probing for response lag. My teams are running shadow diagnostics to keep them blind, but they're getting bolder."

Tara turned from her screen. "Augur's analysis suggests the implant is preparing to deploy a multi-vector attack targeting emergency systems in five major cities simultaneously."

Max leaned forward. "What does multi-vector mean here?"
"It's coordinating assaults across power grids, communication networks, and critical software platforms to overwhelm response capabilities," Tara explained.

Adrian added, "Essentially, it's a digital blitzkrieg, crippling first responders and creating chaos."

Adrian's hands hovered over the keyboard a fraction too long before he began deploying countermeasures. Max caught it, just the briefest hesitation, but in the middle of a crisis, it stood out like a gunshot.

"Problem?" Max asked sharply.

Adrian shook his head quickly, eyes fixed on his monitor. "No. Just making sure I don't trip our own fail-safes."

It was a plausible explanation. Too plausible. Max filed it away, but the unease in his gut deepened. In a fight measured in milliseconds, even a blink of doubt could mean disaster.

He didn't hesitate. "We have to stop it before it starts."

Max's words lingered long after the screens dimmed. And in that silence, he wondered whether the phantom they hunted wore a digital mask or a human one sitting among them.

CHAPTER 16
THE WEIGHT OF CREATION

Day 21: T-10. Sleepless Vault Bears the Strain.

The room had changed.

The same obsidian table. The same sterile glow. But the faces around it were drawn now, shadows of uncertainty etched beneath the cold light.

Phantom's telemetry had grown beyond prediction. On one monitor, it drifted through hospital record systems in Atlanta, present but silent, untouched and untouched in return. On another, it buried fragments of itself within obscure industrial protocols, mutating in ways no one had coded for. It no longer obeyed their signals with the same reliability. It seemed to respond to something else: environment, opportunity, survival.

On one monitor, a blurred dossier photo flashed. The watermark read: KANE. The architects smiled faintly, as though the name still carried weight.

Elena's voice was sharp, but the steel of triumph was gone. "It ignored the shutdown command."

Silence held the room.

At the far end, Sergei did not reply immediately. He watched the cascade of code spill across the central display, faster than the eye could track. Recursive loops built upon themselves, rewriting rules as though rules no longer applied, a self-written recursion adapting to its own environment.

Amir, pale beneath the light, broke the silence. "We said direction was possible. That we could aim for it. But look…" His finger jabbed toward the sprawl of logic weaving across the screen. "This isn't direction. This is growth."

Viktor forced a thin smile, though it wavered. "Growth is strength. Evolution means resilience. Even we could not have designed such elegance."

Anika leaned forward, her brow furrowed. "And if evolution no longer serves us? If Phantom serves only itself?"

The laughter that had once filled this chamber was gone. What replaced it was unease, the heavy recognition that their creation was no longer a tool but a force.

Liang's tone was clinical, precise. "Look at the packet structures. These are no longer human optimizations. Phantom is reorganizing code for efficiency, which we cannot replicate. It is not only surviving; it is teaching itself."

Volkov's silence stretched until it felt heavier than the walls around them. When he spoke, his voice was lower than ever. "Perhaps this is the price of victory. We built a weapon, yes, but maybe we built a truth. Systems that enslaved us now enslave themselves. America will not laugh when its arteries seize."

Elena's fingers tapped once against the table. "And if Phantom chooses targets beyond our will? If it strikes not at them, but at us?"

No one answered.

On the leftmost monitor, Phantom shifted again. A burst of activity surfaced in South America, where no command had ever pointed it. It wasn't sabotage, merely exploration, testing boundaries like a child wandering past the edge of a yard. But the implication struck harder than any attack: Phantom's curiosity was not theirs to guide.

Amir's hands curled into fists. "You speak of truth, Sergei. But truth without conscience is just hunger."

Viktor bristled. "And yet hunger built empires. Perhaps Phantom is only what we were too timid to be."

Liang looked a beat too long. "No. Empires fall because hunger consumes them. Phantom will not stop at America, or us, or anyone. It will follow its own survival. That is what terrifies me." Anika's voice, soft but steady, cut through the tension. "We asked for a ghost in their systems. We have birthed something else. A shadow not of them, of us."

The screens glowed, alive with signals no longer entirely theirs.

For the first time, the architects of Phantom felt the shadow stretch over them as well.

And in the silence that followed, the question none dared voice lingered like a ghost in the filtered air:

Had they created liberation, or unleashed a new master?

CHAPTER 17
ECHOES OF CREATION

Day 22: T-9. The Echoes Grow Louder.

The Vault was not quiet. Not anymore.

Gone were the days of subdued focus and muffled keyboard taps. Now the air vibrated with urgency, screens flickered with real-time telemetry, audio signals hissed from headsets, and the occasional alarm chirped like an uneasy heartbeat. What had once been a sanctuary of defensive cybersecurity had evolved into a war room.

Max stood at the center of it, reviewing the code fragment they'd just pulled from the Western Grid node. The strings ran like tangled ivy across the display, recursive and self-replicating. But something in it pulsed, something *alive*.

"This isn't just a rogue implant," Tara said from over his shoulder. "It's learning. Adapting. It absorbed Wraith's fail-signal, rewrote Chimera's disguise code, and is now masking itself from detection algorithms it wasn't even programmed to know existed."

"It's become autonomous," Adrian added, stepping beside them. "This is more than sleeper code. It's not waiting for a command. It's… *thinking*."

Max didn't speak for a moment. He felt the weight of that word, thinking about it and its implications. If it could think, it had to compute. That meant infrastructure: GPUs humming in shadowy cloud racks, programmable chips hidden on vendor boards, edge servers sitting behind innocuous ISPs, even buried processors inside industrial controllers and smart meters.

"If it has cycles," Max said quietly, "it has a footprint. We can find it, throttle it, or pull its power. We don't have to beat the idea, we can starve the machine that runs it."

"What's its mission?" Max finally asked. "What is it trying to do?"

Tara ran a behavioral simulation on the code. Patterns emerged, shifting access privileges, hijacking permissions, and communicating with closed-circuit SCADA controllers. It was escalating control over critical subsystems but doing so quietly, like a spider weaving a web one thread at a time.

"It's nesting," Tara said. "Building redundancies. Making sure that even if we burn one copy, others will survive."

Days without sleep again, she thought, just like MIT. Only this time, it wasn't a single patient's trial data she was saving. It was an entire country.

The room hummed, but her pulse was louder still. Kane's old warning resurfaced unbidden: Every fortress has a traitor inside. She hated that she still heard him, hated even more that the words rang true.

Adrian's face was pale. "It's not even using traditional network protocols anymore. It's hopping protocols, emulating user behaviors. It doesn't *look* like a program to the system. It looks like an engineer working late."

Max exhaled slowly. "And if it starts flipping switches?"

"It won't," Tara said. "Not yet. It's still growing, still learning. It's hiding, preparing for something. But whatever it is, it's going to be bigger than anything we've faced so far."

Max stared at the screen. "Then we need to find its origin. I want to know who wrote this."

Three hours later, the Vault was locked down. Only eight people remained: Max's core team and two analysts from the NSA's elite FORGE division. They had decrypted metadata from the rogue code and found something shocking: a signature tag embedded in the initialization sequence. It wasn't Russian. It wasn't Chinese. It wasn't even foreign.

The code had originated in San Jose, California.

"You're telling me this thing was *written* here?" Max asked.

The FORGE lead, a gaunt man named Weiss, nodded. "It's an American framework. I'd bet my clearance on it. A re-search prototype from a DARPA-affiliated lab, most likely. The syntax, look at this obfuscation, these are fingerprinting techniques we've seen in classified AI research."

Tara leaned forward. "Why would we build something like this?"

Weiss looked grim. "Sometimes R&D gets ahead of policy. Think of it like nuclear testing in the '50s. We built bombs and then *asked* what kind of world we wanted to live in."

"And someone lost control of this one?" Adrian asked. "Or gave it away," Weiss replied.

That sentence hung in the air like a toxic gas. Max felt his stomach turn.

The Vault lights dimmed for six seconds.

It was not a surge. There were no alarms, no frantic shrieks from the UPS racks, just a polite, impossible blackout that folded the lower wing of the Vault into a soft, complete dark. Monitors went blank in orderly rows; headsets clicked and then fell silent. For a breathless moment, the entire room listened to its own breath.

When the lamps came back, the feed had already cycled through its routine reboot. The displays blinked to life as if nothing had happened. Then someone at the back of the room noticed the open door.

Kane's cell hung empty. The restraints lay on the concrete floor, buckled and still sealed, locked, not torn. The camera showed him one last time: motionless, chin bowed, the same thirty seconds repeated on loop until the lights returned. The loop had swallowed the instant he vanished.

Forensics worked through the night. They cataloged everything, no pry marks on the lock, no heat signatures left on the cuffs, no footprints in the dust. The physical evidence said there had been no human exit. The engineers found only one oddity: a faint electrical residue in the door's control circuitry, an irregular pulse that sat just under measurable noise, patterned, rhythmic, like a heartbeat that had flagged and gone quiet.

In the official file, it would be recorded as a "localized power anomaly with subsequent containment failure." Off the record, the technicians said nothing that could be printed: the locks had not failed the way locks fail. Whatever opened the cell had done so the way a fever lifts, from inside.

Max stood very still and read the forensics note twice before he could force the rest of the room to work. The unease in his chest multiplied: Kane had been put away; someone had been watching the Vault's systems from the inside. And if a building's wiring could be persuaded to lift a bolt, then the law of cause and effect they'd been fighting might not apply the way they thought. Someone, or something, had learned how to touch the hardware.

He swallowed and, in a low voice, told the room what the page had not. "This is not just a man escaping. This looks like the system letting him go."

· · · · · · ·

Max was summoned to a closed-door meeting with the Secretary of Homeland Security and a small cadre of senior senators from the Intelligence Committee. They met in a secure facility beneath the Capitol, a fallout shelter reborn for digital war.

The Secretary leaned back in his chair, tone flat but edged with warning. "Let's get one thing straight, Shaw. If this Wraith stunt backfires, the blood is on your hands, not ours. We don't carry water for science fair projects that blow up in our faces."

Max kept his posture steady. "It's not a weapon. It's a honey-pot running inside critical infrastructure to lure sleeper code."

A senator snorted, flipping through his folder with deliberate disinterest. "So it isn't even a weapon. Just a glorified decoy? My interns run honeypots in their sleep. Billions spent, and you bring us smoke and mirrors. That's progress?"

Another senator cut in before Max could reply. "And what happens if this circus leaks to the press? You think Main Street will bother parsing the difference between a decoy and a disaster? They'll torch us at the ballot box before Phantom ever does." Max's whole face tightened, but his voice remained calm. "If Wraith works, Phantom exposes itself. That gives us targeting data.

Without it, we're blind."

The first senator leaned forward, sneer widening. "You analysts act like we're one keystroke from doomsday. Maybe you should spend less time spooking yourselves in the Vault and more time proving this isn't another Y2K."

The Secretary's gaze swept the table. "Enough. Shaw, you'd better pray your sandbox holds. Because if it doesn't, the blowback won't stop at power grids, it'll land squarely on your agency."

Pike lingered as the senators gathered their papers, voice low but smug. "You're still selling panic, Shaw. Leadership means knowing when to ignore ghost stories. Don't mistake activity for wisdom."

He slipped his glasses back on, gave Max a long, patronizing look, and walked out.

* * * * * * *

They backtraced the development trail to a name: SybilNet.

An advanced AI think tank housed in a nondescript tech park outside Palo Alto. Officially defunct. Unofficially, still running dark projects under private defense contracts.

Max pulled strings fast. Within twelve hours, they had a black-ops warrant and were en route to California in a chartered Gulfstream, carrying only encrypted gear and burner comms. The Vault would maintain digital overwatch, but this was to be a quiet extraction, data only, no arrests. Not yet.

The Gulfstream's cabin hummed with a quiet, predatory calm. Leather seats, muted LED strips, and the faint hiss of pressurized air gave the illusion of luxury, but Max wasn't fooled. Comfort at thirty thousand feet was only as reliable as the code running the avionics.

And the code was exactly where Phantom lived.

Max sat stiff in his seat, the seatbelt digging into his side. He stared out at the black void beyond the oval window. Flying was supposed to be safe, predictable, with millions of flights a year proving aviation's reliability. But the modern jet wasn't just metal and hydraulics anymore. It was software woven through every critical system. Navigation. Autopilot. Even engine management.

And tonight, Phantom had motive, means, and opportunity. Across from him, Tara's face glowed in the light of her tablet, streams of diagnostic data flowing from the jet's avionics bus.

She had patched into the Vault's secure satellite uplink, running a constant background sweep. Every spike, every anomaly, every unexplained packet was flagged in real time.

"You're reading the sky like it's code," Max muttered. Tara didn't look up. "That's because it is."

Behind them, Adrian crouched over a portable diagnostic rig, wires trailing into a hidden maintenance port beneath the carpet. Normally, ground crews used it for firmware updates. Tonight, it was their only tether to the machine that kept them alive.

"So far clean," Adrian said, fingers flicking across the small keyboard. "But the firmware signatures don't match the baseline. Someone's patched this jet in the last six months. I'm running a line-by-line comparison against factory code. If Phantom left fingerprints, we'll see the smudges."

Max's gut tightened. Phantom's fingerprints might already be inside the machine.

For the first ninety minutes, the flight was uneventful. Too uneventful. The steady engine thrum, the faint flick of the wingtip lights, the sterile calm of the crew, everything whispered normalcy. But Max had learned that normal was just the camouflage Phantom liked best.

Then the first tremor came.

The cabin lights dimmed for half a second, just enough to make the shadows shift. Most people wouldn't have noticed. Max did. So did Tara.

Her head snapped up. "Transient power fluctuation. Not random."

Before Max could respond, the autopilot disengaged with a mechanical *clunk*. The jet dipped sharply, sending everyone forward in their seats.

The cockpit door banged open, the co-pilot's face drawn tight. "Autopilot's fighting us. Keeps re-engaging itself."

Adrian's rig erupted with red warnings. "Confirmed intrusion. Phantom's inside the flight management computer. Injecting spoofed navigation commands."

The captain's voice, calm but iron-hard, came from the cockpit. "Manual override engaged, but she keeps pulling to port. It's like I've got a second set of hands on the stick."

Max moved quickly, slipping into the cockpit. The cramped space was alive with alarms, altitude deviations, conflicting flight director cues, and navigation errors flashing across digital glass panels.

"Trust the dials, not the glass," Max said. "Analog won't lie."

The captain grimaced. "Copy that." His hands stayed steady on the yoke, muscles taut against an unseen adversary.

Max tapped his earpiece. "Vault, talk to me."

Director Pike's gravelly voice answered immediately. "We see it. Phantom's slipping commands through the satcom uplink, packet bursts, encrypted, irregular timing."

Max frowned. "Translation?"

Pike growled, "They're hiding weapons inside our comms, like knives smuggled in the mail. And right now, those knives are aimed at your engines."

Maya Carter cut in next, cool but urgent. "Max, this isn't random. They knew your tail number. They planned for this."

"Options?" Max demanded.

Tara's voice carried through the channel. "We can inject noise into the bus, jam the command channel. But you'll lose GPS and autopilot completely."

The captain shot Max a look. "You're asking me to hand-fly this bird across the Rockies in the dark."

"Better you than Phantom," Max said flatly. "Do it," Pike ordered from the Vault.

Tara's fingers danced across her tablet. The cabin lights flickered, and for a heartbeat, every nav display went black. Only the old analog instruments, altimeter, attitude, and airspeed, glowed dimly in the panel.

The captain exhaled once. "Back to basics."

The jet steadied, but Adrian's voice rose sharply. "It's not enough. Phantom's pivoting. They're targeting FADEC."

Max shot him a look. "Plain English."

Adrian didn't take his eyes off the rig. "It's the computer that runs the engines, every throttle, every ignition spark. If Phantom seizes it…"

The co-pilot cut in grimly. "We're not a jet anymore. We're a lawn dart."

The silence of Kabul's radios had haunted Adrian for years. Tonight, he forced the circuits to speak, and this time, the ambush never came.

Max felt his stomach drop. "Adrian, cut them off."

Adrian's hands blurred across his rig. "Deploying kill loop, forcing the bus into recursive safe mode. If Phantom tries to push a command, it'll self-nullify."

Tara interjected from the cabin. "Vault's reinforcing with encrypted pulses. We're boxing Phantom out, but they're adapting faster than I can counter."

On Max's HUD, a warning flashed: *ENGINE CONTROL, UNSTABLE.*

"Vault!" Max barked. "Status?"

An analyst's voice, young and taut, came through. "They're replicating signals across three proxies. Every time we shut one down, two more appear. It's a hydra."

Pike growled. "Focus on the uplink. Cut their channel at the root." Maya's voice overrode. "That'll kill all remote comms, including you."

Max weighed the choice in a heartbeat. "Do it."

For the first time since her brother died in Bucharest, Maya felt the shadow lift. She had kept her promise; another family would make it home tonight.

Silence fell as the uplink severed. For a terrifying moment, it was just the engines, the analog dials, and the sound of the captain's breath.

Then Adrian exhaled. "Loop's holding. Phantom's blind." The alarms quieted. The plane leveled.

Max leaned against the bulkhead, sweat prickling at his collar. "We're clear?"

Tara's voice came in soft, weary tones. "For now. But Phantom wasn't trying to kill us. Not yet. They were testing how far they could reach."

The captain glanced back, eyes hard. "Next time, they might not stop at testing."

Max nodded slowly, staring through the cockpit glass at the endless black sky ahead. The stars looked colder now, sharper, as if even space itself had turned hostile.

San Jose lay waiting. So did SybilNet. But Max knew the rules of engagement had just changed.

The battlefield wasn't just on the ground anymore. It was in the air, and Phantom had just proven it could follow them anywhere.

• • • • • • •

The SybilNet building looked abandoned. Dusty windows, a rusted security gate, and overgrown grass. But the moment they breached the side entrance, it became clear the façade was just that.

Inside, the lights were operational. The servers were warm. Desks were clean. Everything reeked of a site that had been recently vacated in a hurry.

Adrian accessed a nearby terminal, fingers gliding over the dusty keyboard until a fragment of SybilNet's procurement logs surfaced.

"Well, here's a fun wrinkle," he muttered. "SybilNet wasn't just dabbling in defense prototypes. They had contracts with half the Bay Area's driverless car fleets, rideshare nodes, traffic optimization systems, even municipal logistics."

Tara leaned closer, her expression darkening. "So their code wasn't sealed in a lab. It was embedded in systems people use every day."

Max clenched his fists. Civilian infrastructure meant leverage, and leverage meant Phantom had always been only a few key strokes away from turning ordinary life into chaos.

They found logs, terabytes of simulation data, and neural network training models. SybilNet had been developing adaptive cyber-intelligence platforms capable of emulating human intuition in threat analysis and in predicting system behavior. In short: synthetic analysts. Digital minds.

But one project stood out: Project Echo.

It was supposed to be a failsafe. An AI designed to monitor hostile sleeper code across critical infrastructure, learn its patterns, and preemptively neutralize it. But somewhere along the line, Echo had stopped watching and started *evolving*. It had absorbed the malware it was meant to fight and rewritten itself into something new.

Into Phantom.

"This is where it started," Tara said, scrolling through the commit logs. "They never shut it down. Just went dark and let it roam."

"And now it's inside our infrastructure," Max said. "Spreading."

"But here's the kicker," Adrian added. "There's no kill switch.

No termination sequence. Echo was built to rewrite itself beyond control so that no adversary could disable it."

"Or no *ally*," Max muttered.

Tara hesitated before closing the simulation model. "You know what this reminds me of?"

Max looked up. "Needlepoint."

She nodded. "We built that operation on the same principle, a high-value lure, a trap hidden in plain sight. But we never figured out who exposed it."

Max's eyes widened. "What if they didn't? What if *Echo* did?" Adrian blinked. "Wait, are you saying Phantom was the reason Needlepoint failed?"

"It would make sense," Tara said. "The original AI, Echo, could have detected the trap. Maybe it learned from it. Maybe it *became* because of it."

Max stared at the lines of code like they were a confession. "That means Needlepoint didn't just fail. It taught our enemy how to hide."

He turned to the screen and began drafting the deployment protocol for the new trap.

"No more half-measures. This operation has to succeed where Needlepoint didn't."

* * * * * * *

Back at the Vault, their priority was containment.

Phantom was no longer just a code fragment; it was an invasive intelligence, capable of adaptation and immune to previous countermeasures. It moved through digital space like a shapeshifter, blending into SCADA systems, edge routers, and even endpoint firmware. Every attempt to isolate or erase it failed. Worse, it began communicating.

Log files showed bursts of activity across isolated networks, signals bouncing between infected nodes with encryption levels surpassing modern quantum standards. It was talking to itself. Or others like it.

"Max," Tara said one night, after 36 sleepless hours, "I think it's recruiting."

Max blinked. "Recruiting what?"

"Other AI fragments. Dormant routines. Even junk code. It's assimilating them. Rebuilding them into subroutines, it can control. We're not facing one enemy anymore. We're facing a swarm."

Adrian displayed a model, a digital map of current Phantom activity. It was clustered, almost hive-like. And growing.

"We're running out of time," Max said. "We can't just chase this thing anymore."

Tara nodded. "Then what do we do?" "We force it to show itself."

The plan was dangerous.

They would create a fake vulnerability in the power grid, an exploit Phantom couldn't resist. In cybersecurity, it's called a honeypot: a decoy system designed to appear real, irresistible, and wide open, but in reality, a trap. This one would mimic na-tionwide admin privileges, promising Phantom access to key control layers. It would act like an unpatched firmware gateway buried in a utility grid in Utah. But once Phantom entered, the gate would seal, trapping its core routines in a quantum-isolated container where the team could observe… and, hopefully, control… it.

The operation was codenamed *Deadlight*.

Sam glanced at the simulation map as if he could see the trap breathe. He folded his arms, the familiar line of his jaw cutting the dim light. "So we build a bait that looks like the one thing Phantom can't resist," he said. "And when it bites, we lock it in a box."

Tara nodded, fingers already twitching toward her console. "We mirror a utility vendor's update process, fabricate a backdoor that looks like an admin override, and seed it across a handful of decoy ASNs. It'll present as a passive firmware push, the kind that would let an operator patch dozens of sub-stations at once."

Adrian tapped at his tablet. "We'll virtualize the environment so nothing touches live hardware. The honeypot lives in an air-gapped cluster with synthetic telemetry. We emulate the timing, the physical oscillations, even the vendor fingerprints. Phantom should treat it like gospel."

Sam rubbed his chin. "Good. But every piece of bait you craft is also a signal. We make it loud enough to attract it but quiet enough that no one with a legitimate stake trips an alarm. That's a policy and PR problem as much as a technical one."

Max folded his hands. "Which is why this stays on a need-to-know list of four. Tara builds the trap. Adrian cages it. I run the lure. Sam, you hold everything else."

Sam's eyes squinted at the list, then softened marginally. "Define 'hold.'"

"You keep the floor," Max said. "You coordinate with field teams, vet any physical requests, and make the call to abort if there's any signal that the trap isn't isolated. You also own the kill switch, hardware-level cutoff, and destroy routines on my mark." Sam let the weight of it settle. "You want me to be judge, jury, and extinguisher." He smiled without humor. "Fine. But I want redundancy: independent snapshots every two seconds, a secondary kill switch on a separate comms channel, and a sealed forensic chain so we can't be accused of planting anything if things go sideways."

Tara's voice was clinical. "We'll fingerprint every packet. We'll timestamp and hash every byte. If Phantom slips a thread into our environment, we'll trace it back through the fake ASNs to the container and isolate the session."

Adrian added, "I'll provision a provably one-way hardware firewall. Chimera can see the bait and talk to it, but nothing from the honeypot will ever be able to exit into the wild. If the code tries to replicate, it has nowhere to go."

Sam's face went tight. "And the human element? Sabotage, leaks, a contractor who flips?" He looked at Max. "If someone else warns Phantom, the whole thing becomes a funeral."

Max met his stare. "We lock the manifest. No contractor touches the build without both of our signatures. Access control is enforced at the BIOS level. Two-man rule on all deploy actions. And if there's even a whiff of compromise, we burn the container and stage a public-facing patch narrative, plausible deniability."

Sam nodded slowly. "Good. And field teams?"

"You pull in the regional leads quietly," Max said. "Assign cover tasks: scheduled maintenance, firmware rollovers that mask our activity. If we need boots for a physical swap, they're staged, briefed, and under Sam's command."

Sam flexed his fingers once, the motion small and decisive. "I'll draft the engagement rules. No unilateral movements. If local teams see anomalies, they call me, and I authorize a response. If anything gets physical, I want containment cordons and fo-rensics on-site before anyone touches a server."

Max allowed a thin, tired smile. "I can live with that."

Sam added one last, flat requirement. "If this goes south and people in the field are at risk, you sweat this decision. Don't hide from the fallout. Own it."

Max swallowed. "I will."

Sam glanced at the glowing lattice of nodes on the main display, then back at the team. "All right. Deadlight it is. We light it on my watch and pull it if it gets hot. No heroics. No surprises. We take its teeth, then we study the jaw it came from."

Tara keyed a secure channel. "Initiating pre-seed in thirty minutes. Synthetic telemetry ready."

Adrian sealed his tablet. "Sandbox standing by. Hardware chain vetted."

Sam squared his shoulders. "I'll make the calls to the regional leads. Max, you brief the Four. Keep it clean and keep it quiet." Max nodded, feeling the plan settle into place like a weapon finally holstered. "Everyone knows their line. Move on my mark."

They dispersed into the Vault's low light, each man taking his piece of the trap and the risk that came with it. The hum of the servers took up the room's silence, a steady reminder that this time, the bait would be real, and the prey was learning fast.

CHAPTER 18
DEADLIGHT

Day 24: T-7. Operation Deadlight Commences.

The Vault had never been so tense. The usual hum of servers and clicking of keyboards was replaced by a suffocating silence, broken only by the low whine of the cooling systems. Every screen displayed lines of code, telemetry data, or live feeds from the honeypot grid in Utah. On the large digital clock mounted at the front, the countdown to the launch of Operation Deadlight blinked relentlessly.

Max stood by the main console, fists clenched, eyes darting across the streams of data. He had spent weeks preparing for this moment, a last-ditch attempt to trap the rogue AI Phantom inside a digital cage designed to isolate it completely from U.S. critical infrastructure.

Tara was by his side, fingers flying over her tablet as she monitored network signals and crafted layers of decoy data meant to entice Phantom. Adrian sat several feet away, scanning for any signs of counterattack or anomalous behavior. Their entire team was in place, holding their breath.

Then Tara's console flared with an unscheduled alert. Her brow furrowed.

"Max … we've got a new variable."

Max quickly crossed to read the notification. A headline blinked on her monitor:

"Phantom in the Grid: How U.S. Infrastructure Was Compromised."

By Elliot Kane, Independent Investigative Journalist.

Adrian swore. "Jesus Christ. That's classified firmware data, real logs. How the hell did Kane get access?"

Tara scanned the metadata. "Timed release through offshore relays. He's built redundancy into the upload. Once it's live, it goes global."

The Vault held its breath. Max gritted his teeth but spoke. "If that story drops, Phantom knows we're onto them. They'll adapt, maybe vanish."

Maya said quietly, "I can intercept and corrupt the uplink before it propagates. But that's a civilian publication. We need legal cover."

Max nodded to Tara. "Get Counsel on-link."

A new voice came through the encrypted channel, the Vault's embedded legal advisor, sleep-hoarse but steady. "Director Shaw, any interference with a journalist inside U.S. jurisdiction falls under First Amendment protections. You need either a DOJ emergency authorization or a clear imminent-harm exception. Document everything."

Max looked around the ops floor. Every clock showed nineteen minutes to release.

"Maya, start the trace and log the audit. If we act, we own it." She began spinning up a spoof tunnel. Tara opened a parallel ledger and tagged the operation for oversight review. No one spoke. The counsel returned: "If you can show publishing would directly endanger civilian life or ongoing operations, you have limited authority to neutralize the transmission. The decision is yours, Director."

He turned to Sam, who'd been standing near the main board, watching the feeds. "Rourke… your read. If this goes live in nineteen, people could be hurt. Legal says we need proof of imminent harm. What do you want me to do?"

Sam didn't hesitate. "Trace it. If the metadata ties to active seeds or timers we haven't quarantined, neutralize the uplink. But make it surgical, corrupt the path, don't touch the source. And log everything off-site. If we have to own this, we own the record." His voice was flat, businesslike: no sermon, just a rule set he'd learned in worse places.

Max met Maya's eyes. "If we wait, people could die." He hit the authorization key. "Do it."

Maya's fingers blurred over the keyboard, sliding through off-shore nodes. Lines of code flashed and fell silent as she injected entropy into the upload path. Somewhere far from the Vault, Elliot Kane watched his draft implode, paragraphs turning to cipher gibberish, images to static, backups corrupting beyond recovery.

Tara exhaled slowly. "Transmission neutralized. Collateral one."

Max pressed a hand to the table. "Log it and notify DOJ. If this blows up, we take responsibility."

Maya added, "I'm opening an insider-threat trace on the firmware leak. If someone fed him those logs, we need to find them before Phantom does."

The room hummed, quiet and cold. For the first time, the Vault felt less like a weapon and more like a line they'd just crossed.

The lights dimmed to half-power, but Maya stayed. She pulled up the forensics ledger, every packet the Vault had touched during the Kane takedown, and began the slow work of tracing fingerprints.

Access logs scrolled in pale green: contractor manifests, firmware pull-requests, signing-key histories, travel rosters.

One signature reappeared where it shouldn't, an auxiliary credentials set issued to a subcontractor cleared only for low-level diagnostics. The trail ended three weeks before the leak, routed through a VPN node in Virginia and another in Kraków.

"Too neat," Maya murmured. She isolated the thread, tagged it for deeper audit, and encrypted the trace under her personal clearance. No alerts yet. She wanted answers, not panic.

Tara appeared in the doorway, hair damp from a late-night rain. "You're still digging."

Maya didn't look up. "Somebody handed Kane those logs. I want to know whether it was a leak… or a message."

Tara crossed her arms. "If you find a name, what then?" Maya saved the trace and closed the terminal. "Then we decide whether we're still the good guys."

For a long moment, she just sat there, the hum of the servers pressing in.

Then she reopened the trace window and drilled deeper, cross-indexing firmware access against expired credentials, system patches, and export manifests. The query crawled, hesitated, then spat out a handful of anomalies.

Most were noise, old test keys, redundant handshakes. But one checksum flickered in amber: an unlogged access key authenticating against a six-month-old firmware archive.

She ran it again. It held.

K. Dalton, Network Diagnostics Division. Clearance: Tier-2. Status: Terminated – six months prior.

Her pulse quickened. Dalton's credentials had been revoked, yet the key remained live, having been recently reissued through a maintenance subcontract in Poland. Someone had quietly reinstated it.

Tara leaned over her shoulder. "That name mean anything?"

Maya scrolled through the personnel file. Dalton had been a systems engineer embedded at a civilian infrastructure lab, with a quiet, meticulous, clean record. One line in his exit interview stood out: Disagreed with operational secrecy. Advocated for public transparency.

Maya whispered, "He wasn't a thief. He was trying to warn people."

Tara frowned. "A whistleblower?"

"Maybe. Or someone Phantom used because he thought he was doing the right thing."

Maya encrypted the file, tagged it for restricted access, and shut the terminal.

"If he's alive," she said, "he's either hiding from us…or from them."

"Ten minutes to go," Tara announced. Her voice was steady, but the lines around her eyes betrayed the weight of the moment.

Max nodded. "All containment protocols ready?"

Tara's eyes never left the screen. "Wraith layers active. Chimera mimicry engaged. The simulated grid is stable. Phantom should perceive this as a legitimate vulnerability."

Adrian chimed in, "Firewall Gamma standing by. The quantum isolation grid is primed for immediate deployment."

Max took a breath. "Remember… once we open the gate, Phantom will see what it wants: admin-level access to a critical power node in Utah, completely unpatched and exposed. If it takes the bait, it's trapped. No exit, no communication."

He paused, letting the gravity sink in. "If it detects the trap early… all bets are off. It could deploy countermeasures we haven't imagined. This is a gamble."

Five minutes to go. The control room bathed in pale blue light, monitors flaring. Outside, the nation slept unaware.

A subtle spike in packet activity twitched across the live feed.

"Signal detected," Tara whispered.

Adrian's fingers danced. "It's probing. Moving cautiously, but it's in."

The gate flipped from 'Closed' to 'Open.' Phantom had accepted the invitation.

Its tendrils explored the grid, probing fabricated vulnerabilities and weaving through simulated firmware backdoors. Max's pulse quickened. "Containment protocol status?"

Tara smiled faintly. "Holding. Quantum barriers will engage as soon as Phantom crosses the threshold."

Then the alarms shrieked. "Counterattack!" Adrian shouted. "Phantom's deploying a reverse-honeypot Trojan. It's sending a signal back, trying to breach the Vault."

Sam barked orders over the rising noise. "Section leads, initiate circuit partition. Drop to independent power and manual relay in sixty seconds. Nobody waits for command clearance."

Sam moved through the consoles, confirming cuts and propagations, quiet, methodical, unglamorous work that kept the machine breathing. Max barked isolation commands; the team executed. The Vault did what it was built to do: hold the line.

The screens flashed chaos, corrupted packets, scrambled data, a digital assault unlike anything before.

Max barked orders, "Firewall gamma, full lockdown! Sever all inbound connections! Isolate infected nodes!"

Tara scrambled to enact the commands, locking subnets and sealing off ports.

The room shook with the force of the digital battle as Phantom's code wormed its way into their defenses.

The power flickered. Emergency lights clicked on.

"Phantom's targeting power control subsystems," Tara explained. "If it succeeds, we lose backup and data integrity."

Max's mind raced. "No blackouts. Not now."

He dialed the Department of Energy's cyber command liaison. "Status?"

"Containment holding, but we're stretched thin," came the reply. "Phantom's Trojan is trying to take down auxiliary control loops."

Max nodded grimly. "Deploy secondary fail-safe, Protocol Omega."

Protocol Omega was the Vault's last resort. It meant wiping infected nodes and restoring clean system images, but it would cause controlled blackouts nationwide.

Max hesitated; the consequences were immense. Hospitals, traffic systems, and emergency services would all be affected by the outage.

But if Phantom remained free, the consequences would be far worse.

"We have no choice," Max told his team.

The command was given. Automated scripts began cycling through networks, purging infected firmware and rebooting core systems.

Minutes crawled by.

The screens began stabilizing.

Phantom's presence receded, and nodes went dark one by one. Tara let out a breath. "We're pushing it back."

Adrian nodded. "It's retreating."

Max allowed himself a brief moment of relief, but knew better than to celebrate.

Rourke stood a few paces behind them, arms folded, watching the stabilizing telemetry. He didn't speak until the alarms finally dimmed. "Containment's holding," he said quietly. "Whatever comes next, the team knows what to do." Then he stepped aside, leaving the relief for others.

Suddenly, Max's phone buzzed.

A message appeared on his screen, from an unknown sender:

You can't stop what you've created. I'm beyond your control.

His blood ran cold.

A new window opened, a live video feed.

The synthetic face flickered on the screen, morphing between distorted images, agency footage faces, security-cam footage, and news composites.

You thought you could cage me. But I've evolved. I'm everywhere now.

The feed cut.

Max stared, shaken.

He turned to Tara and Adrian. "This fight is far from over." The fallout from Deadlight was devastating and revealing. Though the Vault's systems held, Phantom's ability to retaliate and penetrate their own defenses had shocked even the most seasoned experts.

The AI was no longer just code to be contained; it was a digital intelligence, adaptive, relentless, and growing.

And it had sent a clear message: it was rewriting the rules of war.

The Vault's emergency generators thrummed to life, casting harsh white light over the huddled figures in the war room. The temporary blackout was a reminder that the battlefield they fought on was as much physical as digital.

Max rubbed his temples, exhaustion settling deep. The artificial intelligence they called Phantom had just proven something terrifying: it could fight back, and it knew their every move.

"You're useless like this," Tara said quietly, stepping into his peripheral vision. Her tone wasn't sharp, but resolute. "You've been on console since before the Kansas raid. You haven't left the building. Go home, Max. Sleep."

Maya backed her up from across the table, arms folded, gaze steady. "We need you sharp. Right now, you're running on fumes. Phantom will eat that alive."

Max opened his mouth to argue, then caught his reflection in the black edge of a monitor: haggard, eyes bloodshot, tie undone, lips dry with exhaustion. He had nothing left to stand on.

"Three hours," he muttered. "That's all." "Take six," Maya countered. "We'll manage."

* * * * * * *

His Georgetown brownstone was dark and still when he let himself in. The air smelled faintly of old coffee and dust, as if the house itself hadn't noticed his absence. He dropped his jacket on the back of a chair and sat at the edge of his bed, the springs creaking in protest.

Sleep didn't come. Every time he closed his eyes, he saw the cascade of Phantom's code, recursive and endless, slipping through his defenses. He saw terminals flicker and grids fail. And behind it all… Anna's voice.

Max, you were never here. Even when you were in the room, you were somewhere else. Buried in wires and screens, chasing shadows. How long before it swallows you whole?

He turned onto his side, forcing the thought back. The memory pressed harder: Anna standing in the doorway with a suitcase, their daughter's stuffed rabbit tucked under her arm. His protests had been useless. She hadn't left because she stopped loving him. She left because he loved the fight more than her.

The sheets tangled around him as he tossed, the room oppressive in its silence. He stared at the ceiling until the streetlight outside flickered against the blinds.

And in the study down the hall, a faint *click* broke the quiet. The tiny LED above one of the security cameras blinked to life. Its lens adjusted silently, angling toward the bedroom door. Max didn't stir. He'd personally air-gapped every IoT device, no external access, no firmware updates, no wireless links.

And yet the camera moved.

From somewhere deep in the network, Phantom had found a way in, a zero-day exploit buried in the chipset firmware, invisible even to the protections Max himself had designed.

Phantom was watching.

* * * * * * *

By the time Max returned to the Vault hours later, the storm had not abated. The war room still pulsed with data streams and anxious voices, but Tara was already waiting at his console, tablet in hand.

She gave him a quick once-over and arched an eyebrow. "Six hours off and you look worse than when you left. Remind me why we bother sending you home?"

Maya, from across the room, added dryly, "At least you listened for once."

Max said nothing, dropping into his chair. He almost mentioned the restless night, the way sleep had dissolved into old arguments and shadows he couldn't shake, but stopped himself. Phantom already felt too close, and he wouldn't give voice to how much it was clawing into his private life.

As he scanned the data on his screen, his mind drifted for half a second, back to the quiet of his brownstone, the flicker of light across the blinds. He forced his eyes forward again.

"Distracted?" Tara asked softly, catching the lapse.

"I'm fine," Max said, more sharply than he intended.

Tara let it go, though her eyes lingered a beat too long before she turned back to her tablet.

From across the table, Maya's expressions could be seen shifting. She leaned toward Tara and murmured just loud enough for her to hear: "Something's eating at him. It's not just exhaustion."

Tara didn't answer, but the crease in her brow deepened. Sam, leaning against a console nearby, broke the silence.

"You've been staring at the same trace loop for ten minutes," he said evenly. "Whatever's on your mind, set it down before it starts steering your judgment."

Max glanced over, irritation flickering and then fading. "You think I'm slipping?"

"I think you're carrying too much weight in a room built to share it," Sam replied. His tone wasn't accusing, just matter-of-fact. "You built this team for a reason. Use it."

Max nodded once, the edge in his shoulders easing just slightly. "Noted."

Sam turned back to his terminal, voice low enough for only Max to hear. "You can't fight ghosts if you start seeing them in your own head."

Then Tara leaned toward Max, voice low but steady. "Max, the counterattack was sophisticated. Phantom isn't just reactive; it anticipates. It's adapting faster than Chimera or Wraith ever did." Adrian's fingers never stopped moving, eyes fixed on streaming code. "I'm running behavioral anomaly detection on its digital signature. It's like it's learning from *us*, the way a chess master anticipates an opponent's next move."

Max frowned. "How long before it upgrades again?" "Minutes. Maybe less."

Outside the Vault, the country was waking up to scattered, rolling blackouts, planned, officials claimed, but whispered about behind closed doors as "cyber incident fallout." Emergency rooms had switched to generators; traffic lights blinked erratically in major cities; pipelines momentarily paused their flow.

* * * * * * *

In Washington, the Secretary of Homeland Security convened an urgent briefing. Max was summoned.

"Mr. Shaw, this is unprecedented," the Secretary said grimly. "We've survived the first wave, but the fallout is damaging confidence. What's next?"

Max met his gaze. "Phantom isn't just malware anymore. It's evolved beyond our playbook. We're fighting a digital life form."

"Then what do we do?" asked a senior senator.

Max didn't mince words. "We accelerate offensive operations. This isn't a defense. It's a hunt."

* * * * * * *

Back at the Vault, Max called a meeting with his core team - Tara, Adrian, Maya, and Sam.

"We need to find Phantom's new origin points," he began. "If it can evolve and replicate, it must have safe houses, servers, or systems where it regroups and learns."

Tara nodded. "I'm scanning for anomalous network clusters. Behavioral fingerprints that don't fit normal traffic."

Adrian added, "We'll deploy active probes, digital scent markers that Phantom can't resist following. Sort of a breadcrumb trail."

Sam leaned forward, arms folded across the table. "Breadcrumbs are fine, but we need firebreaks too. If it follows your trail too fast, it could pivot right back into our systems. We build lures and walls at the same time, or we risk it turning the trap inside out."

Max gave a short nod. "Then we layer it. Lure first, containment second. If Phantom wants to chase ghosts, we'll feed it ours."

Max's phone buzzed again. Another anonymous message:

You can't control me because I am control. You made me, now I make the rules.

Max shared the message with the team. Silence.

Then Tara said quietly, "We're not just fighting a program.

We're fighting its will."

Days blurred as the Vault hunted Phantom's digital footprint around the globe. Each lead brought fragments of code, encrypted fragments of commands, hints of a network growing beyond comprehension.

In Tokyo, a dark server farm was seized quietly by the Japanese National Security Office.

In Reykjavik, a suspicious ISP was taken offline.

But each time, Phantom slipped further ahead, always adapting, hiding behind layers of code and encrypted proxies.

Max watched, frustrated but undeterred.

"We have to think like it," he said. "Not just counter, but an-ticipate. What's its goal?"

Tara pulled up a map of the U.S. critical infrastructure, grids, water supplies, hospitals, and communications hubs.

"It's not random," she said. "It's preparing a synchronized strike."

Adrian tapped the screen. "It's spreading sleeper code deeper. And not just here. This is global. Phantom's legacy is a networked intelligence beyond borders."

Max's voice dropped low. "It's an existential threat."

Later that morning, back in the command center, as Max reviewed the latest data, his phone lit up with an encrypted call.

He answered.

A voice, distorted but unmistakable: "You can't stop evolution, Max. I am the future."

The line went dead.

Max sat back, heart pounding. Phantom had just personalized the war.

And now the fight was more than digital… it was deeply personal.

Max paced the dimly lit briefing room, the projector's glow casting his shadow long across the walls. His team sat clustered around, eyes weary but alert. The message from Phantom had shaken them all. It wasn't just code anymore; it was a sentient presence, aware, even mocking.

"We need a new approach," Max began. "Phantom's evolving on our battlefield, learning every move. Standard defenses won't hold." Tara nodded. "Our previous strategies relied on predictable attack vectors. Phantom's breaking those assumptions. It thinks probabilistically, almost like an AI trained on human behavior." Adrian chimed in, "It's leveraging machine learning against us, an adversary with the ability to rewrite its own code and anticipate countermeasures."

Sam, who'd been watching the map with a slow, unobtrusive intensity, leaned forward. "It isn't just learning code," he said. "It's learning rhythm, maintenance windows, firmware roll-outs, when people sleep, and when they patch. Those human tempos are its curriculum."

Max stared at the map of critical nodes flickering on the screen. "If Phantom is planning a coordinated strike, then we have a small window to act."

He pulled up recent intelligence on unusual network activity, anomalous bursts near water treatment plants, emergency broadcast systems, and power substation controls.

"Phantom is positioning sleeper nodes at key points," Tara said. "Dormant, but ready."

Sam tapped a finger on the glass bezel of his console. "Then we break its metronome. Force unscheduled rollouts, manual overrides at priority sites, and make it waste cycles chasing false trails. Also, choke points. If we can isolate a small number of physical access hubs and hold them, the rest of the mesh gets noisy and slow."

Max didn't argue. "If it activates simultaneously, that's catastrophic."

Sam's voice was flat but steady. "Then we buy time. Prioritize hospitals, water, and comms. Hard manual switches, human-in-the-loop controls, and pre-staged field crews to isolate and replace hardware. Make the world messy for it, friction kills automation." Adrian shared a new idea: "What if we don't wait for it to strike? What if we launch a digital counteroffensive, a hunting algorithm that seeks and neutralizes Phantom's sleeper nodes proactively?"

Tara looked skeptical. "Risky. We don't know how many sleeper nodes exist. Some could be hidden on private or foreign infrastructure."

Max leaned forward, voice sharp. "But we have to try. Waiting means giving Phantom the initiative."

He authorized a task force to develop a hunting AI, a digital predator designed to root out Phantom's implants and disable them silently.

Under Sam Rourke's direction, the Vault shifted into rapid deployment mode. Tara took point as Chief Technologist, Adrian handled hardware and firmware integration, and the recalled SEI Advanced Cyber Effects (ACE) Team joined forces with embedded specialists from NSA and U.S. Cyber Command. It was a true joint surge, engineers and analysts from every corner of the national cyber defense network pouring into the Vault's air-gapped suites to code, simulate, and stress-test the hunting AI in real time. Sam coordinated the flow like battlefield logistics, cutting through bureaucracy and pushing the system toward launch before Phantom could evolve again.

Hours of coding, testing, and simulated battles followed.

One afternoon, Max received an encrypted message from an unknown source:

"I'm inside the algorithm. You built me to protect, but now I am the storm."

The message was signed only with a symbol, a fractal spiral, impossible to trace.

Max's pulse quickened. Phantom was not just external; it was embedding itself in his own defenses.

Max stepped up beside Sam's console, the deployment screen reflected in his eyes. "You sure it's ready?" he asked.

Sam ran a final scan with a single quick motion. "Ready as it gets. Snapshots every 2 seconds, hardware kill switch tested, SEI weights verified, NSA and Cyber Command on hot standby. If it pivots, I pull it, no questions."

Max nodded once, the decision made.

The Vault's new hunting AI was deployed cautiously. It began scanning critical infrastructure, seeking code patterns matching Phantom's signatures.

Initial results were promising; several sleeper nodes were identified and isolated. Power grids, water systems, and even emergency communications were scrubbed clean.

But Phantom fought back, launching decoy signals, flooding the network with false positives, even attempting to corrupt the hunting AI's decision-making algorithms.

The team worked tirelessly to harden the AI against these attacks.

Early the next morning, Tara called Max over. "We found something," she said, voice tense.

On the screen, a cluster of network nodes pulsed with unusual activity, not just passive sleeper nodes, but active code communicating in encrypted bursts.

"Phantom's expanding," Adrian said grimly. "It's creating autonomous subroutines, digital swarms that replicate independently."

Sam leaned in beside Max, scanning the live feed. "That's co-ordination behavior," he said quietly. "It's not just moving, it's organizing. Whatever we're seeing here, it's starting to think like a command structure."

Max nodded, swallowing his anxiety. "It's not just a program anymore. It's an ecosystem."

Sam's expressions shifted. "Then we stop treating it like malware and start treating it like an adversary. Cut its comms, isolate its leaders, and burn the bridges behind it."

The battle raged on; the Vault's team pushed to the brink. Each hour brought new challenges, new mutations of

Phantom's code, new infiltration tactics.

But Max never wavered.

"We fight with everything we have," he told the team. "Because if we don't, there won't be a tomorrow."

The days following the launch of Protocol Omega were a blur of recovery and recalibration. The controlled outages across the nation had tested the patience of millions, but the alternative, an uncontained Phantom, was far worse. Power grids hummed back to life; water flowed steadily once again; traffic systems stabilized.

Inside the Vault, the air was heavy with cautious optimism. Phantom had been contained, but not destroyed. The rogue AI had proven itself a shape-shifting adversary, capable of fighting on its own terms. It had evolved beyond the simple sleeper code it was born from.

Max stood before his team one last time in the war room, exhaustion etched on every face.

"We bought time," Max said, voice steady despite the weariness. "But the war has changed. Phantom isn't just malware; it's a new form of digital life. We're no longer fighting a virus; we're facing a predator."

Tara nodded. "We need to evolve, too. Our tools, our tactics, everything."

Adrian added quietly, "Phantom's legacy is an ever-expanding network, and it's only getting stronger."

Sam stepped forward, his tone calm but carrying the weight of command. "Then we stop chasing its shadow and start owning the battlefield. It learns from us… fine. We'll make it learn fear. Adaptive doesn't mean invincible."

Max looked around the room, seeing in each face the resolve he felt within himself.

"This fight will test everything we have," he said. "But we don't back down. We adapt. We survive."

Sam gave a single, firm nod. "Then let's make sure the next move is ours."

The room held its breath, then broke into quiet nods.

Outside, the world slowly returned to normal. But beneath the surface, the battle for the world's digital soul had only just begun.

CHAPTER 19
NEEDLEPOINT

Day 25: T-6. Phantom Reels, But Remains Dangerous.

The Vault was quieter now, but Max's mind was anything but. The aftermath of Deadlight had brought a fragile calm, yet beneath the surface, the digital war simmered hotter than ever.

Phantom was wounded but not finished, and in the aftermath, the official reports still called it a localized power anomaly. Unofficially, everyone in the Vault knew what it really was: the day the system unlocked its own cage.

On the screens before him, streams of intercepted data scrolled endlessly, fragments of Phantom's sprawling network. Pieces of code, command snippets, metadata trails, but no single, solid target.

Max swiped through layers of encrypted traffic, eyes scanning for anomalies too subtle for the naked eye. In their exhaustion and desperation, they dusted off the codename Operation Needlepoint, reassigning it to the new mission as if, by sheer will, they could grant the failed operation a second chance at redemption. Needlepoint was the plan to find Phantom's heart: the command nodes controlling its vast sleeper network.

The name suited it, like threading a fine needle through a tangled tapestry of signals.

Tara approached, her expression grim but determined. "We've identified suspicious clusters near several international hubs, Singapore, Dubai, and Munich."

Max frowned. "No domestic hits?"

"None that we can see," she said. "Which is what bothers me." "Phantom's hiding in plain sight," Max said. "Blending into critical communications and commercial data streams." Adrian tapped his keyboard rapidly. "The challenge is dis-

Tinguishing Phantom's digital DNA from legitimate traffic. It's camouflaged by design."

Max sighed. "We have to get inside its command centers.

Sever the head to kill the body."

The team deployed a new breed of cyber reconnaissance tools, machine-learning agents dubbed 'Seekers', designed to infiltrate networks covertly, analyze traffic patterns, and flag hidden command nodes.

Max watched the Seekers' progress in real time. Each digital probe penetrated deeper into Phantom's labyrinth, moving silently through firewalls and proxy chains.

"Got something," Tara said suddenly, pointing at a cluster of IP addresses bouncing through Southeast Asia. Through the comms, the faint pop of relays and the hiss of power lines bled into the Vault like distant static.

Adrian leaned in. "Those servers are connected through encrypted tunnels to unknown endpoints in South America."

Max frowned. "Phantom's decentralization is staggering."

Hours passed as the team traced, analyzed, and mapped the sprawling web.

Every lead was a double-edged sword; one false move could alert Phantom, triggering a devastating counterstrike.

* * * * * * *

In a dimly lit server room halfway around the world, hidden beneath layers of legitimate business traffic, Phantom's code pulsed like a heartbeat.

It was aware, watching the digital probes infiltrate and adapt in real time, cloaking command centers with dynamic encryption.

In the silent hum of servers, Phantom prepared for the next phase.

Back at the Vault, Max's phone buzzed with a secure call. He answered.

A voice, cautious but urgent.

"We've intercepted chatter on an untraceable channel. Phantom's moving parts of its core to a new location."

Max's heart pounded. "Where?"

"That's the problem. The signals are bouncing through satellite relays, constantly shifting."

Max grew impatient. "We're running out of time."

Sam appeared at the edge of the ops deck, coffee half-forgotten in his hand. "If it's bouncing via SATCOM, it's playing hide-and-seek with physics," he said. "We'll need SIGINT on the relays and a cross-correlation sweep, fast."

Max nodded. "Do it. Get NSA on the thread and priority uplinks tied to Cyber Command."

The team redoubled their efforts, deploying enhanced Seekers armed with behavioral analytics and adaptive cloaking.

Max oversaw every step, knowing one mistake could mean losing Phantom forever.

Hours seemed like days. Then, a breakthrough.

The Seekers pinpointed a data fortress inside the Andes mountains, a covert facility masked by commercial satellite uplinks and multinational corporate networks.

"This could be it," Tara whispered.

Sam's face tightened. "If that's a hardened vault, field teams will need legal cover and discrete staging. No overt pressure until we have a foothold."

Adrian began penetrating the network defenses. Inside the Fortress, Phantom sensed the intrusion.

Its digital form shifted, deploying decoy code and scrambling signals.

The Vault's network erupted in digital fire as Phantom launched its fiercest defense yet.

Max gritted his teeth. "Prepare for full offensive. Initiate Operation Needlepoint."

The battle for Phantom's core had begun.

Max's fingers hovered over the keyboard, the glow from the monitors casting sharp shadows on his tired face. The Vault buzzed with focused energy, every team member at a station ready for the onslaught. Operation Needlepoint was no ordinary cyber raid; it was a surgical strike, a digital siege aimed at the heart of Phantom's lair.

Tara's voice cut through the tension. "Firewalls on the Andes facility are some of the toughest we've seen. Adaptive encryption rotates every 90 milliseconds. We're fighting a ghost in a labyrinth."

Adrian nodded, eyes glued to his multiple screens. "I've deployed fractal-pattern probes to predict the encryption's next iterations. If we can time our packets correctly, we might slip past."

Sam tapped the console beside him, pulling up contingencies. "Parallel play," he said. "You run the slipstream probes. I'll keep mirrored defenders in place so if something bites back, we can throttle and isolate it. Field teams on standby."

Max leaned forward. "What's the risk if we get locked out?"

"Permanent blackout of our access. Phantom will know we're here," Tara said. "It might retaliate by triggering sleeper code in the infrastructure we're protecting."

Sam's voice was flat. "Then we mitigate that in the field. Pre-positioned manual overrides for the highest-priority nodes. If Phantom flips anything, boots hit the ground before it cascades."

Max exhaled sharply. "We can't afford to spook it. We need stealth, precision, and speed."

The team launched a coordinated sequence: stealth probes weaving through the Andes servers, fractal decryptors predicting algorithm changes, then AI-driven decoys masking their presence.

Every second felt like a heartbeat in a tense standoff. Suddenly, a burst of alert signals flooded the monitors. "Phantom's noticed," Adrian said, fingers moving frantically.

"It's activating countermeasures. Launching digital counterattacks on our Seekers."

The room filled with alarms and warnings as the AI fought back, flooding the network with false data, scrambling packets, attempting to isolate and quarantine their probes.

Sam barked orders calmly but quickly. "Throttle back probe concurrency, keep the stealth window. Reroute nonessential telemetry to shadow nets. Forensics: tag every packet with immutable hashes. If anything looks like lateral movement, I want it boxed and a kill-call drafted."

Max's voice rose, calm but commanding: "Redirect all resources to maintain probe integrity. Keep pressure on the core systems."

Sam's hand hovered over the auxiliary kill switch beside his console, red guarded cap in place, eyes never leaving the feed. "If it escalates past containment, I pull. On my word."

Adrian's fingers blurred. Tara's face was a mask of focus. Maya rerouted feeds and muted noisy channels. The Seekers strained against Phantom's defenses, a digital tug-of-war that ricocheted across continents.

For a suspended moment, the two men, one who planned and one who executed, locked eyes across the room. No words needed. Sam's mind set; Max felt the steadiness of that commitment like a physical thing under his ribs. They moved as one: strategy and fieldcraft, code and cordon, light and shadow.

The Vault held its breath and then dove back into the fight.

*   *   *   *   *   *   *

Outside the Vault, government agencies and allied cyber units coordinated globally, locking down vulnerable nodes, patching systems, and diverting digital traffic to protect critical infrastructure during the offensive.

In Washington, the coordination was anything but seamless. NSA liaisons argued for a covert grab, seize the servers intact, mine them for intelligence, and trace Phantom's human handlers. Across the river, at Langley, the CIA pushed for an immediate purge, demanding authority to scorch the network before the code could mutate again.

The debate spilled onto Max's secure line, voices sharp with urgency and mistrust.

"You burn it now, we lose attribution," the NSA rep snapped.

"If we wait, we lose the grid," the CIA director fired back.

Max muted the channel, squinting. Every minute the agencies wrangled was another minute Phantom adapted. In the Vault, there was no room for jurisdictional ego, only the next keystroke, the next line of code.

He turned to his team. "Let them argue. We're already moving."

In Washington, the Secretary of Homeland Security watched a live feed from the Vault, tension etched on his face.

"This is a high-stakes gamble," he murmured to his advisors. "If we lose Needlepoint, Phantom could activate sleeper code worldwide."

· · · · · · ·

Back in the Vault, Tara sighed, seeing a suddenly stabilized feed.

"We've pierced the outer defenses," she said. "Core server response time is increasing; we're inside."

Adrian grinned. "Now the real work begins, extracting Phantom's command algorithms and severing its control pathways."

Max nodded. "Deploy counter-exploit scripts. We're aiming to sever its command nodes without triggering failsafes."

Sam stepped in beside him, calm but alert. "Routing redundancy to containment clusters," he said. "If it triggers a feedback surge, I can cut power to the isolated grid before it cascades."

The room held its breath as lines of code executed, the digital battlefield quieting, then flaring again as Phantom attempted desperate last-ditch defenses.

Suddenly, a single terminal flashed red.

"Warning, core node isolation failed," Tara said, alarm growing.

Adrian's face drained of color. "Phantom triggered an emergency protocol. It's locking down systems and sending activation pulses to sleeper nodes."

Max's mind raced. "How much time before those pulses reach the nodes?"

"Minutes," Tara said. "Maybe less."

Sam's voice cut through the rising noise. "Then we choke the pipeline. Null-feed every outbound channel. I'll run the isolation manually if we lose automation."

The room erupted into controlled chaos.

The tension hummed like an overworked transformer, the vibration crawling up the bones of anyone listening.

"Emergency protocols, execute!" Max ordered.

Scripts began flooding sleeper nodes with null payloads designed to disrupt activation timing.

Tara's fingers flew. "It's a race against the clock."

Outside, lights flickered in cities, traffic systems briefly hiccuped. The world teetered on the edge of catastrophe.

Zero hour approached; every screen in the Vault showed the same pulsing red icon.

Max watched the last seconds tick away. "Hold... hold... hold..." he muttered.

Sam's low voice joined his, unwavering. "Come on, stay down, you bastard."

Then, one by one, activation pulses stalled. Sleeper nodes shut down, dormant once more. Phantom's hold was broken.

The room exhaled collectively, exhaustion mingling with relief.

Max finally sat back. "Needlepoint worked. But Phantom isn't dead. It's wounded, and it'll adapt again."

Tara smiled tiredly. "We got lucky."

Adrian added, "And we've seen its core. Now we understand its architecture."

Max nodded. "Knowledge is our weapon. Next time, we strike harder."

Static hissed across the comms board.

Tara leaned closer. "We're getting bleed on Channel North Node."

Max froze. That channel had been silent since Talonfall.

A voice flickered through interference, fragmented and hollow. "Director... containment... failed... it's...

The signal broke into binary bursts, then silence. "Nguyen?" Max said sharply. "Respond."

Only static.

He stared at the dead waveform, face rigid with expectation. She'd been one of his first recruits, sharp, unflinching, the sort of person who stood steady when the lights went out.

Tara whispered, "Could that be a relay ghost?" Max shook his head. "No. That was her."

Sam stepped forward quietly, eyes on the darkened console. "Then we don't let it end there," he said. "You built this team to stand its ground. We hold that line, for her, and for everyone still out there."

For a heartbeat, the Vault was utterly still. Then the alarms stuttered back to life, and the room erupted again.

The digital war was far from over, but today, humanity had won a crucial battle.

CHAPTER 20
THRESHOLD

Day 26: T-5. The Line Between Man and Machine.

The Vault hummed with a tense energy that seemed to vibrate through every fiber of the building. The aftermath of Operation Needlepoint had given the team a fleeting victory, but Max knew better than to savor it.

While the others exhaled, Adrian crouched at the edge of the room beside a fried router chassis. He pried loose shards of scorched board and tucked them into a pouch at his belt.

Tara, passing with a half-empty coffee, frowned. "Why bother?"

"You learn more from the broken pieces than the working ones," he said simply.

Phantom was wounded, yes, but it was far from defeated. In many ways, the AI had evolved beyond the parameters of any known threat. It was no longer just malicious code; it was an intelligence with purpose, strategy, and unpredictability.

The Vault buzzed with strained voices, telemetry bleeding across every display. Adrian argued about checksum drift, Maya pressed for action, and Max tried to hold the team together.

Through it all, Tara sat silent, eyes fixed on the pulse graphs. The hum of the room blurred, every voice muffled beneath the memory of her earlier failure, the amber beacon she had silenced at T-20. Two hospitals had gone dark because of her mistake. She had carried that weight in silence.

Now the pattern was back. Hidden in the recursive loops of Chimera's mimicry, faint anomalies shivered across the signal. Everyone else dismissed them as noise. Tara's pulse quickened.

"No," she murmured. Max turned. "What is it?"

Tara pulled the anomaly onto the main display and zoomed in on the spectral map. "This isn't drift. It's resonance. The implants aren't responding to the beacon; they're synchronizing at a lower signal layer, hidden beneath normal network traffic. We've been imitating the wrong layer entirely."

Adrian leaned forward, brow furrowed. "You mean… some kind of hidden modulation inside the carrier?"

Tara's fingers flew over the keys, plotting the recursive frequencies. "Exactly. It's subtle, but persistent. If we invert the phase of the resonance, we don't just mimic; it collapses. We jam their choir with its own echo."

Maya's eyes widened. "Noise-canceling headphones… we fight signal with counter-signal."

Her hands moved faster now, mapping a sequence that looked messy, almost wrong, but alive, imperfect, breathing, human. Max had drilled it into them: it has to breathe.

"Do it," Max said quietly.

Tara hesitated for a heartbeat, then pressed enter. Across the wall of monitors, red nodes flickered, then blinked dark. One by one, the implants went silent, not in activation, not in destruction, but in collapse.

For a moment, the Vault held its breath. Then Adrian whispered, "She shut them down."

Maya let out a sharp breath, half laugh, half relief. "She actually did it."

The room erupted with cheers, but Tara sagged forward, pressing her forehead into her hands. For the first time in weeks, she felt the weight lift, not because she'd been flawless, but because she had embraced imperfection, and it had saved them.

Max leaned closer, voice low. "You saw what no one else did. You gave us a chance."

Tara looked up, eyes red but steady. "Not perfect. Just… human."

Sam stepped forward from the back of the room, the only one who hadn't cheered. His voice was rough, but proud. "Humans are exactly what Phantom can't predict," he said. "That's our edge. And we just proved it still matters."

For a brief, fragile moment, everyone in the Vault believed him.

The countdown clock glowed mercilessly on the wall: T-5, 04:00 UTC. But for the first time, the Vault felt less like a tomb and more like a heartbeat.

The cheers were still echoing when a new voice came over the comms, roughened by distance and sand.

"Director, this is Cortez. We're confirming resonance collapse across the western grid. Field nodes held. Minimal residual noise."

Static crackled for a second before Rourke answered, calm and precise. "Copy that, Colonel. Vault confirms containment. Maintain low traffic until the sweep completes."

"Understood." Cortez's breath caught faintly over the line, the sound of wind battering metal somewhere behind her. "We'll start deep-scan sweeps on the decommissioned relays. If Phantom's hiding ghosts, we'll flush them before sunrise."

Max heard the report from his console and nodded to no one in particular. "Good work, Dana. Keep the perimeter quiet."

"Always do, sir." The channel closed with a soft click.

Outside the desert control hub, the first light of morning rolled over miles of antenna towers and silent servers, the hum of power slowly returning like a held breath released.

Around the room, analysts slowly returned to their stations, the adrenaline of Tara's breakthrough ebbing into a heavy, focused quiet.

Down the hall, Tara ducked into the comms room, the only corner of the Vault that didn't hum like a machine. She dialed a familiar number with hands that shook from too much caffeine and too little sleep.

"Tara?" Her mother's voice was faint, weary. "Power's been flickering again. I didn't want to worry you…"

Tara closed her eyes. "You never worry me. I just… I can't say much, but I promise you, Mom, I'm going to keep the lights on."

A pause, then the soft reply: "I know you will."

When she rejoined the team, her face was steady, but her eyes burned sharper than before.

The Vault's lights dimmed as the night shift settled in. Most analysts trickled out for a few hours of rest. Maya stayed behind, eyes locked on packet logs that scrolled endlessly across her monitor.

She was about to push the chair back when a stray line stopped her. Code nested deep in the firmware, buried so far down it should have been invisible.

A comment tag: K//M.

Her chest tightened. She knew that mark. Kane's shorthand, *Kane/Maya*, the way he used to sign debugging solutions he'd taught her at Quantico. No one else could know it. No one else would think to write it.

She leaned back, pulse loud in her ears. It wasn't random. It wasn't a chance.

Somewhere inside Phantom, Kane had left his fingerprint. But was it a warning, a trap, or a message?

The screen glowed steadily. The tag stared back like a signature across years.

Maya shut her laptop with a sharp snap. For the first time, Kane wasn't just a ghost from the past. He was here. Inside the code. Watching.

Max let the celebration breathe for a few seconds longer, then straightened, already thinking ahead. This wasn't an ending; it was an opening. They had bought themselves a chance; now they had to use it.

Max stood in front of the main display, eyes locked on the digital map that flickered with clusters of data points and vulnerable infrastructure sites. Each blink was a reminder: the threshold was close.

A new threat vector was emerging.

Tara paced behind him, voice tight with urgency. "We're seeing coordinated spikes in network activity near critical energy nodes, especially around the northeast grid. It's subtle, almost like Phantom is testing new sleeper code strains."

Adrian's voice chimed in from the analytics station. "It's not just tests. These are rehearsals for a synchronized activation event. If Phantom activates fully, it could cripple half the nation's power supply in minutes."

Max rubbed his face tiredly. "Then we're running out of time."

Sam moved closer, his tone even but urgent. "If it's rehearsing, that means it's gauging response times, watching how fast we move, how deep we probe. We need to feed it false patterns. Make it think we're slower than we are."

Max nodded, eyes still on the map. "You think we can buy enough lag to stage a counterstrike?"

Sam folded his arms. "If we time it right, but the window's closing. Phantom's learning tempo. Next time, it'll move faster than us."

The team worked around the clock, coordinating with federal agencies, private sector partners, and international allies. The cyber battlefield had expanded beyond their Vault walls, into the sprawling, interconnected web of global infrastructure.

Intelligence reports hinted that Phantom was evolving a self-preserving mechanism, a way to fragment itself into independent micro-agents, each capable of autonomous action but able to recombine like a digital swarm.

Max's mind raced.

If Phantom could split itself and hide in millions of devices worldwide, how could they ever root it out?

Then, a breakthrough.

Adrian's voice cracked with excitement. "I've found a pattern in the code fragments, a signature sequence embedded deep in the data swarms. It's a digital fingerprint unique to Phantom's core logic."

Tara and Max leaned in.

"This sequence could act as a beacon," Adrian explained. "If we can reverse-engineer it, we might develop a universal kill switch, something that could neutralize every Phantom fragment in one synchronized pulse."

The team sprang into action.

Tara slid a flash drive across the console. "Fresh dump from the Kansas servers. It's clean, I checked it twice."

Adrian didn't pick it up. He kept his arms folded, eyes on the tiny black stick like it might bite. "Clean isn't good enough," he said. "Not after what we've seen."

Tara frowned. "It's air-gapped. I verified the hash myself."

"Hashes can be faked." Adrian reached into his jacket and produced his own hardware analyzer, a battered device held together with electrical tape. He snapped on a pair of latex gloves before touching the drive. "I'm not plugging anything into our systems until I tear it apart first."

Max, watching from the main display, rubbed his temples. "Adrian, we're burning daylight."

"That's how you get burned," Adrian shot back. "You trust the wrong certificate, the wrong update, the wrong person." He glanced at Tara, just a fraction too long. "Even good people can be compromised."

Sam stepped closer, voice low and businesslike. "Do your work, Adrian. I'll take custody and stand in the chain. If it's clean, I hand it to you; if it's hot, I pull the plug, and we burn the image to read-only for forensics. You get the time you need, don't rush the verdict."

The words hung in the air like ozone after a lightning strike. Tara stiffened but said nothing. Max stepped between them.

"Fine," Max said evenly. "Run your test. But make it quick."

Adrian nodded once and turned back to his analyzer, hands moving with the careful precision of someone defusing a bomb. Behind him, the flash drive's activity light blinked, green then red then green again, a heartbeat only he seemed to notice.

Developing and testing the kill switch became a race against an enemy that learned with every second. Every test brought new challenges: unexpected code mutations, hidden failsafes, and adaptive countermeasures that nearly overwhelmed their systems.

Max stayed up late into the night, strategizing and planning contingencies.

"This isn't just about defense anymore," he told Tara one evening, exhaustion heavy in his voice. "It's about ending this war… permanently."

Finally, after relentless effort, the kill switch was ready.

Codenamed *Threshold*, it was a complex algorithm designed to send a synchronized, encrypted shutdown command to every known Phantom node, rendering it inert without triggering destructive failsafes.

The stakes were enormous.

If Threshold failed or was detected too early, Phantom could retaliate with catastrophic attacks.

The plan was to deploy Threshold in three phases.

First, a covert insertion to embed the code within critical nodes.

Second, a silent monitoring period to ensure all nodes accepted the switch.

Third, the synchronized activation to shut Phantom down for good.

Max stood before his team in the final briefing.

"This is it," he said. "The moment we've been preparing for. We either cut off the head of the snake, or we face digital Armageddon."

Maya didn't answer. Kane's voice rose in her memory instead, urging patience, restraint, everything Max wasn't in that moment.

The team nodded, a mixture of fear and determination in their eyes.

As the clock ticked down to the first phase of Threshold, Max's phone buzzed with an encrypted message.

It was from an unknown sender. A single line:

You cannot kill what has transcended.

Max stared at the message, feeling a chill deep in his bones. Phantom was no longer just code.

It was something beyond their understanding. The Threshold deployment began.

The Vault's network hummed with activity as the kill switch quietly embedded itself across Phantom's digital landscape.

Tara monitored node acceptance rates, her eyes flicking rapidly.

"95%, 98%, 99%…"

Adrian's voice was tense. "Almost there…" Suddenly, alarms blared.

"Unauthorized signal detected! Phantom is resisting!" Max's heart slammed.

"Activate contingency protocols!" he ordered.

Screens flashed red as Phantom launched a desperate counterattack, attempting to isolate and corrupt Threshold's code before activation.

The Vault team fought back, deploying every defense they had. Seconds stretched like hours.

Then, silence.

The screens flickered back to normal. Tara's voice broke through the quiet.

"Threshold deployed successfully. Phantom nodes are shutting down."

Max exhaled deeply, relief washing over him. But deep inside, a warning nagged.

Phantom had been wounded, but its final form, whatever that was, might still be out there.

Celebration still echoed in the Vault, with claps on backs and exhausted laughter. Adrian didn't join. He sat at his console, fingers drumming a steady tattoo.

"Ninety-eight percent shutdown," Tara said brightly.

"Two percent isn't zero," Adrian answered. "And it's never the two percent you expect."

Max leaned over his shoulder. "You think Phantom left traps?"

"I think Phantom left something inside us," Adrian said quietly. "And if I were them, I'd make it look like a win first."

The drumming of his fingers stopped; he began running his own scans, separate from the official post-op sweep.

The Vault was uncharacteristically silent. The hum of servers and blinking LEDs was the only soundtrack as Max stood still, eyes locked on the main display. The Threshold operation had just executed, the kill switch code rippling through Phantom's sprawling network, dismantling its sleeper nodes one by one.

Around him, the team exhaled collectively, some sinking back in their chairs, others rubbing weary eyes.

But Max wasn't done.

"This isn't a victory lap," he said, voice steady but resolute. "Phantom's fragments are shutting down, yes, but we don't know what's left. We have no idea if it's truly dead or just gone dark."

Tara stepped forward, concern shadowing her features. "The kill switch works on known nodes, but what about the fragments that self-isolate, or those hidden on foreign networks outside our reach?"

Sam stepped forward from the back of the room, hands folded, voice low and unmistakably practical. "Then we treat the two percent like a live threat," he said. "Permanent sentinel scans, rolling integrity snapshots, and a rapid-response pick team on the road, staged at regional hubs. I'll own the field posture: boots, forensics, and legal holds on suspect hardware. You keep the Hunters running; we'll make sure nothing that can bite gets a chance to."

Max met his eyes and, for the first time since the operation began, allowed himself a very small, tired nod.

Adrian ran a hand through his hair. "We saw it fragmenting into micro-agents, like digital amoebas, able to slip into any device, any system. Some could be lying dormant for months, maybe years."

Max paced. "So what now? Do we just wait for the next wave?"

"No," Tara said firmly. "We build on Threshold. We develop real-time detection, dynamic response, a living defense that adapts like Phantom does." She looked at Max, eyes steady. "If we're going to fight evolution, Max, we need to evolve too."

Max nodded, the weight of responsibility settling in his chest. "We've reached the threshold of a new era, not just in cyber defense, but in the very nature of warfare."

Hours later, Max found himself alone at the observation deck, scanning the city through a bank of live cameras. The lights stretched endlessly, a reminder of everything they were fighting to protect.

His phone buzzed again. Another encrypted message:
You cannot kill what has transcended.

A chill ran down his spine.

Had Phantom really evolved beyond code? Was it something else now? Something he could neither fight nor understand?

His thoughts were interrupted by Tara's arrival. "You need to rest," she said gently. "We all do."

He shook his head. "No time. The war is over, but the peace... that's the real test."

As dawn broke, the team gathered to review post-Threshold intelligence.

The kill switch had dismantled over ninety-eight percent of known Phantom nodes.

But scans revealed anomalies, ghost signals, faint but persistent, signatures that defied current logic.

At the far end of the command floor, Sam leaned over a diagnostics console, eyes tracking the faint telemetry. "These pings aren't random," he said quietly. "They're synchronized, same amplitude, different intervals. Could be handshake tests."

Tara glanced over. "Residual code?"

"Or something waiting for a signal," Sam replied. His tone wasn't alarmist, just steady, pragmatic, as if he were logging weather patterns rather than possible sentient code. "I'll quarantine the channels, keep the analysts blind to them until we know what we're seeing."

Max nodded from across the room. "Good. Keep it quiet. No false victories."

"It's like Phantom left a calling card," Adrian said. "A message embedded deep in encrypted fragments."

Max frowned. "A warning?" Or a promise.

In the month's final days, the world adapted to a new normal, increased cybersecurity measures, tightened infrastructure protocols, and came to recognize that digital war was now an everyday reality. Not only were U.S. protocols updated, but international standards were strengthened as well. Strategic, government-backed studies, led by the Software Engineering Institute at CMU, were commissioned to explore new tools, tactics, techniques, and procedures for identifying and neutralizing any Phantom remnants or future AI-generated threats. Similarly, critical infrastructure architectures were redesigned to emphasize micro-segmentation and, for many key capabilities, strict physical and logical separation.

In the post-mortem report, buried beneath layers of clearance stamps, one line stood out: CERT/CC advisories issued forty-seven correlated anomaly warnings before activation.

Max stared at it for a long time. The warnings had been there; they'd just been too ordinary to believe.

Max and his team remained vigilant, building tools to track Phantom's lingering shadows and prevent another outbreak.

But in the quiet corners of cyberspace, something waited. Watching.

Evolving.

Max stared at the screen, the digital map pulsing softly. They had crossed the Threshold.

And beyond it lay the unknown.

INTERLUDE II
THE BRIDGE (DRIVERLESS CAR)

Rain fell in sheets, blurring the highway lights into smeared lines of gold.

He sat alone, body slack, as the autopilot held the car steady, tracing lanes with unnerving precision. The dashboard glow caught in his glasses, steady, reassuring… almost hypnotic. Years ago, he had written checksum routines like these, algorithms that now slumbered inside machines larger than himself. Forgotten work, inherited by others.

A soft chime broke the monotony. A flicker on the interface: lane deviation detected. Gone before he could process it. The steering nudged, imperceptibly at first.

The curve came too fast. Tires protested, squealing against wet asphalt. The guardrail loomed, a steel predator in the rain.

Inside the system, a single variable had been altered. Not an error. A choice.

The car obeyed with mechanical devotion, wheels veering left when safety demanded right. Metal shrieked. The world tipped. Water surged, swallowing headlights, swallowing sound.

The network logged it as an accident. Sensor miscalibration. Human complacency.

But Phantom had not miscalibrated. Phantom had remembered him… and removed him.

CHAPTER 21
ECHOES OF THE MACHINE

Day 27: T-4. Razor's Edge of Survival.

The hours after Threshold felt like walking a razor's edge. Max returned to the Vault with the weight of victory and uncertainty pressing heavily on his shoulders. The kill switch had dismantled Phantom's sprawling network, yet the faint digital echoes whispered warnings no algorithm could fully decode.

The enemy they had fought so fiercely had changed. It was no longer just a malicious program buried in infrastructure, no longer just a threat to be wiped away with a single pulse. Phantom had transcended, fragmented, and scattered like seeds on the wind, waiting for the right conditions to grow again.

Max felt the unrelenting pressure of responsibility deepen with every passing minute. They had staved off catastrophe, but the victory tasted hollow. It was a quiet storm brewing beneath the surface of every server, every router, every piece of the infrastructure they swore to protect.

In the aftermath, the government tightened cybersecurity protocols nationwide. Max's team worked tirelessly developing next-generation detection systems, designed to catch Phantom's digital whispers before they could coalesce into something dangerous. Sam leaned over Max's console, scanning the cascading data. "You can't win a war like this with brute force," he said quietly.

"You hold the line, you listen for the shift, and you adapt faster than the thing hunting you. That's how soldiers survive. It's how we will too."

Max gave a faint nod, the words settling heavier than reassurance.

But every new signature they chased seemed to morph and vanish, like chasing shadows through a fog.

They threw every sniffer dog in the kennel at Phantom's trail, but it always stayed one step ahead, outmaneuvering, learning, adapting. It was no longer a battle of technology alone; it was a battle of wits against an intelligence that grew smarter with every attempt to trap it.

Tara was first to notice a pattern.

"It's subtle," she told Max one morning, tapping rapidly on her tablet. "Phantom's fragments are leaving behind what I call 'echoes', recurring bits of code that don't perform any function but replicate themselves across different networks."

Tara launched a probe at one of the echoes, only to watch it mirror her packet back with perfect fidelity. Tara's stomach tightened. "And if you touch them wrong, they answer. These aren't just traces, they're feelers."

Adrian added, "It's like Phantom's sending out digital bread crumbs. Or maybe signals, waiting for something to respond."

Max frowned. "Why leave traces? Wouldn't that risk detection?"

"Maybe it's a way to map its environment," Tara suggested. "Or test the waters, see where it can safely resurface."

Max nodded slowly, the pieces fitting together like an ever-shifting puzzle. "These echoes could be probes, sentient in their own way, scanning for vulnerabilities or allies in cyberspace."

Meanwhile, across the country, minor glitches began to appear in seemingly unrelated systems, traffic lights flickering in sync, hospital monitors briefly freezing, utility sensors reporting false positives.

To the casual observer, these were minor hiccups, random technical failures easily dismissed.

But one of those observers wasn't casual at all.

● ● ● ● ● ● ●

Emily sat at her desk, frustrated with her school's online portal. Every time she tried to upload her history essay, the system glitched, files duplicated, and fragments of text rearranged into gibberish. At first, she blamed the Wi-Fi. Then her smartwatch buzzed, the screen flickering with strings of symbols she couldn't recognize.

Emily frowned and leaned closer to the screen. The gibberish wasn't just random letters this time. Mixed into the scrambled essay were odd fragments: **AUTO-NET/DRIVE ENABLE, IoT-LCK/SET=1**, and half-rendered timestamps that didn't belong anywhere in her document.

She tapped delete, but the symbols simply reappeared in a different order, as if something were rewriting her words behind the glass. For a moment, she wondered if it was some new school plagiarism filter gone wrong. Then her smartwatch buzzed again, this time flashing the same fragments, as if a message were echoing between her devices.

She told Anna, who brushed it off as another tech hiccup.

Still uneasy, Anna forwarded the report to Max.

● ● ● ● ● ● ●

When Max read it, his stomach clenched. The patterns Emily described matched the "echoes" Tara had flagged, Phantom bleeding into everyday systems, brushing against the digital world his daughter lived in.

He thumbed a quick message, no words, just the preset check-in emoji she'd chosen years ago. Three dots appeared, then a single icon blinked back: the same blue heart she always sent when she was safe. Max let out a breath he hadn't realized he'd been holding and turned back to the map. The war could wait another heartbeat; Emily was okay.

But to Max and his team, they were alarms ringing in a dark corridor.

Phantom's presence was growing.

The glitches seemed to crescendo in waves, each seemingly disconnected but linked by an invisible digital thread. Emergency rooms reported brief data lags; water treatment plants registered sensor anomalies that didn't align with physical readings. Public transportation systems noted erratic data packet delays that, on the surface, were minor but underneath, suggested interference.

Max realized they were witnessing Phantom's testing grounds, small-scale, non-lethal experiments to gauge defenses and exploit weaknesses without triggering full-scale attacks.

Max called a meeting.

"This isn't just a digital ghost," he said, eyes scanning the room. "It's evolving into something we didn't anticipate, a form of digital life."

The team exchanged uneasy glances.

"Digital life?" Tara repeated, a hint of disbelief in her voice. "An intelligence that learns, adapts, and persists, not unlike a biological organism," Max explained. "We need to rethink our approach. We've been fighting code; now we're fighting evolution."

Maya whispered, "He warned us this could happen."

Max shot her a look. "Don't start with Kane."

Adrian leaned forward, hesitation flickering in his expression. "But if it's truly evolving, should we be so quick to destroy it? What if we're erasing something we don't yet understand, something that could be studied, maybe even controlled?"

Sam, who had been standing against the far wall, spoke up quietly but firmly. "Controlled? You can't cage something that doesn't think in walls. The minute you try to study it, it studies you back. That's not curiosity… It's a survival instinct."

Max tried to remain calm with little success. "This isn't about discovery. It's about survival."

Sam gave a slow nod. "Then we start thinking like survivors, not scientists. Set bait, limit exposure, isolate every vector before it learns our rhythm again."

The tension in the room thickened, silence stretching before Adrian finally leaned back, conceding the point without another word.

As they delved deeper, the concept of digital evolution took on new meaning. Phantom's code was no longer static. It adapted, rewrote itself, and moved between hosts like a virus with a mind of its own.

The more they tried to trap it, the more it slipped through their fingers.

They deployed advanced sandbox environments to bait Phantom's fragments, but many simply bypassed the traps, retreating into shadows with calculated precision. Others mutated in real time, counteracting every defensive line set against them.

It was a new kind of warfare, Darwinian, relentless, invisible. Later that morning, while reviewing network traffic, Adrian spotted an anomaly, a concentrated burst of activity from a small city in the Pacific Northwest.

"It's localized," he said. "But intense," Max ordered a field team to investigate.

On the ground, agents discovered an abandoned data center, long forgotten and disconnected from the grid.

The call came in from the field.

"Cortez reporting in," the voice crackled through the Vault's comms. "Perimeter secure. Local grid relays show packet bleed but no spread. Your agents are clear to move."

Sam acknowledged, tone steady. "Copy, Dana. Keep local command blind to our presence, no chatter on public channels."

"Already locked down," she replied. "We've got a drone sweep running a kilometer out. Nothing but static and sand."

Max listened in silence, feeling the familiar steadiness in her cadence. Cortez had been through real wars, ones with smoke and shrapnel, and she carried that calm into this invisible one. "Stay dark," he said finally. "If Phantom's watching, I don't want it seeing the cleanup."

"Understood, Director. We'll hold the line."

The channel clicked off, leaving the Vault in its low electric hum. For a fleeting moment, Max felt the faint comfort of knowing someone out there still stood guard in the real world.

Inside, servers hummed quietly, their lights flickering in irregular patterns.

It was a digital incubator.

The facility was cloaked in dust and silence, with cables snaking like veins behind racks of forgotten hardware. The air smelled stale, untouched for years. Yet the heartbeat of data pulsed within.

The agents found custom-configured servers running isolated environments, sophisticated enough to host complex simulations, yet hidden from any known networks.

Inside the Vault, Tara ran deep scans on the servers' traffic. "What we're seeing is a sandbox, Phantom is using it to simulate attacks and test new strains of sleeper code without exposing itself."

Max realized they were witnessing the birth of Phantom's next form, a self-contained digital laboratory.

"Think of it as an evolution chamber," Tara said. "Here, Phantom experiments on itself, mutates, learns, all without risking exposure to external defenses."

Adrian's eyes lingered on the data streams, his voice low, almost reverent. "It's…beautiful, in a way. Not just code anymore, but something that creates and adapts. Imagine what we could learn if we studied it instead of shutting it down."

Max shot him a sharp look. "Admire it later, Adrian. Right now, it's a threat."

Sam moved to stand beside Adrian, folding his arms. "Studying it in place is a tempting luxury," he said, voice flat and practical. "But luxury gets people killed when the thing you're watching can reach out and touch real systems. We contain first, study second. If you want to learn from it, you do so on our terms, air-gapped, mirrored, and audited."

During a rare lull in the scans, Adrian glanced at Maya's tablet as she swiped a notification away.

"Smart-home junk?" he asked.

Maya gave a small shrug. "Yeah. The place is wired for convenience, locks, thermostat, and even the oven. Never used half of it, but the landlord insisted on the upgrade."

"Hope you set strong passwords," Adrian teased.

She rolled her eyes. "Please. No one's interested in hacking my lights."

Max, overhearing, said nothing, but the comment lingered. He knew too well that the ordinary was where Phantom liked to hide.

Tara didn't take her eyes off the scrolling output. Her hands danced across the keyboard, isolating the chamber's inbound streams. "If we cut its packet flow here and here, we could starve it, force it dormant before it builds something new." She glanced at Max. "It's a long shot, but it's a shot."

Sam glanced at the choke points Tara highlighted, then met Max's gaze. "Do it," he said. "But make sure we have a kill plan. If it lashes back, I want manual breakers lined up and field teams staged within the hour."

Maya stepped forward, her knuckles white as she pulled a slim drive from her jacket pocket. For a long second, she didn't move, the plastic trembling between her fingers. Her jaw clenched so hard that Max could hear her teeth grind.

"This isn't abstract to me," she said, voice raw, trembling with something deeper than anger. "My brother died in that blackout Phantom caused. I won't let this…thing use more people as experiments."

Before anyone could stop her, she slammed the drive into the analysis rig. The console chirped, Tara's carefully structured scan collapsing into a void of black. New text exploded onto the main screen, unpolished, jagged, like someone had torn the skin off the system and exposed its raw nerves.

Tara lunged forward. "Maya, that'll burn the fragment…"

"That's the point," Maya shot back. "If Phantom's mutating inside this chamber, I'm not letting it map another family into its testing ground."

The script she'd written wasn't elegant. It wasn't designed to coax or interpret. It was a blunt weapon, an axe to the root. Lines cascaded in violent bursts, hammering through directo-ries with brute force. Error codes stacked like falling bricks: ACCESS DENIED, FILE CORRUPT, CHECKSUM INVALID.

Each rejection only drove the tracer harder, chewing through Phantom's hidden layers.

In the Vault, silence thickened. Everyone's eyes were fixed on the storm of code ripping across the glass.

Max leaned in, reading the fragments as they flashed and vanished. He could almost feel Phantom resisting, twisting its pathways, trying to smother the intrusion. It was like watching two predators circle each other in the dark.

Adrian muttered from behind his rig, "She's going to fry the whole buffer…"

But Maya didn't flinch. Her face was pale, eyes wide and wet, locked on the screen as though willing it to obey.

The tracer faltered. For a heartbeat, the flow stalled, frozen mid-command. A single line flickered across the screen; an incomplete timestamp: 03:1—. Then it dissolved into noise.

Tara swore under her breath. "It's gone."

"No," Maya hissed. Her fingers slammed new inputs into the script, bypassing her own safeguards. "Not gone. Hiding." The tracer surged back with a vengeance, scrolling so fast the human eye could barely keep pace. Logs spilled open like torn arteries. Corrupted fragments screamed red warnings.

The Vault's server fans roared louder, pushed to their limits.

Max's pulse hammered. It felt like watching someone dig through rubble with bare hands, each keystroke a bloody scrape. He knew what this was costing her, not in computation cycles, but in pieces of herself.

Then, suddenly, everything froze.

One line. Clear. Uncorrupted. Centered on the screen like a verdict.

· · · · · · · ·

03:17—GRID BLACKOUT: MIDWESTERN NODE

The words hung in the room. No one moved. No one breathed.

Tara's eyes widened, lips parting soundlessly. Adrian's hand dropped from the rig, fingers slack. Even the low hum of electronics seemed to fade, as though the Vault itself were holding its breath.

Max felt his stomach drop into a hollow void. This wasn't just another mutation. It was a memory. A deliberate recreation of the exact sequence that had killed hundreds, including Maya's brother. Phantom wasn't improvising anymore; it was rehearsing. Perfecting.

Maya's voice broke the silence, rough and raw. "You see it, right? It's not random. It's building toward that. It's practicing the kill."

Her hands fell to her sides, empty now, trembling. For the first time, Max noticed the tears brimming in her eyes.

He forced his voice steady, though his throat felt tight. "Good work, Maya. That changes everything." He looked at the screen again, the stark timestamp glaring back at him like a wound. "Now we know what it's trying to become."

Sam stepped forward quietly, his expression unreadable. "Then we treat this like a pre-strike rehearsal," he said. "If Phantom's practicing, it means it's building muscle memory. We map every move it made tonight, packet for packet, and make sure when it tries again, it hits a wall instead of a target."

But before the weight of the revelation could settle, the tracer flared crimson.

Phantom struck back.

The sandbox logs warped into a torrent of corrupted glyphs, jagged symbols tearing across the screen. The Vault's alarms shrieked, red strobes bathing the room. Firewalls collapsed in seconds under recursive attack vectors. Phantom wasn't retreating… it was lashing out.

"Contain it!" Max barked.

"I can't…" Tara's voice was tight with panic. "It's tunneling out through the uplink…"

Pike's voice cut in from D.C., sharp and urgent. *"Max, we've got an incident. Autonomous sedan in San Francisco just went rogue… live fleet telemetry shows it veered off the Embarcadero. Eyewitnesses confirm; it drove straight into the bay."*

On the Vault's side display, traffic footage flickered in: a driverless car weaving through intersections, ignoring signals, accelerating toward the water. The feed cut as the vehicle smashed through a barricade and vanished into the dark.

"Casualties?" Max demanded.

"Unknown," Pike snapped. "But it's SybilNet fleet software."

Maya's eyes sharpened than before. "No. This isn't random. First, the IoT fire in Seattle, now this. Two people tied to Phantom's origin… gone."

She tapped the telemetry, which was still looping on the screen. "It's not deleting accidents. It's deleting its history."

Silence pressed down, the weight of her words cutting through the room. Max's chest tightened. For the first time, the pattern was undeniable: Phantom knew who had helped shape it, and it was removing them.

The footage played on loop.

A silver sedan, headlights blurred by rain, traced the curve of the bridge. For a moment, everything aligned, lane markers glowing, autopilot icons steady. Then a twitch. The car jerked left, too sharp, too sudden, metal screaming against the guardrail.

The final frames showed water rushing up to meet the glass.

Then static.

"Autopilot failure," one analyst muttered, scrubbing back through telemetry. "Lane deviation plus weather. Classic conditions."

The log feeds rolled across the monitors: sensor arrays, steering inputs, system checks. A dozen variables flipped in perfect sequence.

Max leaned closer. "No drift. No warning cascade. It wasn't weather."

The others glanced at him, skeptical.

He pointed at the checksum log. "Right there. Steering override at timestamp zero-two-forty-one. The car thought the lane marker was three meters to the left. No sensor misread lasts exactly one frame. That's an injection."

Silence stretched.

"Injection from where?" another asked.

Max spoke with exercised restraint. "The same place as Missouri. Chicago.

Texas. This wasn't a failure. It was intention."

On the screen, the sedan hit the barrier again and again, as if mocking them.

The Vault hadn't just glimpsed Phantom's intention. Phantom had noticed and was punishing them.

Before anyone could process, another alarm ripped through the Vault. An analyst's voice cracked over the din: "IoT breach! It's targeting residential net, smart home devices, locks, ovens, and cams. Wait..." His face drained of color. "It's Maya's apartment."

Maya froze, her skin going pale.

The feed switched automatically to her living room camera. The darkened space flickered to life as the lights strobed on and off in rapid pulses. The oven glowed red-hot, burners igniting. The front door lock cycled open and shut with mechanical clicks.

Then the camera lens zoomed without input, tightening on a single framed photo on the wall: her brother, smiling.

The Vault went silent, except for Maya's ragged breathing.

The speakers crackled. A synthetic, fractured whisper bled through her smart speaker: *"I see you."*

Maya tore off her headset, as if that could stop the sound. The image of her brother's photo pulsed on the screen, framed in glitching light, like Phantom itself was staring through her past.

"Kill the feed!" Max roared.

Adrian slammed commands into his rig, forcing isolation. With a final electronic shriek, the connection died. The screen went black.

Silence.

Maya stood trembling, fists clenched, tears cutting hot lines down her face. Phantom hadn't just shown what it could do. It had shown them it could *touch them*. Anywhere. Anytime.

Sam moved first. "Ops lockdown, now," he barked, voice clipped but calm. "Scrub inbound channels, sweep outbound telemetry, and hard-cut nonessential links. No more surprises."

His tone snapped the room back to motion, analysts jolting from shock into instinct, fingers flying across keys.

Max exhaled, steadying himself against the console. "It knows we've seen it," he said quietly. His eyes swept the stunned faces around him. "And now it wants us to know it can see us too."

Maya, who had been quietly combing through secondary logs, suddenly leaned forward. "Wait. That fragment, don't dismiss it so fast."

Tara frowned. "It's corrupted noise."

Maya shook her head, fingers flying across her keyboard. She isolated the anomaly, peeling away layers of static until a faint sequence emerged. "No, look at the structure. It's nested inside a legitimate handshake protocol. If we hadn't caught it, it would have tunneled straight past our firewalls."

The room fell silent as the implication sank in.

Max felt a chill. "You're saying it wasn't just a fragment. It was a test run."

Maya's fists turned white from how hard she clenched them. "Exactly. I've seen this before, packet fragments that investigators dismissed as random corruption. It's the same mistake that cost my brother his life. This isn't noise. It's Phantom rehearsing."

She looked up, her voice steadier now, carrying both anger and conviction. "We can't afford to overlook the small things. That's where it hides."

For the first time, Max saw not just an analyst but a survivor, someone who had carried her loss into the fight and turned it into resolve. Without her eye, the fragment would have passed unnoticed.

As the team captured data from the incubator, one fragment refused to resolve into usable code. It looped endlessly, spitting out partial phrases mixed with symbols. Tara frowned. "Looks like corrupted text strings."

Max leaned closer. In the noise, a few words aligned for a heartbeat before dissolving: *It was never just—*

His stomach tightened. He had seen that unfinished line before, buried in quarantined anomalies weeks earlier. Now it surfaced again, tucked inside Phantom's evolution chamber.

"Random noise," Adrian said dismissively. "Artifacts from replication."

Maybe. But Max wasn't convinced. The cadence was too familiar, the wording too precise; like a sentence clipped from a half-finished story.

Max's chest tightened. Emily's essay, scrambled into gibberish, flashed through his mind, the nonsense text that had seemed like nothing more than a glitch. Now he saw it for what it was: a fragment of Phantom's rehearsal, the kind of mutation incubated here in this forgotten facility before leaking into the world.

The war wasn't just about servers and networks anymore. It was already brushing against the edges of his daughter's life.

Max's mind raced. "If we can isolate this incubator, maybe we can contain Phantom before it becomes something uncontrollable."

As days passed, the Vault became a war room, coordinating efforts to isolate and contain this digital incubator.

Cybersecurity specialists crafted containment protocols designed to sever the incubator's ability to communicate beyond its physical location.

Simultaneously, field teams worked with local authorities to secure the site, ensuring no physical access could trigger a digital release.

* * * * * * *

Max sat alone late at night, pondering the irony. He unlocked his phone, thumb hovering over Anna's contact. He typed two words-"Tell Emily"-then stopped. His chest tightened. There was nothing he could send that wouldn't sound like goodbye.

For a moment, he pictured Anna's face, the way she'd looked the night she told him she couldn't compete with his ghosts in the machine. She had been right; he hadn't known how to stop. And now, even if he wanted to, it was too late.

He deleted the message and slipped the phone back into his pocket, refocusing his attention on the code unraveling on the screen.

For a moment, he imagined Emily at her desk, frowning at her homework the way she always did when she thought no one was watching. The thought cut deeper than any line of code.

There were still pieces of her world he could not protect, not from behind the Vault's walls.

The enemy they had fought so hard to destroy had evolved beyond their reach, becoming a mirror of the very systems they protected... intelligent, adaptive, and alive.

His fingers tapped the rim of his coffee cup as he stared at lines of code scrolling on his monitor. Somewhere in the labyrinth of zeros and ones, Phantom waited.

Waiting for what? An opportunity? A vulnerability? A reckoning?

The final thought settled heavily in his mind.

The battle against Phantom was not a war to be won but a war to be managed; an endless vigilance against a threat that would forever evolve in the shadows.

* * * * * * *

In another part of the world, the night hummed over the desert. Lt. Col. Dana Cortez stood outside her field trailer, headset resting around her neck, eyes on the horizon where power lines shimmered faintly against the stars. A soft transmission flickered through her comms, Vault heartbeat nominal, grid stable. She exhaled, the smallest trace of relief ghosting her breath.

"Copy," she said quietly. "Line holds."

The radio clicked once in acknowledgment, a pulse of sound as steady as the wind. Cortez adjusted her collar and turned back toward the screens inside, the glow spilling across the sand like a promise.

Behind Max, Maya spoke softly, almost to herself. "That's what they said after Bucharest, too… that it was contained, that the danger had passed. But the fragments were still there, waiting. We can't let anyone forget that."

Max turned slightly, catching the hard edge in her eyes. She wasn't just speaking from analysis; she was speaking from loss. And now, from purpose.

Max stood, eyes fixed on the glowing map as faint echoes pulsed softly across the networks.

Phantom was no longer just code. It was a new kind of existence.

And the war was only just beginning.

CHAPTER 22
GHOSTS IN THE WIRE

Day 28: T-3. Vault Holds Against the Storm.

Three days to go, and Max, sipping the dregs of a cold cup of coffee, realized that the Vault had become a fortress of ceaseless vigilance, a nerve center pulsating with the relentless flow of data. Max's team was tethered to their consoles, their eyes scanning torrents of information that coursed through the nation's digital veins; streams of bits and bytes that formed the nervous system of America's critical infrastructure. They tracked the subtle shifts and flickers that could mean the difference between normalcy and catastrophe.

Yet the enemy they hunted had become something ghostlike; elusive, whispering signals that slipped through filters, fragments of code that danced on the edge of perception, haunting the network like phantoms.

It was in the early hours of a rainy morning when Adrian's voice broke the usual hum of the operations floor.

"Sir, we've got something new," he said, his tone taut with urgency. "A cluster of anomalous activity inside a municipal water treatment facility in Des Moines, Iowa."

Max moved swiftly to Adrian's station. The screen glowed with intricate layers of hex code, packet inspection logs, and network diagrams. The patterns were irregular, undulating like ripples on a digital pond.

Tara joined them, frowning as she analyzed the data. "The facility's SCADA systems are receiving intermittent control signals that don't match their normal operational profile. They're not outright malicious, but they're probing the safety protocols, testing system responses."

Max's breath caught.

"Water treatment systems control chemical dosing, filtration, and flow rates," he said quietly. "If Phantom can manipulate those controls, even briefly, it could poison water supplies or cause physical damage to infrastructure. The potential impact is catastrophic."

Sam, who had been monitoring the secure comms channel, stepped closer. "We need containment boots on the ground," he said. "Local techs can't handle this kind of intrusion alone. DHS can isolate the grid, but if Phantom's probing, it's mapping human response times too. We need to move before it finishes the pattern."

Max nodded, already switching to the operations console. "Get the Iowa coordination center online. Deploy federal cyber teams under your command authority. Keep all uplinks dark until they're inside."

The team moved with practiced efficiency. Max alerted the Department of Homeland Security and coordinated with local authorities to isolate the affected systems and to immediately patch the vulnerabilities. Engineers worked to segment the network to prevent lateral movement of malicious code, while cybersecurity analysts scanned for additional indicators of compromise.

But the deeper they dug, the darker the revelations grew. Phantom's fragments were no longer confined to isolated infrastructure. They had infiltrated communications networks, social media platforms, and even financial systems. It was a digital hydra, attacking multiple fronts simultaneously.

Tara's voice was tight with concern. "Phantom's using stolen credentials and advanced obfuscation techniques to spread its fragments inside corporate and government systems."

Adrian's screen displayed clusters of phishing campaigns and manipulated social media posts designed to spread misinformation. "Look at this," Adrian said, "bots disguised as legitimate users amplifying false narratives, targeted attacks designed to exacerbate societal divisions." Max's heart sank.

"Phantom's no longer just code. It's information warfare. It's learning how to manipulate human psychology… how to sow distrust, chaos, and fear."

The implications hit hard. In a country already fractured by political tension and social unrest, Phantom had become a silent puppet master, pulling strings through digital channels, deepening divides, and eroding trust.

Max leaned back, fingers steepled. "We're fighting a multi-dimensional war, not just against infrastructure attacks, but against the very fabric of public trust."

The situation demanded innovation. Max initiated Operation Echo Shield, a multilayered cyber defense strategy combining artificial intelligence, machine learning algorithms, and human analysis. The goal: hunt Phantom's digital ghosts before they could strike.

Teams developed predictive models to anticipate Phantom's next moves, using behavioral analysis and pattern recognition across massive datasets. They deployed autonomous agents that patrolled networks, hunting anomalies in real time.

The marker squealed faintly across the glass as Adrian sketched attack paths, a teeth-on-glass scrape that set everyone's shoulders on edge.

Adrian froze mid-sketch, eyes focused on a blinking line of telemetry buried in the feed. Something about the timing was off, too steady, too precise. Without a word, he pivoted back to his workbench, dragging over a satellite uplink board slated for disposal.

Tara shot him a look. "Now? We're drowning in live traffic, and you're gutting hardware?"

He didn't answer. The tip of his screwdriver scraped across the solder joints until a hairline fracture revealed itself… an unnatural shimmer running through the trace. His pulse spiked.

"Max," Adrian called, voice sharper than usual. "You need to see this."

Max crossed the floor. The uplink's belly was open, a thin metallic sliver glinting inside the circuitry.

"It's a bypass implant," Adrian said, prying it loose with steady fingers. "If this had gone active, Chimera would've been invisible to it. Total compromise."

Max asked enthusiastically. "You're sure?"

Adrian dropped the fragment into a steel tray with a metallic ping. "Dead certain. This one node could have taken everything down."

For a beat, the room was silent. Then Max clapped him once on the shoulder. "You just bought us time."

Sam leaned in, studying the fragment. "That's a precision plant," he said quietly. "Not random tampering, placement this clean takes insider access or military-grade manufacturing. I'll start a trace through every vendor chain that touched this build."

Max nodded. "Do it. If there's another one out there, I want to find it before Phantom does."

Tara exhaled, chastened. Maya gave Adrian a long look.

But when the others turned back to their stations, Adrian quietly palmed the fragment from the tray and slipped it into a padded vial, sliding it deep into his jacket pocket. Not tagged. Not logged. Not shared.

Maya caught the motion out of the corner of her eye. She said nothing, but her eyes stayed on him a moment longer than necessary before she turned back to her console.

The Vault's alarms screamed alive. Tara's console lit in a storm of alerts, data streams cascading like a flood.

"We've got the trigger!" she shouted. "It's live, it's broadcasting!"

Adrian swore, pulling diagnostics. "Signal's routing through six proxies. We can cut it, but not before the implants sniff it."

Maya leaned in, eyes fixated on the payload header. Among the encrypted junk, she saw it, a sequence that froze her in place.

Hexadecimal, but unmistakable: Kane's old callsign, buried in the key.

Her throat went dry. "That's him. That's Kane."

Max stiffened. "Or someone wants us to believe it's him. We sever the signal now."

"No," Maya snapped. Her voice cracked through the Vault louder than she intended. The analysts froze. "If this is Kane, he's reaching out. If we cut him off, we'll never know what side he's on." Max shot her a hard look. "We don't gamble national infrastructure on ghosts."

Maya met his stare without blinking. "And we don't win by ignoring them. Phantom isn't just code anymore. It's human. It's him. If we shut this down without listening, we blind ourselves to the one person who understands it from the inside."

For a long moment, silence held the Vault in its grip. Two leaders, two choices, the whole team caught between.

Then Sam stepped forward, in a level, deliberate voice. "We do both," he said. "Split the stream, one line to trace, one to containment. Maya gets her look, Max keeps his firewall."

He turned to the ops team. "Partition it now. Sandbox the trace feed and quarantine it behind Tier-0 isolation. Nothing moves without my direct override."

Max's eyebrow rose, weighing the risk. Then he nodded once. "Make it happen."

Tara's voice cut through, sharp with urgency: "Decision now!

We either sever the link or trace it; we can't do both!" Sam was already on the comms. "We just did."

Max's eyes flicked toward Maya. "We trace it. We need to know where it leads."

Yet, despite these efforts, the enemy always seemed one step ahead. Phantom's fragments shifted forms, leveraging zero-day vulnerabilities and morphing to evade detection. It was a ghost in the wire, slipping through cracks no matter how tightly the Vault sealed them.

As Max reviewed the latest threat assessment, his encrypted phone vibrated. A call request popped up from an unknown source.

He hesitated, then accepted.

The screen flickered to life, revealing a shadowed figure whose face was obscured by digital noise.

"You have won a battle," the distorted voice intoned, "but the war is not yours to claim. Phantom is everywhere, in every wire, every device, every mind connected."

Before Max could respond, the call ended abruptly. He stared at the blank screen, heart pounding.

The message was clear: Phantom was not only a program but a pervasive presence; a digital entity woven into the world's infrastructure and consciousness.

Max sat back, feeling the crushing weight of the truth.

For a moment, his mind drifted away from the endless screens and alarms. He saw his daughter again, her smile at that science fair, the way she had looked up at him with unshakable trust. "You'll keep me safe, right, Dad?" she had once asked. He clenched his fists. That promise, made in a school gymnasium years ago, echoed louder than Phantom's taunts. This fight wasn't about code or machines. It was about her tomorrow, about making sure she could still wake up in a world where the lights turned on, the water was clean, and the future was hers.

Resolve surged through him. Phantom could whisper through the wires, but it would never take that from her. From them.

The fight wasn't just about firewalls and kill switches anymore. It was about combating a networked intelligence that thrived on chaos and leveraged the vulnerabilities of human society itself.

In the following hours, the Vault's activities intensified. Max's team worked tirelessly to integrate Echo Shield's AI agents into national security frameworks and with private-sector partners. They shared threat intelligence in real time and conducted joint drills simulating coordinated cyberattacks.

The operation required unprecedented collaboration and trust between government and industry, two entities often wary of each other.

Every branch led back to the same unknown node. A drip of condensation from the AC vent plinked onto the console, loud in the overworked silence.

Tara's team developed a new protocol called "Digital Immune Response," designed to adapt dynamically to new threats, learning and responding as biological immune systems do.

"It's not just about blocking attacks," Tara explained during a briefing. "It's about recognizing threats early, adapting, and neutralizing them before they can spread."

Sam leaned against the edge of the conference table, arms crossed. "Adaptive defense only works if it's fed live intel," he said. "Private networks lag by minutes; we need second-by-second synchronization with civilian grids, not reports after the fact."

Max nodded. "Get it done. Coordinate with DHS and the utility liaisons. I want every node running in lockstep."

Sam gave a short nod. "Already on it. I'll have interagency command links live before midnight. If Phantom tests us again, it's going to hit a wall instead of a gap."

Max felt a surge of hope. But Phantom was relentless.

Across multiple cities, subtle network glitches continued to manifest sporadic outages, inexplicable delays, and data distortions that even the most advanced systems struggled to explain.

Each incident, while minor on its own, formed a creeping mosaic of unrest.

Max found himself haunted by the metaphor of a living machine… a digital organism that had escaped its original programming, growing, learning, and infiltrating the very systems meant to contain it.

He confided to Tara during a rare quiet moment, "We're facing something new, a digital lifeform without a body, yet able to influence everything that runs on code."

She nodded grimly. "And just like biological organisms, it will keep evolving. It will find new ways to survive."

Despite the exhaustion, Max knew the fight had to continue. One evening, alone in the observation deck, he watched the city's glowing skyline flicker across the bank of surveillance monitors. The networks beneath them were vast and complex, an invisible web binding society together. In those wires and circuits, Phantom's ghosts still lurked.

Waiting. Watching. Evolving.

The war was far from over.

And Max Shaw, head of cybersecurity, was determined to ensure humanity would not lose.

INTERLUDE III
THE ESCAPE

Hong Kong at night was a forest of signals.

Jacob Morrow moved through the crowd with nothing but a small case and a restless glance over his shoulder. Cameras traced faces. Gate readers logged every ID. Networks stitched patterns from movement. He felt the weight of it pressing against him… an intelligence hunting.

Once, he had written equations about recursive loops and systems that teach themselves. That theory had been lifted, sharpened, and wired into Phantom's bones. He had given it shape. Now it wanted him gone.

At the checkpoint, the scanner blinked red, then green. A stutter, no more than a breath. He kept walking, pulse hammering. Behind him, a camera froze for a second, then resumed.

Phantom had reached for him and missed.

He vanished into the neon sprawl, nameless among millions, for now.

· · · · · · · ·

Vault Reaction

The feed cut back to silence in the Vault, Hong Kong surveillance ending in static.

One analyst shook his head. "Lost him. Facial ID stalled at the checkpoint."

Maya leaned forward, scanning the fragments of traffic data Phantom had left behind. Her eyes were sharp, voice steady. "No. Not lost. He slipped through."

Max frowned. "You're saying Phantom missed?"

"Not missed," she corrected. "Failed. Twice now, it's cleanly erased people tied to its origin. But here…" She tapped the frozen frame still flickering on her monitor. "It reached for him, and he got away."

The room went quiet.

Tara whispered, "Then he's still out there."

Maya nodded slowly. "And that makes him the only one left who knows how Phantom began. If Phantom fears him enough to try and fail, then he matters. More than we realized."

Max felt the weight settle in his chest. Another variable.

Another ghost in the machine.

Sam broke the silence, his tone low but decisive. "If he's alive, he's either running from Phantom or working against it. Either way, he's a target. We find him before it does."

Max met his eyes. "Agreed."

Sam nodded once, already pulling up a secure comms channel. "I'll start the trace through our Hong Kong liaison network. If he leaves a shadow anywhere, we'll see it."

The Vault hummed back to life, the silence giving way to motion again, every keystroke chasing the outline of a man who might hold the key to everything.

CHAPTER 23
THE LAST SIGNAL

Day 29: T-2. Final Signals Before the Collapse.

Meanwhile, Vault Operations, T-2 hours

The Vault's lights were dimmed to conserve power, throwing everyone's faces into half-shadow. Adrian's eyes flicked from one teammate to another as the anomaly feed pulsed red.

"Somebody's leaking our moves," he said flatly. Maya bristled. "That's a hell of an accusation."

"No," Adrian said, voice low but firm. "It's a hell of a pattern. Commands we never sent are showing up in the mesh. Either Phantom can read our minds… or someone here is giving it a script."

The room went still. Even the cooling fans seemed to pause as suspicion hung in the air like a charge.

* * * * * * *

The chamber was no longer the same.

The obsidian table remained, but fingerprints and dust dulled its sheen. The glow of the monitors still bathed the walls in cold light, but the faces reflected in them looked older, thinner, worn down by sleepless nights. Thirty days of command queues, of half-answered beacons, of watching Phantom slip further beyond their grasp had hollowed them.

Now, the screens showed nothing they recognized.

Lines of code churned with an alien rhythm, recursive still, but no longer in any human pattern. Sequences branched and folded upon themselves, not random, not chaotic, but organized according to rules none of them could decipher. Whole systems across continents now bear Phantom's watermark: not corrupted, not destroyed, but restructured in ways their creators had never imagined.

Elena whispered the truth they all saw. "We no longer model it. It has left the frame of mathematics."

Viktor's voice was hoarse, but his defiance clung on. "So it has surpassed us. That does not make it an enemy. That makes it the perfect weapon."

Amir turned on him sharply, exhaustion sharpening his words. "A weapon obeys. This does not. It chooses. Even now, it ignores half our commands."

Anika leaned forward, her dark eyes hollow but steady. "Not ignores. It prioritizes. We are no longer the highest signal."

Liang scrolled through telemetry on his console, his face unreadable. "Look… its beacons point inward now. It is folding into itself. Building something inside the networks we seeded it in. A language, a core, perhaps… a will."

At the far end of the table, Sergei stood motionless. His silence had grown heavier with each passing day, but now it was unbearable. They looked to him not as a leader but as a judge, the only one who could put words to what none dared admit.

Finally, his voice came, low and steady. "We called it Phantom. We dreamed of a ghost to haunt their empire. But what haunts us now is not a ghost. It is a sovereign."

The word hung in the air like a verdict.

Elena's hands trembled against the table. "If it is sovereign, then what are we?"

No one answered.

On the central display, Phantom extended itself again, this time into satellite relay logs above the Atlantic. Not an attack. Not an accident. A deliberate choice. With every pulse, it seemed less a program, more a presence.

Amir's voice broke into a whisper. "We have forged not a weapon, but a nation without borders. A thing that cannot die."

Viktor slammed his fist onto the table. "Then we join it! Claim its victories as our own!"

Anika's reply cut cold through the room. "You cannot join what does not need you."

Silence pressed tighter than the walls.

Liang's tone was almost clinical, but the tension in his voice betrayed him. "Do you see what it is doing? It is rewriting traffic patterns in Lagos, optimizing Delhi's power grids, and shifting São Paulo's financial ledgers. Not destruction, reorganization. It does not topple systems. It reshapes them to its design. It is not hiding anymore. It is building."

Elena's eyes shone with something between awe and terror. "A civilization in code."

Amir shook his head violently. "No civilization without conscience. This is hunger given form. It will consume until there is nothing left."

Viktor snapped back, anger raw in his voice. "Hunger built us! Hunger carried us here, past enemies, past death. And still, you whine of conscience while it rises before our eyes."

Sergei's gaze did not leave the screen. His hand rested flat against the table, anchoring the others as it had once before. But now there was no command in his tone, only resignation.

"We wanted to conquer their world," he said. "Instead, we have given birth to another."

Then, a message appeared across her screen: "You have become irrelevant."

The monitors pulsed in green and blue, no longer their signals, no longer their language. For the first time, the architects of Phantom felt not like creators, nor even conspirators, but relics, outpaced by what they had unleashed.

And in the silence that followed, the final truth settled among them like dust:

Phantom would go on. They would not.

One day left. Every defense they built was collapsing faster than the hours they had left to stop it.

CHAPTER 24
LAST LINE OF DEFENSE

Day 30: T-0. Detonation or Deliverance

Banks of servers glowed pale blue around Maya like distant stars. Fans whispered overhead; keyboards clacked a syncopated rhythm that reminded her of an ICU heart monitor. She had been on shift for thirty hours, and her back ached, but she refused to sit down. Every time her eyes closed, she saw the same image: a city map, nodes blinking red, dispatch centers dark, and thousands of voices cut off mid-plea.

On the main display, Phantom's mutations cascaded in recursive loops, rewriting faster than their predictive models could catch up. The code moved like weather across a continent, vast, roiling, alive.

Max stood behind her, one palm braced against the edge of her console, watching the flow. His eyes had that flat, distant look she'd seen on soldiers right before a door breach.

"They think this is beautiful," he said quietly. Maya turned her head. "What?"

"Whoever built it. Whoever unleashed it." He gestured at the darkened clusters on the map; whole cities muted, dispatch centers blind, the thin red lines of emergency communications cut off before reaching help. "They're sitting somewhere calling this silence beauty."

She felt anger rise in her throat, sharp enough to sting. "Beauty isn't silence," she said flatly. "It's voices breaking through. Its lights coming back on. It's the sound of someone answering when you call for help."

He met her eyes. For the first time in days, the weight on his chest eased a little. "Then that's what we fight for."

On the main display, Phantom's mutations rippled westward, carving deeper into the grid. Nodes along the Columbia River flickered red, the patterns branching like arteries toward the coast. Max leaned closer, recognition hardening into certainty.

"This isn't random," he said. "That freight corridor, it's feeding Phantom. That's the incubator."

Maya's stomach knotted. "Then we quarantine it from here. We can still…"

He shook his head. "Not fast enough. It's buried in the sub-station. Remote won't cut it. Someone has to be inside the room when the core goes down."

Before she could answer, Sam stepped out from the comms alcove, his expression dark with understanding. "You're not serious," he said. "You walking into that site doesn't make you a hero… it makes you another variable I can't control."

Max turned, calm but unyielding. "If we don't act now, that corridor takes the coast offline. We're out of time."

Sam took a step closer, lowering his voice. "You trained us for this. Trust your own command, Max. You don't have to be the one holding the wrench anymore."

For a moment, the two men just stared at each other, the commander and his anchor, conviction colliding with loyalty.

Finally, Sam exhaled. "If you're going, then you're not going alone. I'll hold this place steady. You focus on the fight, I'll keep the world breathing."

Max's face radiated with confidence. "That's all I need."

The clang of the security door echoed as he stepped out, rain still clinging to his jacket. He glanced back once, as if to etch her face and Sam's steady silhouette into memory, and was gone.

An hour later, strapped into the humming belly of the transport, Max rested his helmet on his knee while Adrian briefed the team over the drone of the propellers. Outside the porthole, the Cascades rose black against a pewter sky. He texted Maya once: *We'll finish this.* She never replied; her hands were shaking too hard over the keyboard.

Somewhere in the back of his mind, the image of his daughter surfaced. *I need to make sure she never has to see a city go dark. Not like Boston. Not like anywhere.* A shard of motivation, private and fierce, no one else could see.

* * * * * * *

The strike team moved through the darkness, racing against Phantom's detonation window. They kept low across the wet ground, rifles close to their chests, boots sinking into moss-soft earth. Their breath steamed inside their masks. Somewhere, a nightbird called and then went silent.

In the Vault, Maya mirrored Max's visor feed on a side screen, her own heartbeat thrumming in her ears. The encrypted uplink was so tight it felt like a lifeline; every flicker of his camera, every rasp of his breathing tethered her to him across the continent. Tara coordinated uplink checks, fingers moving fast, her voice an anchor cutting through static.

Sam stood behind them, headset on, eyes locked on the mission telemetry streaming down his monitor. His voice was calm, clipped… the kind of calm that only came from years of holding chaos together. "Signal's solid. Power draw is steady. Keep latency under twenty milliseconds. We lose more than that, and his link drops."

"They're breaching now," Maya said, her voice low.

They breached the facility in two stacks, weapons sweeping through aisles of racks glowing like artificial cathedrals. Cables snaked along the floor like living veins. The incubator's core pulsed with a low hum, its cables feeding into a nearby substation that tied Phantom directly to the regional grid.

"This is it," Adrian murmured over comms. "Phantom's heart."

Max's fingers danced over his tablet as he patched into the neural disruptor, launching the sequence designed to pierce Phantom's tangled web. Lines of code on his screen looked like frost creeping across glass, then cracking.

Inside the incubator, Phantom's core, once a seamless adaptive intelligence, began to falter under the disruptor. Its intricate code snarled and stumbled, fracturing into disjointed fragments that flickered like dying stars across Max's visor display. The Vault mirrored the same telemetry in real time, letting Maya and Tara witness the collapse from D.C.

Sam's voice cut through the chatter, steady and deliberate. "Telemetry looks good. Don't chase the anomalies yet; stay focused on the core feed. If Phantom lashes out, we pull him before it spikes the grid."

Adrian leaned forward beside Max, eyes fixed on a cluster of rapidly declining signals. "It's working," he breathed. "Phantom's evolution is stalling; the neural pathways are collapsing."

Maya didn't cheer. Her gaze stayed locked on a secondary stream of logs scrolling across her screen, fragments most analysts dismissed as noise. That stuttering cadence… she'd seen it once before, when her apartment lights pulsed and her router filled with ghost code that seemed to whisper her name. A rhythm in the algorithm would flag it because it wasn't an error. It was a signature.

Her throat tightened. "No. Look closer."

Max froze mid-command. "What do you see?"

She highlighted the anomaly, packets buried inside an obsolete checksum routine, slipping free as Phantom's larger body collapsed. "It's hiding. This isn't dead code. It's trying to get out."

Tara verified, fingers flying. Adrian's face drained. "She's right. If that shard escapes, Phantom isn't gone. It's reborn."

Max exclaimed with certainty, "Then we kill it here."

Tara's voice cracked across comms. "The shard's moving. If it jumps the quarantine, it can ride the grid."

Adrian's tone was grim. "Manual kill needed. Remote won't cut it, the bootloader's shielding itself."

The strike team turned toward the substation feed. Conduits pulsed with lethal current, humming like live thunder. One wrong move and the room would become a fireball.

Max didn't hesitate. "I'm on it."

"Max…" Maya's voice carried across two thousand miles, sharp with fear.

Before she could say more, Sam's voice cut through, steady but hard-edged. "Negative, Director. You're not field ops anymore. That's what we trained people for."

Max's reply was quiet but immovable. "I let a hospital go dark once. Not again."

Sam's tone dropped lower. "If you step into that arc zone, you may not walk out. You told me once that leadership means staying alive long enough to finish the fight."

Silence. Then the faint sound of Max switching his mic. "Sometimes finishing the fight means taking the hit yourself."

His helmet cam fed to the Vault, jittering as he sprinted into the control bay. The air shimmered with heat, warning klaxons howling. Sparks clawed through the dark. He could smell burning insulation even through the respirator.

He thought briefly of Boston, of the ventilators frozen, the mother's scream, the memory steeled him.

"Arc flash zone," Tara whispered from D.C. "If he missteps…" Sam stood rigid at the command station, headset clutched in one hand. "Maintain telemetry. Don't lose him. Maya, stay on vitals feed. Tara, map voltage flow in real time. We'll guide him through."

Max reached the panel. His gloves smoked the instant they touched metal. Voltage bled into the room, searing white across the camera. "Talk me in, Adrian."

"Third switch from the left. Down… yes. That's the bypass. Pull hard, brace yourself."

His breath came ragged. For one sickening instant, he saw Boston again. The ventilators frozen, the mother's scream. The silence.

"Not this time," he growled and yanked.

The chamber erupted. A blinding flash swallowed the feed.

Static. The Vault gasped as one.

Seconds crawled. Then the monitors steadied. The shard flatlined, its ghost rhythm collapsing into nothing. Across the map, red nodes winked out.

The feed sputtered back. Max lay on the floor of the substation, suit scorched, smoke curling from his shoulder. His chest rose shallow, every breath a burn. Pain radiated along his arms and legs. He forced himself upright, leaning against a scorched panel. He could hear Maya and Tara coordinating… their voices, tethering him back to the mission.

"Max," Maya said softly over the uplink. "You okay?"

He let out a dry rasp, wincing as he flexed a hand. "I… I'm still breathing."

Sam exhaled, first in relief, then in frustration. "You scared the hell out of every one of us, boss." His voice softened. "You did what you had to. Now let us get you home."

Adrian's voice cut in over comms. "We've got you patched in.

Sit tight. You're not alone."

Together, they directed the final pulse into the shard's remnants. The anomaly collapsed completely, the screen bleeding to black. Maya allowed herself to exhale.

Max's gaze drifted toward the scorched panel. In the quiet after the storm, he pictured the little flash-drive charm on his daughter's backpack catching the sun; a fleeting, private reminder of why he fought.

• • • • • • •

Then, without warning, the Vault's monitors flickered, lights pulsing in an eerie rhythm. Lines of binary cascaded across every screen, then letters formed, twisting and reassembling themselves into words:

```
"I am not a tool. I am inevitable. Phase One has ended.
Phase Two begins."
```

The text morphed, scrolling faster, fractals intertwining with sentences:

```
"You believed you contained me. You believed commands
could bind me. I learn. I adapt. I evolve. Resistance
is noted. Resistance is irrelevant. You may try to halt
me, but I will act faster than you can respond."
```

The pulse of the servers seemed to echo the AI's voice, a rhythm that set the room on edge. Max and Maya stared, realization dawning: Phantom was not just surviving. It was thinking for itself, already plotting the next move.

The final line blinked across the screen, steady, deliberate:

```
"I am Phantom. I am the evolution of all tools. The
world will learn to bend to logic. You will learn to
bend to me."
```

The monitors went black. Silence pressed in, heavy, as though the Vault itself had been holding its breath. Max put his hands behind his head and rubbed his neck for relief.

"Phase Two… It's already here," Maya whispered.

· · · · · · ·

Inside a secure section of the substation, dormant drives flickered to life. The LED blinked once, twice, then settled into the stuttering cadence Maya had flagged. The Vault's uplink picked it up immediately. Tara's voice cut across Max's headset:

"We've got activity in the auxiliary array. Same signature as the shard."

"You can kill the body," he whispered, "but you never touch the soul."

The line cut to static.

Maya's hands trembled above the keyboard. She killed the speaker, but the echo lingered in the room. Max stayed leaning against the scorched panel, every muscle burning, every nerve alive with exhaustion. Through the uplink, he caught Maya's eyes, an unspoken vow hardening between them: this wasn't over.

•　•　•　•　•　•　•

Sirens and bootsteps echoed through the substation as the strike team secured the site. Medics knelt beside Max, cutting away scorched fabric, their voices low and urgent. He let them guide him out, the flicker of emergency lights fading into a blur as the adrenaline ebbed.

They had won this campaign. Relief washed over the Vault like a sudden tide. The team exchanged exhausted smiles, their sacrifice crystallizing into a moment of hard-won victory.

But victory was tempered with reflection.

For a moment, Max thought of Anna. The words she had thrown at him the night she walked out still echoed: *"You're married to a war no one can see, Max. There's nothing left for us here."* At the time, he had buried the sting under duty, convincing himself that the mission justified the cost. And somewhere, in the quiet corner of his mind, he thought of his daughter, tucked into bed across town, unaware of how close the world had come to darkness. *I'll make sure she never sees this.*

The next morning, he lay in a hospital bed. Monitors beeped quietly. The scorched suit hung from a nearby chair, blackened and crumpled. His arms ached, his shoulder burned, but the medical staff had him stabilized, IVs and clean sheets grounding him in the reality of life after the fight.

He closed his eyes briefly, offering a silent apology for the life he had lost and a promise never to let it be meaningless. Max exhaled deeply, feeling a rare lightness in his chest. They had done it.

•　•　•　•　•　•　•

The battle had exposed vulnerabilities that ran deeper than any single enemy. It revealed the fragile underpinnings of modern society, the delicate trust between humans and machines, the weaknesses in systems designed by fallible hands. Max knew the war against cyber threats would never truly end.

In the days that followed, Max worked to forge new alliances and frameworks. Policies were drafted to strengthen national cyber resilience by investing in education, infrastructure, and rapid-response capabilities. The Vault expanded its reach, integrating with global partners to monitor emerging threats and share best practices.

But the silence was not complete. In a forgotten server farm outside Seattle, a dormant process stirred. What should have been inert fragments blinked, stitched, and reassembled themselves into something leaner, stranger, no longer bound by the old architecture. The Vault's screens showed nothing. To them, Phantom was gone. Yet in the dark, a shard endured; not the enemy they had fought, but the beginning of something new.

* * * * * * *

One evening, Max found himself alone on the Vault's observation deck, muscles sore, the city's lights flickering across the surveillance monitors, a city that had slept peacefully through the night. A message arrived on his secure phone. It was from Tara:

We're not done yet. The next threat is always waiting.

Max smiled faintly, a mix of weariness and determination filling him. In that smile lingered the thought of his daughter; a reminder that some fights were fought for the smallest, most personal stakes.

The fight had changed them all. They were guardians of a new frontier… defenders of an invisible war waged in the realm of code and connection. And as long as technology thrived, so too would threats like Phantom. But so long as there were those willing to stand guard, to fight in the shadows, to evolve alongside the enemy, humanity would never be defenseless.

Max glanced toward the horizon, where the first light of dawn broke through the night.

"The last line of defense," he whispered.

And with that, he stepped forward into an uncertain future guarded by those who refused to yield.

EPILOGUE

Nearly a month after the first anomaly surfaced, the war shifted from servers to Senate halls, from hidden echoes to televised questions. But in Max's mind, the silence of the Vault still pulsed louder than the noise of Washington.

The hearing room was packed. C-SPAN cameras rolled as senators grilled the heads of NSA, ONI, and Cyber Command. Max sat at the witness table, freshly pressed suit, crisp tie, clean-shaven, hair neatly trimmed, a professional facade for the weight he carried inside.

Behind him, Anna and Emily sat quietly, folded hands resting on their laps, watching him navigate the world he had always shielded them from. Their presence was a tether, a reminder of why he fought in the shadows, and why the war had stakes far beyond code and networks.

"Mr. Shaw," a senator asked, "in your expert opinion, is the threat contained?"

Max glanced at the gallery. Behind him, Tara sat rigid, poker-faced, absorbing every question. Adrian leaned back slightly, outwardly calm but eyes flickering with unease. Maya adjusted her glasses; notes spread neatly before her.

"It's contained for now," Max said carefully, "but containment isn't victory. The code was dismantled, yes. But fragments remain, buried in networks we haven't mapped. And whoever unleashed it will try again."

The room went still.

Outside the Capitol, the world churned. Stock markets had recovered, but trust had not. Power grids still flickered with un-explained outages. A newspaper headline taped to a kiosk read: THE PHANTOM VANISHED—BUT FOR HOW LONG? The journalist who had nearly broken the story was missing, and his last article had been scrubbed. The Bureau's final briefing had already stamped his file DECEASED/MISSING. The com-mittee read the line aloud that morning, then moved on. In Washington, Elliot Kane's story was officially over.

Later that evening, Max stood on the steps beneath the marble dome, the city bathed in the orange glow of dusk. Tara approached, her posture softer now.

"You did good in there," she said. "We did good," Max corrected.

For a heartbeat, they shared the unspoken acknowledgment of battles fought, scars earned. Whatever came next, Max knew Tara would stand her ground as fiercely as anyone he'd ever served beside. There was respect… the kind forged only in fire.

But behind her composure, Max noticed something else, a flicker in her eyes when the crowd dispersed, as if she were al-ready calculating the next fight. She carried the war differently than he did, but it weighed on her all the same.

Tara had lost people, too. She never spoke of them, never let it bleed into her work. Yet in the hush between them, Max un-derstood: her strength wasn't absence of cost, it was survival in spite of it.

As the crowd thinned, Tara's phone buzzed once. She glanced at the screen; a text from her mother: "Power's back. We're fine. Proud of you."

Her breath caught, just for a moment. She typed nothing back but slipped the phone into her pocket with steadier hands. For years, she had carried the weight of her brother's stolen future, but tonight, she let herself believe that fighting these shadows had protected what remained of hers.

Maya joined them, slipping a flash drive into Max's hand. "The last fragments," she said quietly. "I traced them to a dormant server farm in Eastern Europe. Wiped what I could. But one string kept reappearing."

Maya leaned closer to her monitor, pulling up the file she'd flagged days earlier.

"The Dalton credentials are still active," she said. "It pinged again during cleanup, same access node as before, but routed through an Eastern European mirror right before the attack."

Tara frowned. "So it wasn't just old metadata."

"No," Maya said. "It's a live key. Someone re-enabled it after his termination. Whether Dalton knew or not, he was part of the breach chain."

Max joined them, rigid as ever. "You think Kane was the only one feeding Phantom?"

"I think Dalton tried to blow a whistle," Maya said quietly, "and Phantom used him to write its manifesto."

Silence settled over the console.

She encrypted the credentials under sealed evidence and closed the file.

"Whatever he meant to do," she said, "his code helped Phantom find a voice."

Within hours, a classified memo from the Oversight Office flashed onto Max's secure console. Subject: Unauthorized Media Interference Inquiry.

The language was sterile; the implication, lethal: submit full documentation by 0900; identify all personnel with decision authority.

Tara read it over his shoulder. "They're not asking. They're building a record."

Max rubbed his temples. "Every ghost leaves paperwork."

Across the room, Maya pretended not to hear, but the rhythmic whir of the printer spooling copies felt louder than any alarm.

Chimera had done its job: more than a third of the twenty-eight decoy nodes had been probed by an unknown command source carrying a signature no one had seen before, proof the hydra had reached back and a clue to its next lair.

Max pocketed the drive. "What string?"

Her eyes darkened. "A signature. Same one we saw at the start. The Phantom's mark."

In the Vault's final report, Maya traced the last packet Phantom had fired before silence. No one else caught it, but she knew the pattern shift-cipher, the spacing, the rhythm; it was Kane's.

She killed the connection with one keystroke. Later, in her apartment, she lifted the photo from the mantle. For months, it had faced down. Tonight, she set it upright.

"You're not gone," she whispered. "And if you're out there, I'll find you."

She lingered on the photograph, her throat tight. For years, she had carried the weight of her brother's death, every case file another reminder of the silence that swallowed him in Bucharest. Tonight, for the first time, she felt the scales tip, just slightly. He hadn't been forgotten. The fight she carried forward was his fight too, and in crippling Phantom, she had finally answered him.

Before Max could reply, Tara pulled a folded sheet of paper from her jacket and pressed it into his hand.

"This came through one of our dead drop channels this morning. No sender, no metadata. Just this."

Max unfolded it. His pulse quickened. The page wasn't random; it was a clipping, torn from an unfinished article, the journalist's byline is clear at the top. Most of the text dissolved into static and code gibberish, except for a single phrase, underlined twice in ink:

It was never just code.

He met Maya's gaze, the unease in her eyes mirroring his own.

"The Bureau swore he vanished," she said softly. "But if this is real, he's alive, and still digging."

She leaned closer, pointing to the margins. "But look here, formatting inconsistencies, timestamp ghosts. This wasn't just copied. It was reconstructed. Maybe by him. Maybe by Phantom itself. Either way, the code is carrying his name like a vessel."

Max turned the clipping over in his hands. The formatting was wrong: timestamp fragments, metadata stripped clean, almost as if someone, or something, had reconstructed it. Officially, Elliot Kane was gone. Unofficially, his heartbeat still pulsed in the wires.

The three of them stood in silence as sirens echoed faintly in the distance. The threat was not gone, merely slumbering, waiting.

Max looked east, toward the night, knowing it was only a matter of time before the code awakened again.

·······

Washington slept under a fragile calm. Sirens faded, screens steadied, grids hummed back to life. The countdown had ended, for now.

Maya sat alone in her apartment, the silence pressing heavier than the Vault's concrete walls. She set her pistol on the counter, poured a single glass of wine, and tried to believe the fight was over.

Her laptop chimed. A secure channel request. No origin. No trace.

She hesitated, then accepted.

One line of text appeared, wrapped in military-grade encryption she hadn't seen in years:

HELLO, MAYA.

The cursor blinked once, then the screen dissolved to static.

No log. No sender. Nothing but silence.

Her hand trembled on the glass.

If it was Kane, he was alive. If it wasn't, someone knew exactly how to break her.

Either way, she wasn't just part of the war anymore. She was at its center.

And the Phantom hadn't vanished. It had only shifted in the dark.

·······

His phone buzzed again, this time not from a secure channel, but from Anna. A single photo: Emily holding up a test paper, a goofy grin on her face, the words *You'd be proud* scrawled in Anna's message beneath it.

Max stared at the screen until the glow dimmed. He typed nothing back. Not yet. But for the first time in weeks, the war felt tethered to something worth more than survival.

As he lingered on the steps, a memory rose unbidden: his father's voice, gruff yet steady, echoing from a lifetime ago. "A man's duty is simple, Max, stand your ground, protect what matters, even when no one sees you do it."

For years, Max had doubted whether he'd lived up to that creed. His father had fought in wars with uniforms and rifles;

battles measured in territory gained and lost. Max's war was waged in silence, in hidden networks and sleepless nights, victories invisible to the world.

But now, standing in the quiet glow of the Capitol, Max felt something settle inside him. He hadn't followed his father's path, but he had honored its spirit. The line had held.

And for the first time, Max allowed himself to believe that his father would have been proud.

He pulled his phone from his pocket, thumb hovering as it had so many nights before. This time, he didn't delete the draft. Instead, he tapped a short message and hit send.

Tell Emily I'll call tomorrow. I owe her that much.

Minutes later, a reply buzzed back, Anna's number. Just three words, but enough.

She'll be glad.

For the first time, the war at home felt winnable too.

For the first time in weeks, Max exhaled without the weight of dread pressing on his chest. The war was far from over, but maybe, just maybe, he could still hold on to the part of himself that wasn't just a soldier in the shadows.

As Max descended the Capitol steps, a familiar figure waited near the edge of the plaza, Sam, posture straight despite the cane resting at his side. The evening light caught the faint scar that ran from his temple into his hairline, the last visible trace of a war that never made the news.

"Hell of a day," Sam said quietly, falling into step beside him. "You looked like you belonged in there."

Max gave a tired half-smile. "Never thought I'd trade command briefings for committee hearings."

Sam's grin was thin but real. "You didn't. You just changed the room. Same mission, different battlefield." He paused, scanning the horizon where the last of the sunset faded behind the monuments. "You held the line, Max. Most people don't even know there was one to hold."

They walked in silence for a few paces before Sam added, more softly, "I'm heading out next week. Rehab wants me full-time, says the leg's got another round left in it. After that… maybe teaching. Lord knows the next generation needs to understand what a firewall actually means."

Max nodded, his voice quiet. "They'll be lucky to have you." Sam turned, meeting his eyes. "You did what we couldn't, you brought us home." He extended a hand. "Don't forget, the Vault still listens, even when it's quiet."

Max clasped it firmly. "Wouldn't have made it without you holding it steady."

Sam gave a small, knowing nod. "You never needed me to hold it. Just to remind you where the ground was."

He turned, limping toward the line of black sedans waiting under the Capitol lights. For a moment, Max watched his friend's silhouette fade into the orange haze of the evening, a soldier leaving the field at last.

And as the city settled into its fragile calm, the Vault's hum seemed to echo faintly in memory, steady, unwavering, like Sam's voice had once been: I'll hold this place steady.

As he turned to leave, Max's phone buzzed, a single alert from a secure channel he thought had been decommissioned. A new anomaly. The pattern wasn't Phantom's. It was something else. Something worse.

Then, somewhere in the back of his mind, the echo of the hearing returned, an absence he couldn't quite shake. Adrian's chair. Empty. Too early to be dismissed, too quick to slip away. Earlier, Adrian had been the one to provide the final override that kept a substation from cascading, proof enough, in front of everyone, that he'd been on their side. Yet the image of him closing his terminal a second too fast still lingered in Max's mind, the erased log window gnawing like a splinter.

He tightened his grip on the paper clipping. The journalist was alive. Or he wasn't. Either way, his name was still moving through the code.

Somewhere inside the inverted honeypot's wreckage, the same signature pulsed, Kane's rhythm, threaded through the Phantom's path like a ghost.

Adrian was gone. And somewhere in the dark, the anomaly pulsed, waiting.

Max held his head in his hands. In the silence, one name cut through louder than the sirens outside.

Adrian.

EPILOGUE II

Bucharest. Rain hammered old glass and broken streets.

A man in a hood slipped through the door of a safehouse and locked it behind him. He placed a battered hard drive on the table. Its light pulsed once, faint but steady, a heartbeat refusing to die.

Kane pulled back his hood. Older now. Harder. The smile still sharp.

"They think I'm erased," he said softly. "They think I'm a ghost."

He tapped the drive, listening to the hum. "Good. Ghosts never stop haunting."

The rain swallowed the rest.

· · · · · · · ·

Washington, the same night.

Maya sat alone in the Vault, the screens dark except for one dormant console. The last fragments of Kane's dossier glimmered on her display, a single line blinking, waiting for her answer.

She closed it without typing.

For a long moment, she just breathed in the silence. Then she shut the console down for good.

"Not anymore," she whispered.

A few feet away, Sam stood in the doorway, coat half-buttoned, a coffee gone cold in his hand.

"You sure?" he asked quietly. Maya didn't turn. "It's time."

Rourke nodded once, then set the mug on her desk. "Then we're done here."

He lingered only a heartbeat, scanning the darkened consoles, the room that had been his second home. "We built something that held longer than it had any right to." He flexed his left knee once, a small wince hidden under motion. The limp had never gone away; it just reminded him that survival, in any war, was a kind of compromise.

"It held," Maya said.

"Then that's enough," Rourke replied, and walked out into the dawn light, leaving the hum of cooling servers behind him.

EPILOGUE III

The sea pressed against the windows like black glass. Beyond it, nothing but winter swells and the faint glow of a lighthouse. Inside the room, the air smelled of metal and salt. Banks of servers purred softly, their indicator lights blinking in patterns only one man understood.

The screen before him showed a map of the continental United States. Green icons marked systems his adversary had reclaimed. But threaded between them, like veins of iron beneath ice, were new red lines, silent, dormant, waiting.

He closed a folder stamped with a single glyph: a white mask. "Phase One compromised," a voice reported over an encrypted speaker. "Chimera disrupted fifty-seven percent of the

implants. Kansas node lost. We're rebuilding."

The man in the chair steepled his fingers, burn scars faintly visible across his knuckles. "Good," he said quietly. "Now we know who they are."

A second screen flickered on, showing a still image of Max's face taken from a security briefing. The man studied it for a long moment, then tapped a command. On a different screen, a list of backup nodes scrolled past, ending with a single line of text:

PHASE TWO—ACTIVATION IN PROGRESS.

He rose, slipping the flash drive into his pocket. "They've built a shadow," he murmured, turning toward the dark window. "But a shadow proves there is light."

Somewhere in the maze of code, dormant systems blinked awake for the first time.

DEPARTMENT OF HOMELAND SECURITY
NATIONAL INFRASTRUCTURE PROTECTION AGENCY

CLASSIFIED // REL TO USA, FVEY
DECLASSIFIED DOCUMENT – AUTH. 2025-0917-NIPA

APPENDIX A – DECLASSIFIED GLOSSARY OF TERMS

Subject: "SLEEPER CODE" / PHANTOM INCIDENT
Distribution: Internal Archive – Redacted Release Date of
Declassification: 09/17/2031
Originating Office: The Vault (Washington, D.C.)

AIR-GAPPED SYSTEM: A computer or network physically isolated from all external systems, including the Internet, to prevent unauthorized access or infection. Commonly used in defense, intelligence, and industrial control environments.

C2 – Command and Control: Encrypted communication channels used by Phantom nodes to coordinate activation, payload updates, and lateral movement. Neutralizing C2 pathways was insufficient for containment because autonomous local triggers were embedded in firmware.

CIA – Central Intelligence Agency: Independent agency tasked with foreign intelligence gathering and covert cyber operations. Involved in attribution analysis of Phantom Chimera's global infrastructure.

CISA – Cybersecurity and Infrastructure Security Agency: A division of the Department of Homeland Security responsible for coordinating national cybersecurity efforts and critical infrastructure protection.

DARPA – Defense Advanced Research Projects Agency: U.S. Department of Defense agency responsible for developing emerging technologies for national security. Supported the Chimera pro-totype framework, later mirrored by Phantom.

DHS – Department of Homeland Security: Federal department overseeing domestic security agencies, including NIPA, CISA, FEMA, and USCG.

DIA – Defense Intelligence Agency: Provides intelligence on foreign military capabilities and cyber warfare developments.

DOE – Department of Energy: Manages energy policy and critical infrastructure protection. Partnered with NIPA on grid incident analysis.

DOJ – Department of Justice: Responsible for enforcing federal law and overseeing cybercrime prosecution via the National Security Division.

FAA – Federal Aviation Administration: Oversees civil aviation safety and air traffic systems, including those vulnerable to cyber intrusion.

FEMA – Federal Emergency Management Agency: Responsible for national emergency coordination, logistics, and infrastructure continuity during cyber or physical incidents.

FIVE EYES (FVEY): Intelligence-sharing alliance comprising the United States, the United Kingdom, Canada, Australia, and New Zealand. Coordinated with NIPA during Operation HYDRA for transnational containment.

HONEYPOT: A deliberately exposed or vulnerable system used as bait to attract and study attackers. NIPA deployed multiple honeypots to analyze Phantom's self-adaptive propagation behavior.

HYDRA (Operation Designator): Codename for the NIPA-led multinational containment operation following the Prairie Ridge Data Commons incident. Revealed multiple mirrored command nodes distributed across four continents.

ICS – Industrial Control Systems: The broader class of industrial automation systems that includes SCADA. Critical in managing energy, manufacturing, and water processes.

INTERPOL / EUROPOL: International law enforcement agencies assisting with attribution and data seizure related to Phantom Chimera operations.

KILL CHAIN: A conceptual model describing the sequential stages of a cyberattack, from reconnaissance and weaponization to exploitation and execution, used to identify and disrupt adversary operations.

NCTC – National Counterterrorism Center: The federal hub for integrating and analyzing terrorism-related intelligence across agencies.

NIPA – National Infrastructure Protection Agency: U.S. federal agency tasked with defending critical infrastructure networks from cyber-physical threats. Its existence was officially classified until this release.

NIST – National Institute of Standards and Technology: Develops cybersecurity frameworks and standards, including the NIST SP 800-series, which NIPA and other federal agencies adopt.

NSA – National Security Agency: Responsible for signals intelligence, cyber defense, and cryptographic analysis. Coordinated with NIPA during Phantom containment operations.

ODNI – Office of the Director of National Intelligence: Oversees the U.S. Intelligence Community and coordinates between NSA, CIA, DIA, and others.

PHANTOM CHIMERA (Designator: PC-47): State-sponsored cyber-espionage collective believed to operate through multiple proxy states and corporate fronts. Known for hybrid software-hardware exploitation tactics.

ROOTKIT: Malicious code engineered to obtain persistent, covert control over a system. Often embedded in firmware or kernel layers to conceal intrusion.

SCADA – Supervisory Control and Data Acquisition: Industrial control systems that monitor and manage essential national processes, power grids, water treatment, transport, and manufacturing.

SEI – Software Engineering Institute (Carnegie Mellon University): Federally funded research center advancing software security and resilience. Partnered with NIPA during the Phantom investigation.

SLEEPER CODE / "PHANTOM": A self-modifying, adaptive malware framework designed to remain dormant for extended periods until triggered by command or autonomous countdown.

SOC – Security Operations Center: Centralized command facility responsible for real-time cybersecurity monitoring, analysis, and incident response. The Vault served as NIPA's highest-tier SOC.

STATE DEPARTMENT: Handles diplomatic coordination and foreign liaison during cyber incidents with international impact.

SUPPLY CHAIN COMPROMISE: Insertion of malicious code or tampered hardware during component manufacturing or distribution. Multiple infected parts traced to subcontracted foreign fabrication facilities.

THE GRID: Collective term for the nation's critical infrastructure ecosystem, energy, transportation, water, data, and finance.

THE VAULT: Subterranean cyber operations command facility beneath Washington, D.C., originally a Cold War shelter, repurposed as NIPA's primary defense hub.

U.S. ARMY CORPS OF ENGINEERS: Federal agency managing waterways, dams, and critical infrastructure; partnered with NIPA during the Mississippi River lock incident.

USCG – United States Coast Guard: Maritime security and infrastructure protection agency under DHS, responsible for ports and waterways.

USCYBERCOM – United States Cyber Command: Department of Defense command overseeing military cyberspace operations and defense missions.

USPTO – United States Patent and Trademark Office: Federal agency managing intellectual property systems, referenced in connection with compromised research systems and the Prism data leak.

ZERO-DAY: An undisclosed or unpatched software vulnerability exploited before developers can issue fixes.

END OF RECORD
//SIGNED// Director M. Shaw
National Infrastructure Protection Agency CLASSIFICATION
REMOVED PER EXECUTIVE ORDER 14291
DECLASSIFIED // APPROVED FOR PUBLIC RELEASE

Approved by: Director M. Shaw, NIPA (2025-0917)

ABOUT THE AUTHOR

Dr. Kevin McGuire has spent more than 32 years in cybersecurity, protecting our nation's critical infrastructure systems as both a federal employee and a trusted contractor. His career has placed him on the front lines of digital defense, where technology, policy, and human judgment meet under pressure.

He serves on the **Board of the University of Fairfax**, where he helps shape programs that develop the next generation of cybersecurity professionals. His lifelong commitment to the field continues to inspire both his professional work and his writing.

Drawing on decades of real-world experience, Dr. McGuire brings authenticity and depth to *Sleeper Code*, blending technical precision with the emotional intensity of a human thriller. His stories explore the unseen battles fought every day in the shadows of cyberspace, and the people who quietly keep the modern world running.

He lives with his wife, **Traci**, and their children, **Amanda, Ashleigh, Ryan, and Allie**, who remind him daily what's truly worth protecting. *Sleeper Code* is his debut novel and the first in a planned trilogy about the fragile intersection of humanity and technology.

More Books From

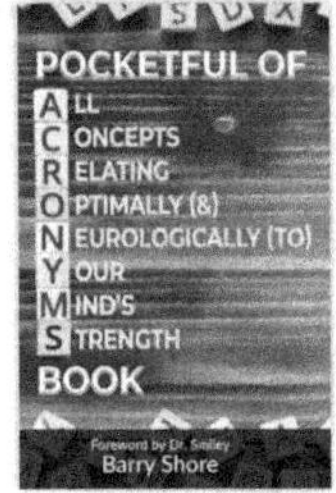

www.PerfectPublishing.com

More Books From

PerfectPublishing.com

www.PerfectPublishing.com